"You tremble," he murmured

"There is no reason, Glenys. Can you think I would ever bring you harm?"

"Nay," she said weakly, hearing how badly her voice shook, "but I am not...I have no...skills or... knowledge. I know nothing."

"And I know everything," he said softly, rubbing his thumb lightly across her lips. "We are not well matched. I vow I wish I could be as you are again, but 'tis impossible." He lifted his other hand, sliding his fingertips slowly down the side of her neck. "Have you ever been kissed, Glenys?"

"N-nay," she whispered, filled with both terror and anticipation.

He smiled. "Good. 'Tis most selfish of me, but I confess that I am glad to be the first."

With his thumbs he carefully tilted leaning toward her slowly...so but a breath away....

THE
Prisoner Bride

Susan
Spencer
Paul

HARLEQUIN®

TORONTO • NEW YORK • LONDON
AMSTERDAM • PARIS • SYDNEY • HAMBURG
STOCKHOLM • ATHENS • TOKYO • MILAN • MADRID
PRAGUE • WARSAW • BUDAPEST • AUCKLAND

ISBN 0-373-29187-6

THE PRISONER BRIDE

Please address questions and book requests to:
Harlequin Reader Service
U.S.: 3010 Walden Ave., P.O. Box 1325, Buffalo, NY 14269
Canadian: P.O. Box 609, Fort Erie, Ont. L2A 5X3

Dedicated with love to my wonderful uncles

Richard Alton Walls
Who, even when I was very young,
encouraged me to follow my dream of being a writer

Charles Yancy Walls
Whose support these many years
has meant more than I can put into words

Alton Emmett McQueen
The true writer in our family, who taught me a great deal
about my craft and saved me from making many
embarrassing mistakes in my earliest books

And, finally, in memoriam, to
Morris Neil McQueen
Whose letters still inspire me in so many ways, and
whom I miss even more greatly with each passing day

Prologue

London, May, 1440

"I'll not kill the girl, if that's what you're asking."

"Nay, nay, of course not," Sir Anton Lagasse assured his guest at once. "You misunderstand me completely. I *love* Glenys, and she loves me. I should never want any harm to befall her. I only want her taken and kept fully safe until her family agrees to let us marry."

Sir Anton looked about nervously at the depraved assortment of villains filling the tavern, and prayed that he'd not have to remain much longer before his business was concluded. The Black Raven wasn't the sort of place he normally visited. It was, however, a favorite haunt of thieves, whores, and murderers—all of whom could be found here and hired for a price. Withdrawing an expensive handkerchief from his tunic, he mopped his sweating brow before turning back to the man who sat opposite him at the table, a man who was as comfortable among these people as Sir Anton was uncomfortable.

"Against her will, you said," his guest replied, setting his tankard aside with slow deliberation. "A woman who loves a man would willingly be secreted away in order to marry him. I can but wonder at how greatly this Glenys of yours cares for you if she must be taken by force and imprisoned until you come to fetch her."

Sir Anton considered his companion with care. Kieran FitzAllen was well known as a man who could be trusted to complete unpleasant tasks for pay and afterward keep silent, but he was also known to be particular about the work he accepted. He was willing to steal, thieve, thwart intentions and fight like the very devil, but he refused to harm women. Though that was hardly to be wondered at. FitzAllen was a handsome knave, and women, young and old, married and unmarried, pure and impure, had an unfortunate tendency to throw themselves at him. He repaid such adoration with equal admiration, mainly of a physical nature, or so Sir Anton understood it. Kieran FitzAllen, it was rumored, had lain with more women in his twenty-nine years than most men could hope to merely meet in a lifetime. Nay, he would never harm a woman, not even for a fortune in gold. Sir Anton knew he must find the way to convince this man of his sincerity.

"Glenys's family is what lies between us," he told him, leaning forward, "and what keeps her from coming to me freely. 'Tis difficult for any who are not acquainted with the Seymours. She fears death if she tries to leave them."

"Death?" Kieran FitzAllen regarded him with suspicion. "How so? You do not mean that they would kill the girl for wedding you?"

Sir Anton sighed and nodded. "'Tis what Glenys believes, no matter how I strive to reassure her. Her family has chosen another for her to wed, and will not even let her see or speak to me. But such is the measure of our love that she, in turn, has refused the marriage they have arranged.''

"This would seem a foolish course," Kieran FitzAllen told him, taking up his tankard to drink from it once more, "since the family has turned your suit aside.''

"But you do not understand! They have only refused me because I have not yet come into my inheritance. But my uncle, the Duc d'Burdeux, is very ill, and not expected to live long. I have been called to Normandy to attend him until his death, and once he has gone to heaven and I have gained the title and lands, I am certain the Seymours will agree to let Glenys become my wife.''

"Then tell them what you have told me," Kieran FitzAllen advised, "and ask them to wait. I do not see why you should want the girl kidnapped and held against her will if she has already refused the other suitor, and if you are but weeks from obtaining your goal.''

"But her family will *force* her to wed this other man," Sir Anton insisted. "You cannot begin to know what they are like. Glenys is terrified of them, and I cannot make her understand that I can keep her safe, that they will not even know how to find her once you have taken her away.''

"*If* I take her," Kieran FitzAllen corrected. He lifted a finger to summon one of the serving maids to refill his tankard. The girl, who with every other woman in the tavern had been staring at him without ceasing, rushed to fulfill his bidding. Her reward was a lazy smile and a pat on her ample behind, which nearly made the foolish girl drop the heavy pitcher she carried. Sir Anton felt slightly ill as he watched Kieran FitzAllen's dealings with the maid. He would probably take the filthy, sluttish creature upstairs and tumble her the moment their business was completed. He looked to be the kind of man with just such lowly appetites.

"You have not yet explained why your beloved must be held against her will," Kieran said once the girl had gone away and he had turned his attention back to Sir Anton. "If I tell her that you have sent me to take her away and keep her safe, she should become instantly agreeable—if all that you say is true."

Sir Anton gaped at the man sitting across from him. "Do you accuse me of speaking falsely?" he demanded.

"Not in the least," Kieran FitzAllen replied easily. "Do you accuse me of being a fool? For only a complete lackwit would accept such a tale without some manner of reasoning. Tell me plainly why you wish me to take this woman against her will."

"I have told you already that she fears her family," Sir Anton said, struggling to contain his anger at such insolence. "Even if you tell her that you have taken her at my command, she will never believe that she can be kept safe from them. But there is, I admit, another reason. Glenys is…I suppose you might say she is on a quest."

Kieran FitzAllen looked amused. "A quest?"

"Aye," Sir Anton said wearily, nodding. "Her family—the Seymour clan—is Welsh, and descended from a noble Celtic lineage. This is their greatest pride, and they yet cling to many of the old beliefs, strange and profane as that may be. The head of the family, Lord Aonghus Seymour, who is Glenys's uncle, even claims to possess certain powers.'' He leaned closer and lowered his voice. ''Mystical powers.''

Kieran FitzAllen seemed unimpressed by this. ''And does he? Possess such powers?''

''Of course not!'' Sir Anton replied, much flustered. ''He's half madman. The whole lot of them are—all of Glenys's strange uncles and aunts. She's the only sane member of the family, despite her insistence upon regaining the Greth Stone at all costs—even that of her own life.''

''Greth?'' Kieran repeated. '''Tis the ancient word for grace, is it not?''

''Aye, and that is just what it means. The Stone of Grace. 'Tis a ring that has been in Glenys's family for many generations, most beautiful, with a large, dark sapphire set in the midst. To see it, one would admire the ring's beauty, but for all that 'tis merely a common family heirloom. I have seen many rings possessing far greater loveliness and value. But the Seymours will have it that the Greth Stone is blessed with great powers—more of their foolishness about all things mystical—and they crave its return to them. It was stolen some months ago by a man named Caswallan, and taken back to Wales. Glenys is determined to find this knave and have the ring again, but Caswallan has not been heard of since he took it. No one knows where he is, or what he has done with the ring. 'Tis a foolish quest she follows, and a dangerous one, but she is set upon it. And I,'' Sir Anton added, sitting back in his chair, ''am determined to keep her safe, even from this. But I confess…she will not like it.''

Kieran FitzAllen emptied his tankard for the third time that day and set it aside. Wiping his lips with his fingers, he said, "So. You desire that I steal Mistress Glenys and take her to…"

"A small keep that I hold in York. 'Tis an insignificant dwelling, uninhabited for many years now, but stout enough that you can surely keep her well and secure. And her family will never find her there."

His guest gave a curt nod. "And you want me to keep her there—against all her protests and fears of her family and her desire to follow her quest—until…"

"Until I am able to come for her," Sir Anton replied. "'Twill be no more than a few months—mayhap weeks, for I vow that my uncle is gravely ill. You will have enough gold to supply all your needs even for a year, if need be, and to keep Glenys in every comfort." Looking about the tavern to see whether any watched what he did, he reached into an inner pocket in his tunic and pulled out a leather bag. "I have come ready to make part payment, you see. Fifty pieces of gold now, fifty pieces on the day you take Glenys, and a hundred when I come for her."

He had expected Kieran FitzAllen—or any knave like him—to leap at the chance to earn so much gold, but the other man merely sat in his chair, looking at him thoughtfully.

"A year is a long time to hold an unwilling woman prisoner, regardless the payment. I am not yet certain 'tis even necessary. Her family must be odd, indeed, if they will not even wait a few weeks for your uncle to die so that you may be deemed suitable."

"I've already told you they're half-mad," Sir Anton said with a growing sense of desperation. If this man wouldn't accept the task of stealing Glenys, he'd have to find someone far less becoming. The thought of having to endure any more time in such places as this was truly distressing. "Even her brother, Sir Daman, is a vicious lunatic. He's tried to kill me—*twice*—simply for meeting Glenys in secret..."

His guest leaned forward, fully attentive now.

"Sir Daman Seymour? *He* is your lover's brother?"

"Aye. Do you know him?"

"Of a certainty, I do." The smile on Kieran Fitz-Allen's face slowly became feline. "So, 'tis his sister you want me to steal, eh? I believe I suddenly understand why you are loath to do it yourself. Daman will kill the man who dares such a thing. Or attempt to, anywise." He laughed in a way that made Sir Anton shiver. "You should have mentioned his name before now," Kieran told him, "and our business would have been concluded the more quickly." Reaching out, he pulled the leather bag from Sir Anton's trembling fingers. "I agree to do as you ask. And soon—within the week. My manservant, Jean-Marc, will let you know the day. Make certain that you have the second payment ready, as you have promised, and give him directions to your keep in York. If all goes well, Mistress Glenys Seymour will be ensconced within its walls before a fortnight has passed."

Chapter One

"Uncle Aonghus?"

Glenys lifted the cellar door a bit higher, peering through the dim candlelight in the room below. Fragrant blue smoke, sparkling with whatever chemicals her uncle had mixed, wafted upward into the hall. Glenys waved the substance away and called more loudly, "Uncle Aonghus?"

"Mayhap he's drunk one of his potions again," Dina, Glenys's maid, suggested, her eyes widening at the thought. "Do you not remember what happened when last he did such a thing?"

"May God forbid," Glenys said fervently, remembering the event—and all the others that had come before it—all too well. "Here, hold the door and I will go down."

The steps leading down to the hidden cellar were both narrow and short, and Glenys tread them with care, lifting her heavy skirts high to keep from tripping.

"Uncle Aonghus? Are you well?" The moment she gained the floor she made for the long table where he kept all of his powders and potions. Furiously waving sparkling blue smoke aside with both hands, she said,

"You promised me faithfully that you'd *never* drink any of your experiments again. And thank a merciful God you've but made more smoke this time, and not caused another explosion."

She coughed as the smoke grew heavier near the table, and heard an answering cough coming from somewhere behind it. Uncle Aonghus, she discovered, was lying on the floor, arms splayed wide as if he'd been knocked back by a large fist.

"God's mercy!" Glenys cried as she knelt beside the elderly man, setting her hands on his shoulders. "Uncle Aonghus!"

He coughed again and, with her help, sat up. "I'm well," he insisted. "I've come to no harm."

"No, stay there a moment," she said, holding him still when he would have risen. "I'll fetch a glass of wine. Only rest until you've recovered."

Moving quickly, Glenys gained her feet, but found that the smoke was thicker than before, and glittering more violently. A few sharp sparks nipped her face and hands, irritating but not painful. A short search revealed the source of the mischief to be a small glass jar set upon her uncle's worktable.

She quickly put a lid over the jar, bringing an end to the smoky outpouring. Then, blindly feeling the tabletop with seeking hands, she at last found another jar of equal size and unlidded it. Scooping up a small handful of the cool, crystalline mixture within, Glenys reached back and flung it into the air. More sparkles filled the chamber, purple and white this time. Almost at once the smoke began to dissipate, and within moments was gone altogether. Behind her, she heard Uncle Aonghus give a sigh of relief.

"I was so close this time," he said. "I wish I knew what element is missing. I'm so very close."

Glenys had already moved to another table to pour her uncle a glass of wine from the decanter set there.

Returning to kneel and give it to him, she replied, "I'm certain it will come to you soon, Uncle, but you must use greater care. If 'tis reported to the sheriff that more colored smoke has been coming from the chimneys, we will find ourselves in great difficulty. I do not know how I can explain it again in any reasonable manner."

Uncle Aonghus drained the cup she'd given him and handed it back to her. He smiled and patted her hand, saying, "Such a good girl you are, Glenys. If not for you, we'd all have been burned at the stake years ago."

"Nay, that is not so," she assured him at once, though her heart knew that he had spoken the truth. She was twenty years of age, and had spent many of those years keeping her aunts and uncles safe. They were as harmless as could be, but so very strange in their ways that she had no doubt they would readily be burned as witches and warlocks if any of those ways became known. She would have kept them all at their ancestral estate in Wales throughout the year, if she could, for in Wales they were always safe. But they insisted upon accompanying Glenys to London for six months out of each year while she took care of the many Seymour businesses. And in London, her aunts and uncles were as vulnerable as newborn rabbits to skilled hunting hawks.

Glenys had only two defenses in keeping them safe while at Metolius, their palatial dwelling on London's Strand. The Seymour family was wealthy enough to buy favor from both the church and crown, which

Glenys made certain to do. And her brother, Daman, who was a famed knight of the realm, rode throughout the country with his army, gaining goodwill and setting the Seymour name in a favorable light. As long as both the tributes and Daman's good works continued, the Seymour family was safe, but Glenys was the first to admit that it was a most wearying task. She often longed to be free of it, knowing full well that 'twould never be. She and Daman had long since devoted themselves to the good of the Seymour family name, regardless of what it cost them.

"Now," Uncle Aonghus said with renewed energy. "I can't sit about all day." Taking the arm she proffered, he let her help him to his feet. "There is much to do before you go. But, oh," he said with open affection, squeezing her hand, "'twill will be so strange and difficult with you gone." Releasing her, he returned to his table, his beautiful, long-fingered hands reaching out to rearrange several bottles there. "Metolius will be terribly lonely. Indeed, I hardly know how we shall go on. But that can't be helped," he stated with all practicality. "And you must not worry o'er us, my dear. I shall make certain that Mim and Wynne behave themselves until you've returned from retrieving the Greth Stone. And I shall strictly forbid your uncle Culain to leave Metolius, save to attend Mass."

Glenys smiled at him. "I'm only going to the bank to speak to Master Fairchild, Uncle Aonghus, just as I do every Thursday. I'll settle the matter of our next shipping venture and return home within two hours. And as for the Greth Stone, you know full well that I'll not set out for Wales until Daman has returned with his men. 'Tis already planned that they will escort me.''

"Yes, dearest, I know what's been planned," Uncle Aonghus assured her as he scooped up a large handful of the crystals that she'd earlier used to stop the smoke, pouring it into a small leather pouch, "but you must be prepared, nonetheless. Now, here, tie this to your belt and make certain not to lose it." He pulled the drawstrings to the bag tight and brought it to her.

Glenys gazed at the offering and gave a slight shake of her head. "But I'm sure I won't need this for such a short visit, Uncle. Can you think it wise to allow one of your mixtures out of the dwelling? Especially this one? I know 'tis not truly magical, but if it should somehow happen to become lost and fall into unknowing hands…" The thought was too unpleasant to finish aloud.

"Have no fears for that, Glenys." He placed the pouch in her hand and curled her fingers about it, smiling at her warmly. "You'll have need of it in future. Trust what I say, dearest. Now come. We'll go upstairs together so that I may see you off."

He led the way toward the small, child-size stairs, climbing them with nimble grace ahead of Glenys. She watched, amazed, as she ever was, at the elegance and ease with which her elderly uncle moved. He was tall, slender and small-boned, as were his sisters and brother, reminding Glenys not so much of an ordinary human being, but of a creature that might be half human and half animal. Precisely what kind of animal, she wasn't sure. Her aunts and uncles were as quick and sure-footed as mountain goats, as delicate and careful as great-eyed deer and as difficult to make behave as a group of highly independent cats. Their coloring and features were remarkably similar, as well, although since Aunt Mim and Aunt Wynne were twins that wasn't so unusual a thing. They all had white hair and blue eyes and remained as beautiful—aye, beautiful, even her uncles—as they had ever been. Sometimes, when Glenys looked at them, she found it impossible to believe that she was in any way related to such wonderful and unusual creatures as her aunts and uncles were. Both she and Daman possessed none of their daintiness or otherworldliness, and Glenys, of a certainty, knew that she possessed none of their beauty.

"Come along, dearest," Uncle Aonghus called from the midway point, beckoning to her. "You must be on your way soon, lest you miss your opportunity."

"I'm only going to see the banker," she repeated, dutifully following behind.

"Here's Dina, holding the door for us," Uncle Aonghus said cheerfully as he gained the hallway, wiping small remaining bits of dust and powder from the long purple robe he wore. "You'll need a much warmer cloak, Dina," he said, taking the door from her as Glenys reached the last step. "Go and fetch your heaviest one."

"But, my lord," Dina said shyly, "'tis not so cold a day. Indeed, 'tis quite warm for May."

"Oh, but it will grow cold in the evening," he told her, patting her arm. "Hurry now. Run and fetch it, just as I've said."

Dina looked at Glenys, who sighed and nodded. With a slight bob of her head, Dina left to fetch her cloak.

"And you'll be needing warmer clothes, as well, Glenys," Uncle Aonghus told her, reaching to curl his long fingers gently about her arm, "but your aunt Mim has already thought of that. Come into the great room and tell them all goodbye, dearest. And do tie that pouch to your girdle. I shouldn't want you to lose it."

And neither would I, Glenys thought silently, looping the strings about the leather belt at her waist and securing them tightly.

"Uncle Aonghus, I'm *only* going to the bank."

"Yes, yes, of course you are," he said kindly as he led her along. "And a very good thing it is, too."

The great room of Metolius was a large, warm and inviting chamber. It was the very heart of the entire dwelling. The walls were beautifully paneled with gleaming cherry wood and the floors covered in soft, richly colored Italian carpets. Tall windows along the length of one wall allowed light to fill the room on sunny days, and a multitude of Danish lamps set at intervals about each wall did the same during the night. Six large, handsome hearths kept the room warm the year round, most especially when the weather grew chill.

The family spent every evening together in the great room, and much of the rest of the day, as well. Each member had a favorite spot. Uncle Aonghus liked to sit near the shelf that was set against the far wall and read from one of his favorite bound manuscripts, which were always kept there. Glenys sat near the fire, usually plying her needle on whatever needed mending, from clothing to curtains, and across from her, also near the fire, Uncle Culain would be sitting at the chess table, moving from one chair to the other, playing a game against himself, just as he was doing now. Aunt Mim and Aunt Wynne liked to sit near the tall windows, gazing out into the gardens and courtyard, chattering away and looking into their special box, giggling and exclaiming over each new discovery. They were in their chairs now, bent over the plain wooden box, gazing at the contents within.

"What could this be?" Aunt Mim said wonderingly, lifting a small, thin package up into the light, showing it to Aunt Wynne. "What do you think, dear?"

Aunt Wynne examined the papery object more closely, squinting to read the red letters printed boldly across it. *"B-a-n-d–A-i-d,"* she spelled slowly. "Hmm. But I'm sure we've seen this before…whatever it may be."

"No, dear," Aunt Mim chided, setting the object back into the box and closing the lid. "The box never offers the same article twice. You know that." She lifted the lid and looked inside. "Oh, look! Now isn't this pretty?"

"Oh, in truth, Sister, it is," Aunt Wynne agreed, reaching one beautifully delicate hand into the box to lift out a long strand of pearls. "How lovely. Such a shame we can't keep them for Glenys. She has the coloring for pearls. We've never looked well in them," she said woefully, then, with a sigh, let the luminous strand slide back into the box. "When will we ever get the key?"

The key was what Aunt Mim and Aunt Wynne spent hour upon hour, day upon day searching for. The wooden box offered up mysteries that Glenys felt uncomfortable thinking upon—of all the oddities at Metolius, it was by far the most unsettling—but its real purpose, she had ever been told, was to one day offer up an ancient key that, like the Greth Stone, had been lost to the Seymour family. It had been hundreds of years since the mysterious key had been placed in the box and sent…well, to wherever it was that things disappeared to when placed there…and various Seymours had been trying to get it back ever since. The key box was opened and closed dozens of times during a single day, offering up small, strange objects for observation, but it hadn't yet yielded the key. Glenys didn't even know what the key was for or what it was meant to unlock, and she wasn't entirely certain that her aunts and uncles knew, either, but the quest was a pleasurable way for them to spend their afternoons, and the anticipation of one day finding the key never seemed to wane.

"Mim," Uncle Aonghus said gently as his sister began to open the box once more. "Glenys is about to leave us."

Aunt Mim, Aunt Wynne and Uncle Culain all stopped what they were doing and stood.

"Oh, Glenys, dearest," Aunt Mim said with distress, moving toward Glenys with one of her long, elegant hands stretched out. "Must you go now? It will be so long a time before you come back to us."

Glenys took her aunt's hand with care, feeling, as she ever did, the great difference between her own sturdiness and the delicate loveliness of her relatives. "There's no need to be overset, Aunt Mim," she reassured her. "I'm only going to the bank, and Dina with me."

Aunt Wynne joined them, tears filling her bright blue eyes. In her hands she held Glenys's warmest cloak. "But we shall miss you so greatly," she said, setting the heavy woolen garment about Glenys's shoulders. "You must take care in all things, dearest, and never forget that you're a Seymour. A *true* Seymour, even though your mother was of the northern people and, like them, so very practical. But that couldn't be

helped, and a dear, good wife she was to our brother
Arian.'' She nodded, and Aunt Mim and Uncle Aonghus and Uncle Culain, who had left his chess game
to join them, all nodded, too.

''But—'' Glenys began, only to be interrupted by
Aunt Mim, who'd begun to lace up the collar of
Glenys's cloak.

''Your aunt Wynne is quite right,'' she said, sniffling
and clearly striving not to weep. ''You and Daman are
Seymours in every way that matters, though you can
be so stubborn about accepting that certainty,'' she said
chidingly, reaching up to adjust the plain silver circlet
that sat atop Glenys's braided auburn hair. ''But you
can't run away from the truth forever. Oh, Wynne,
where is the stone? She cannot go without it.''

''Here, in my pocket.'' Aunt Wynne fished about in
the apron that hung from her girdle, at last producing
a small, white stone that Glenys recognized at once.

''Oh, no,'' she murmured, ''I can't take it with me.
Please, don't ask me to do so.'' She looked pleadingly
at her aunts. ''I'm only going to the bank, and once
I've spoken with Master Fairchild I'll return home—
long before the evening meal, I vow. And you know
how greatly it worries me to take anything…special…
out of Metolius.'' Merciful God, the very last thing she
needed was to have one of Aunt Mim's and Aunt
Wynne's stones glowing on her person. Despite their
small size, the white rocks could put out an astonishing
measure of light. Glenys had even taken to searching
her aunts before each outing just to make certain they
didn't have one absentmindedly hidden somewhere.
She could only envision the trouble that would ensue
if one of her aunts' pockets should start glowing in the

midst of St. Paul's during Mass. "I'd not be able to forgive myself should I lose it."

"Oh, we won't mind," Aunt Wynne said cheerfully, bending to slide the stone into a small pocket within Glenys's cloak. "We have so many of them, and you'll need this while you're gone." She leaned forward to kiss Glenys on the cheek. "Oh, it's *such* an exciting time, dearest, but we *will* worry for you so. Come home to us soon."

"Yes," Aunt Mim agreed, kissing Glenys's other cheek and hugging her. "Just as soon as you possibly can."

"I'll be home in two hours," Glenys murmured helplessly as she was enfolded in the embrace. "Less than two hours, I vow."

"Leave her be a moment, Mim," Uncle Culain chided, moving forward. "Glenys can't leave without my gift."

Another offering? Glenys's heart sank, especially when she saw what Uncle Culain held in his hand. It was his most prized possession, the lone remaining piece of an ancient chess set—the queen. It had been a very odd set, if the intricately carved lady was anything to go by. She was fashioned out of dark red wood, and looked much more like a pagan goddess than a proper queen, with her hair unbound and flowing down to mingle with her long, druidic robes. Her feet were bare, her crown was a wreath of twined flowers and leaves, and her eyes, made of amber, glowed as if a candle burned behind them. Uncle Culain carried the piece with him everywhere, speaking to her as if she could hear him, and even kept her beneath his pillow when he slept. It was impossible that he would part with the chess piece, even for the short while that Glenys would be gone.

"No, Uncle Culain," she said desperately, pushing his hand back. "I could *never* take your good lady, not for any reason."

"But you must," he insisted. "You must, for she is the only treasure Caswallan will bargain for. He would not part with the Greth Stone for any measure of wealth or fear, but for her," he said, gently placing the small wooden figure in Glenys's palm, "he will gladly give it to you."

"Caswallan?" she said with confusion. "Uncle Culain, I'm *only* going to the bank. I'll not be journeying to Wales for another month at the very least. I've already arranged to wait for Daman and his men. You know that." She looked about her at each delicate, lovely face, aunts and uncles alike. "You *all* know that."

They nodded and smiled, and began to walk her toward the great room's entryway, where Dina stood waiting for her. After hugs and kisses from all four of her elderly relatives, she was bustled out of doors, with Dina right behind, and was soon stepping into the waiting carriage with the help of one of the house servants. She looked back, out the open window, as it pulled away, to find her aunts weeping and waving and her uncles nodding sagely and waving.

After so many years, Glenys would have thought that she would be well used to her relatives' unusual ways, but, presently, she was thoroughly bewildered and amazed. The items they'd given her felt far more like terrible burdens than loving gifts, though she knew in her heart that they'd been given as the latter. The chess piece felt as warm as life in her hand, and Glenys pulled her gaze from the sight of her waving aunts and uncles to look down at it, slowly uncurling her fingers to reveal the little treasure. The beautiful lady was face-up in her grasp, and her amber eyes glowed with that odd, peculiar light that had always unnerved Glenys.

''God's mercy,'' she murmured, quickly pushing the piece into the same pocket as the white stone, praying that neither would cause any trouble at the bank. She looked across to the seat where Dina sat. ''Perhaps we should wait until the morrow to visit with Master Fairchild. I vow I am full discomfited.''

Dina's gaze was sympathetic. ''Twill be well, mistress. The white stones never glow when 'tis so light as today, and the others...you must simply keep them hidden. All will be well,'' she promised once more, so convincingly that Glenys believed her. Almost.

They passed the courtyard gates and were soon on the main street heading toward the center of London.

''Pray God you are right, Dina,'' she said fervently, sitting back. ''I have a most unsettled feeling that we would do very well to finish our business and return home as quickly as may be.''

Chapter Two

"I thought you said that Glenys means 'fair one,'" Kieran said, folding his arms across his chest and leaning indolently against the cool bricks of the tavern wall. The wind gusted and the folds of the heavy woolen cape he wore flapped against his leather-clad legs. Casting a glance upward, he saw that the clouds had grown darker, thicker. The day had started as both warm and clear, but a storm was on its way.

"And so it does," Jean-Marc replied, setting his empty tankard aside on the ledge of the tavern's open window. "Mistress Seymour was sadly misnamed, I fear. Her parents must have hoped for a different manner of daughter."

Kieran smiled. "Not with Daman for a son." He eyed the tall, stately figure of Mistress Glenys Seymour as she made her way from her carriage and into the building where her banker kept his business. "She is just the sort of sister such a brute would have, though her coloring is far milder."

"Not very mild," Jean-Marc retorted. "Her hair's as bright as a sunrise."

"Nay, 'tis softer, more like a sunset," Kieran corrected, "though the rest of her appears to be more formidable. I have a great deal of difficulty imagining a soft fellow like Sir Anton scaling that particular fortress, even for love."

Jean-Marc snorted. "What you mean," he said, "is that you can't imagine such a female letting a simpering fool like Sir Anton make the attempt."

"Nay," Kieran murmured thoughtfully, "I doubt that, too. She's not beautiful, of a certainty, but neither is she painful to gaze upon. And her figure is pleasing, i'faith, despite her height. S'truth, Mistress Glenys could do far better for a lover than so delicate a lordling as Sir Anton."

"I little doubt he cares what she looks like," Jean-Marc stated, "or whether her figure is pleasing or no. She's wealthy—*that's* what the scoundrel's thinking of." When his master made no reply, Jean-Marc glanced up at him and asked, "You didn't believe Sir Anton's foolish tale any more than I, did you?"

Kieran shook his head. "I didn't believe a word of it. He was as clear a liar as I've ever set eyes upon."

"Yet you're still determined to take Mistress Glenys away and hold her prisoner in York, waiting for Sir Anton to fetch her?"

"Aye."

Jean-Marc spat on the ground and uttered a sound of unhappiness. "'Tis a fool you are, by God! You risk your neck—*and* mine—only to spite Sir Daman. And to what purpose? Naught that you do to him can give your sister back all that she's lost because of him, or return the joy he took from her."

"Mayhap not," Kieran said softly, his gaze held fast to Mistress Glenys's carriage, most specifically on the coachman and lone manservant, who already began to look weary and bored with their waiting, "but I can make him know misery, as he made Elizabet know it, and I can make him know what 'tis like for his beloved sister to be in the power of another. But never fear, Jean-Marc," he added, glancing at his companion, "I mean Mistress Glenys no harm, and well you know it. Her heart and person will remain untouched and pure— at least until Sir Anton comes to take her away. After that, Daman must worry anew."

Jean-Marc uttered a loud snort. "You? Turn a woman over to a knave who might do her harm?" He laughed. "Never. Not even a woman like that who's tall enough and surely strong enough to bash Sir Anton on his puny head. Gawd's mercy. Tell me another tale, m'lord."

Kieran scowled at his grinning manservant, but said nothing. The truth of it was that Jean-Marc knew him too well. The thought of leaving Mistress Glenys prey to whatever Sir Anton desired—her fortune, gained through forced marriage, most likely—tickled at the edges of what there was of Kieran's small conscience. Not enough, howbeit, to keep him from carrying out the plan Sir Anton had laid before him. The chance at having revenge on Daman Seymour was far too compelling to make Kieran change his mind.

There were few people that he had loved in his life, but among those dear few, and assuredly most prominent, were his parents and brothers and sisters. He was, he supposed, a fortunate bastard, if any man basely born might be called thus. His parents—both mother and father—openly acknowledged him, as did his various grandparents, aunts, uncles and half siblings. Indeed, he knew himself to be well loved by all sides of his family, and had been raised by his stepfather as if he were his natural child. Aye, Kieran was fortunate, especially after his many years of wandering and troublemaking. Time and again his family had rescued him from imprisonment, hanging or worse. Time and again they'd pleaded with him to put his restlessness aside and settle down at the small estate that had been provided for him. And time and again, when he disappointed them, they continued to wait with open arms. He didn't deserve such a family, and certainly not such a long-suffering one. There was only one way in which he was able to make himself worthy, and that was by his loyalty and his own love for them.

This was what drove him to seek revenge against Daman Seymour. Sir Daman, so handsome and celebrated, had caused Kieran's youngest sister, Elizabet, to fall so deeply in love that she had set all of her usual good sense aside. She had believed that Daman would wed her; Kieran knew full well how easy it was to make a sheltered young maiden believe such as that. In her innocence, love and trust, Elizabet had given herself to Daman, and Daman, the accursed knave, had soon thereafter abandoned her, despite knowing that she had conceived his child. Not even the fear of Kieran's powerful stepfather, Lord Randall, had kept the fool from so ignoble a deed, though perhaps Daman had known, and rightly so, that Elizabet's pleading would keep her father from having Daman run to ground and thrown in prison. Shame had done its equal share in convincing Lord Randall to leave the matter be. Elizabet's pregnancy had been well hidden, though that, in the end, hadn't been necessary. Grief over the abandonment of her faithless lover had driven her to illness, and she'd lost the child but a few months after it had been conceived.

That had been five months ago, yet Elizabet remained inconsolable. During the few days Kieran had spent with her at his stepfather's estate, she'd done naught but weep, so wretchedly miserable that Kieran's own heart had felt riven. He'd sworn then that he would repay Daman Seymour for what he'd done to the dearest, sweetest girl on God's earth, and had been searching for a way to fulfill that vow since. Sir Anton and his offer of employ had fallen like a gift into Kieran's lap.

"Aye, you'll never let Sir Anton take Mistress Seymour away," Jean-Marc said with surety. "Especially not once she's fallen in love with you and pleads with you not to abandon her."

"I've abandoned a great many others, despite their pleading," Kieran replied evenly, not contesting the fact that Mistress Glenys Seymour, and her little maid, Dina, as well, would fall in love with him. Women—no matter their age, birth or status—always fell in love with him, and had been doing so since before he'd turned fifteen. It couldn't be helped, only acknowledged and dealt with. He had known when he'd accepted Sir Anton's task that Mistress Glenys's certain passion for him would complicate things. Just as Jean-Marc had said, she would most likely do as others before her and plead with Kieran not to leave her, especially if he held her prisoner in York for more than a few months. But his heart, despite his intense admiration of females in general, had never been swayed by any woman's words, except perhaps for those spoken by his mother and sisters. He was well used to gently turning ardent females aside. It would be an outright falsehood to say that he'd avoided breaking more than a few hearts during his years of wandering, but Kieran had been careful never to leave a woman as Sir Daman Seymour had done, either with child or in such despair that death seemed preferable to life. And Daman's sister was no exception.

Nay, Kieran's revenge must be upon Daman alone, else it was of no value. As to Mistress Glenys, he would keep her safe and comfortable while she was imprisoned in Sir Anton's keep in York, and he would make certain that Sir Anton treated her well afterward, neither forcing her into marriage nor keeping her from her family. As for himself, Kieran would rebuff her declarations of love as gently as he might and do whatever he could to discourage such feelings from the very start.

Fortunately, Mistress Glenys herself would make the task easier. If he'd been attracted to her, Kieran would have found it difficult indeed to keep from seducing her. He'd never fallen in love, but women were assuredly his weakness. Mistress Glenys, however, had the look of a safe woman, which was to say that she wasn't the kind of female Kieran usually preferred. She was…square, he supposed one might say. Angular. It was an odd way to describe a woman, but very apt for Mistress Glenys. And despite the evidence of delightful curves beneath her surcoat, she was also too thin. Unless her clothing possessed some kind of magical powers in hiding what lay beneath, Kieran could detect none of the sweet, soft plumpness that he best loved in his women. Nay, Mistress Glenys was all tallness and bones and strength, a stout, healthy female who looked as if she could put the fear of God into a great many men—though Kieran didn't count himself among them.

"She'll be out soon," he said.

"Aye, in but a few minutes," Jean-Marc agreed. "Very prompt is Mistress Glenys Seymour."

It was true. They'd been watching her, as well as ferreting out information from those who gladly imparted it for gold, for only three days, yet already Kieran knew a great deal about her life—and none of it very exciting. She was twenty years old, almost beyond the acceptable age of marriage, and living with her elderly relatives in one of the stately palaces built on the Strand. She attended Mass with her aunts and uncles each morning, and each afternoon went out into London's center to direct the many Seymour family businesses, always devoting at least one day each week in speaking to their banker, Master Fairchild. Each evening she returned to her grand family dwelling, the main gates shutting firmly behind her, locking her and her family and servants safely inside until the following morn.

He'd seen no visitors arrive in that time, no suitors, no neighbors or acquaintances. In three days nothing about Glenys Seymour's life had varied. Indeed, it had all been so incredibly, unrelentingly dull that Kieran couldn't help but wonder how a young woman—even a serious, modest young woman like Mistress Glenys—could bear it. As well, it wasn't very wise for a wealthy young woman to keep such a regular and expected schedule. She made it almost too easy for kidnappers to take her. He was surprised that no one had tried it before now, for surely her family would willingly pay a large ransom for her return. There was, of course, the thought of the lady's brother, Sir Daman, to dissuade most knaves from even contemplating such a crime. The thought made Kieran smile.

"It's time," he said, casting one last glance at the ever darkening sky overhead.

Jean-Marc nodded and began to unlace the cloak he wore. "I'll be waiting around the corner, then, ready to trade clothes with the coachman."

"And I'll go and fetch him and the manservant," Kieran replied, adding as he walked away, "Don't strike too hard this time, Jean-Marc. I want neither of them hurt. There's no need to rush. We've plenty of time. Everything will go off most easily, I vow. Trust me."

Jean-Marc's low laughter filled the increasingly chilly air, accompanying Kieran as he made his way.

"Hurry, Dina," Glenys said insistently as they made their way out of the building where Master Fairchild kept his banking business. A servant held the large wooden door open for them, bowing as they passed. "I want to be home as soon as we may."

Picking up her skirts, she hurried out to the street toward their waiting carriage. Dina's rapidly following footsteps spurred her on, and Glenys barely cast a glance at their manservant, John, as he opened the door, lowering his head and tugging his forelock.

Despite the brief exchange, Glenys knew at once that something was wrong. But she had already stepped into the carriage before her body responded to what her brain had told her—that John wasn't that tall *or* well-muscled.

"Dina," she said, turning to step back down again, only to have Dina shoved so forcibly inside that they both fell against the seat. Dina screamed loudly in Glenys's ear and clutched at her tightly in panic, making matters worse.

Everything happened so quickly that by the time Glenys had righted both herself and Dina, it was too late. The imposter who'd taken John's place had lifted himself easily into the carriage and shut the door behind him, and the carriage had been set into motion.

"What—!" Glenys uttered.

The man sat in the seat opposite them, pulling a long, sharp, shining knife from beneath the folds of John's tunic—for he wore it over his own clothing—and held it up.

"Be quiet for now, mistress," he said in a calm but commanding tone. "Have no fears, for if you do as I say, no harm will come to you or your maid. If you refuse to obey, I'll make you insensible. And her, as well." He nodded at Dina, who made a gargled, choking sound and promptly fainted on Glenys's shoulder.

"We have no money," Glenys told him, pushing Dina upright with both hands to keep her from sliding to the floor. "I've brought nothing from the bank."

The fiend merely smiled at her—in a ridiculously charming manner that Glenys felt belied the situation entirely.

"I've no care for your money, Mistress Glenys," he replied. "Now heed me, and keep quiet. We'll be at the city gate soon, and then you'll have enough to say. Once we're safe out of London, I'll explain the matter most fully."

"At the city gates, I'll have you—and whoever is driving our carriage—arrested," Glenys vowed angrily. "What have you done with John and Willem? For that is surely not Willem atop. He'd never—"

The stranger held up a staying hand. "They are both well and unharmed. A little tap to the head, I promise you, is all they suffered. I've already arranged for them

to be found and safely returned to Metolius. Have no
fears for them, but for yourself and your maid. I dislike
harming women, but I will do so if I must. We *will* get
through the city gates, either with your aid or without,
though you'll far prefer the outcome if you freely lend
your assistance. Understand me well, Mistress Glenys,
for I mean what I say. I've killed a great many men in
my life, and adding two London guards to the number
will mean very little to me. I suspect, howbeit, that you
would prefer not to be the cause of such bloodshed.
Nay, be still.'' He held up the knife. ''You may speak
as much as you like...later.''

Chapter Three

Glenys folded her arms across her chest, leveled her gaze directly at her abductor and stared. He stared back with that same charming smile on his face, seemingly content to remain silent and match her in a contest of wills.

Glenys's eyes narrowed. He was just the sort of man she despised. Handsome and so assured of his own charms that he thought a mere smile could make a woman melt in adoration. Especially an unattractive female, such as she was. Well, he *was* handsome, she would give him that, perhaps the handsomest man she'd yet set sight upon—and probably as charming as could be—but that mattered for naught. If he believed Glenys would fall prey to such foolish tricks, he was far, far wrong. She'd learned very well how to protect her heart. Ill-favored girls learned that early on, and very quickly.

His eyes were stunningly blue and very clear against the light golden-brown of his overlong hair. His face was aristocratic and finely boned, with a long, aquiline nose and high cheekbones. His mouth—well, Glenys wouldn't let herself dwell upon that particular feature

too long. It was purely sensual, especially smiling at
her in that certain manner. He must have used that
smile to great effect in the past. How foolish he was
to think that Glenys was as simpleminded as so many
other females, though she admitted, grudgingly, it
was...rather unsettling to be looked at just so. She'd
never been smiled at in such a way before, not by any
man, least of all one so well-favored as this thief.

They were well out of London now, several miles,
at least. She'd meant to cry out for help at the city
gate, God's truth she had. But Dina still lay so limply
against her, so entirely vulnerable, and the knave had
secreted his knife with such obvious meaning that
she'd decided it would be best to do as he said for now
and deal with getting rid of him later. Once he realized
that she had no money and that her relatives wouldn't
begin to know how to ransom her—for they had little
practical knowledge of the world, and no knowledge
of how to access their own fortune—he'd let both her
and Dina go. There could surely be nothing else he
wanted, unless it was from Dina. Glenys knew herself
to be thoroughly undesirable, despite the practiced
smiles the rogue was yet sending her way.

And so, resigned to at least obey the man until she
was able to reason with him, Glenys had repeated exactly what he'd told her to say to the guards, and they,
recognizing her, had opened the gates and let them
pass. Almost immediately thereafter Dina had begun to
come to her senses, and Glenys had been busy dealing
with her maid's incoherent fears and fits of weeping
for the next quarter of an hour. Only now had Dina
subsided, reassured by Glenys—and also by the
stranger, though Glenys had bid him to the devil when
he'd spoken—that no harm would come to her. The

younger girl sat, dazed and frightened, with her hands folded in her lap, sniffling and wiping away silent tears. Glenys, certain that she could at last now deal with the matter at hand, crossed her arms over her chest and prepared to reason with their captor. His insolence had held her silent, daring him to speak first, but now that several stubborn moments had passed between them, she at last gave way.

"You will have no money from this venture, I promise you," she told him. "Indeed, you will be fortunate if your only recompense is escaping a fitting punishment at the hands of the king, which would be, most like, nothing less than being drawn and quartered. But you will escape that fate *only* if you cease this venture now, sir. If you do not, I can make no promise that you will evade your just due."

He appeared to be entirely amused at her pronouncement, and nodded at her regally.

"You are kind to think on my safety and well-being, mistress," he said, "but I fear I cannot put an end to this…venture, as you term it…even for the sake of my own life, and that of my companion. I have already accepted payment for the deed and, having done so, I cannot now give way for the sake of my honor, as little of it as I possess."

Glenys's eyes grew round with surprise. "Someone paid you to kidnap me? Who was it? And to what purpose? I tell you there will be no ransom, even if you should threaten to kill me."

His eyebrows rose at this. "Your family holds you far more dearly than you think, mistress. I'm certain they would pay well indeed to secure your return, and most especially to make certain of your life. But you have not been taken for that purpose, for the sake of a ransom. I was hired by your lover, Sir Anton Lagasse, to secret you away and keep you safe in a place where your—"

"*Sir Anton!*" Glenys cried, interrupting him.

Beside her, Dina groaned out loud and said, "Oh, no!"

The stranger regarded them with bemusement. "He isn't your lover?"

Glenys had set a hand to her forehead in distress and briefly closed her eyes. She opened them now and said, far more loudly and irately than she'd meant, "Nay, you God-cursed fool! He's my direst enemy. The very man who means my family naught but ruin and misery."

The knave at last lost his smile. "I'm very sorry then, for 'tis clear that he lied to me about his intentions. But I thought it might be thus, for he seemed a feckless knave. Still, I have taken you as I agreed to do, and will hold you captive until he comes to fetch you."

"Hold me? Until he comes to fetch me for *what?* What lies did he tell you?"

"Sir Anton told me that he is your lover, but that your family refuses to recognize his request for your hand in marriage because they deem him unsuitable. Howbeit, he is shortly to become both landed and more highly titled, and believes that your relatives will thereafter find him acceptable. He fears, however, that you will be forced to marry another before he can attain this goal, and therefore hired me to secret you away at his keep in York, safe from your family, until he can come to claim you in all his splendid glory. I have already admitted that I found the story foolish," the stranger said without shame, "but I had reasons of my own for accepting the task. For those same reasons I will see it through, and we must both set our minds to it.''

"He must have paid you well," Glenys said with disgust, "for, in truth, he has good cause to want me out of his way. And what a fine jest to make himself out as my lover. He must have known you would realize the truth once you set sight upon me.''

To his merit, the thief didn't laugh, as she'd expected him to do. He gazed at her with measured calm and replied, "If this was indeed his thought, then he was far mistaken. I understand what it is that you say, mistress, but you merely prove once more that you realize very little of the truth.''

"I realize perfectly well that no man would claim me as his love unless in jest," Glenys retorted angrily, furious that they even spoke of such things. "Many, however, might be willing to make such a claim for money, and as that is the heart of this matter, then I pray we speak of it now. Clearly and plainly. Sir Anton paid you well, but I can pay you far more. What amount will you require to stop this foolishness and release us? I vow, upon my honor, that I'll make payment and let you go peaceably on your way. I'll say nothing of the matter to anyone, and will make certain that John and Willem are silent, as well. Only stop the carriage now and we'll speak terms.''

"I'm sorry to be so disobliging, Mistress Glenys," he said, "but no amount of gold could cause me to turn this task aside. Apart from Sir Anton's desires, I have reasons of my own for taking and holding you, as I have already said. Mayhap we should begin again. Let me introduce myself to you. My name is Kieran FitzAllen, and I am pleased to be known to you, Mistress Glenys and Mistress Dina." He sat forward and regally bowed his head.

Glenys wished she had something to bash him with in that vulnerable moment, but there was nothing to be had. She threw her hands up in the air, instead, in a gesture of the fury she felt. "I care not who you are, idiot knave! How can I make you see reason? Sir Anton will not come to fetch me. He has sent you on a fool's errand only to keep me out of his path."

Kieran FitzAllen's gaze sharpened.

"Then why would he hire me, if not at least to try to force you to wife? Even if he is not your lover, do you not think it likely that he desires your fortune?"

"'Tis no fortune of gold that he desires," Glenys told him, "but a treasure that rightly belongs to the Seymours. He seeks to find this treasure, which has been lost to us, before I can do so."

"Ah," her kidnapper said with sudden understanding, "the Greth Stone. Is that what we speak of?"

Glenys was so surprised he knew of it that she was momentarily stunned into silence. Beside her, Dina stiffened and whispered fearfully, "He knows, m'lady! He's in league with Sir Anton!"

"Nay, that I am not," Kieran FitzAllen said at once, directing his attention to Dina as he strove to allay her fears. "Sir Anton's reasons for having your mistress taken and held are as nothing to me, though I admit they provided me with the opportunity for doing so. I know of the Greth Stone because he warned me that Mistress Glenys would resist being taken for the sake of her own quest to regain it." He looked at Glenys. "In this matter, at least, 'tis clear he spoke the truth."

"Not the truth, but cleverly enough," Glenys admitted, her spirits sinking by the moment. Each sentence that passed in their conversation set an ever increasing distance between them and London. The carriage rattled along at an alarmingly brisk pace, and the sky grew ever more dark with storm clouds. Her aunts and uncles would begin to worry if she didn't return soon. Or perhaps not, she reasoned, as they seemed to have known that she would not be returning to Metolius anytime soon. The memory of their parting made Glenys inwardly groan. Why couldn't they just *tell* her outright when these things were going to happen? Why did everything always have to be such a mystery?

"Please," she begged, "listen to me, sir, and understand what I say. The Greth Stone is naught but a very old ring, passed through many generations of my family, from as far back as Roman times. It bears no great value save to the Seymours, and only for the sake of sentiment. But there are some who say that it possesses mystical powers, and despite the foolishness of such a claim, there are many more who believe it. Sir Anton is among them. The ring was stolen from our London home, Metolius, while we were gone to our family estate in Wales from Michaelmas until Twelfth Day. The man who stole it is...well, that doesn't matter. What matters is that I know who he is, and 'twas my intention to set out next month in order to search the thief out and reclaim the ring. Sir Anton knew of my plans and has clearly determined that he must stop me."

"He means to find Caswallan before you do, eh?" Kieran FitzAllen asked. Again, Glenys was stunned.

"He *told* you of Caswallan?" she asked, utterly amazed. "God's mercy, but Sir Anton Lagasse must be a greater fool than I had believed." She looked at her captor more closely. "You *are* in league with him, aren't you? You must be, to do his bidding in this fruitless matter."

"I am only concerned with Sir Anton because he hired me to kidnap and hold you, mistress. There is nothing more. I have no interest in your Greth Stone, whether it exists or has magical powers."

"Of a certainty it has no magical powers," Glenys said, scoffing. "'Tis naught but a very old ring of little value. But I will not allow Sir Anton to hold aught that belongs to my family. He sees himself as a conjurer, possessed of great skill, and believes the Greth Stone will make him the more powerful."

At this, the knave finally laughed, throwing his head back and showing teeth that were white and even. Glenys noted, much to her aggravation, that even in mirth he was almost too handsome to look at.

"Sir Anton!" he declared, grinning widely. "A skilled conjurer? I vow, 'tis too much to bear!" He laughed again, fully amused. "By the rood, he seemed more like a well-dressed mouse than so powerful a man." He laughed all the harder.

Glenys frowned darkly. "It matters not what he may seem to be, but only that he has succeeded in keeping me from reaching Caswallan first. I tell you, Sir Anton must not be allowed to get the Greth Stone in his grasp. There will be no chance for my family to regain it if it falls to him. You *must* end this foolishness now and let us go!"

He sobered only slightly, enough to stop laughing and say, grinning, "Nay, that I cannot do."

"But why?" she demanded. "Now that you know 'tis but a fool's errand, you have no cause to continue! I have already said that I will pay you far more than

Sir Anton promised. And surely you must realize that regardless of what he has already paid, there will be no more. He'll not keep his word and come to fetch me. I'faith, 'twill be far more likely that we'll be greeted by worse knaves than you and your accomplice at some point upon our journey, set upon killing us all.''

Kieran FitzAllen looked at her with pure disbelief. "How so? Sir Anton has no reason to want you dead, even if all you say is true, and a less likely murderer I've e'er set sight upon."

"Then you are naught but a fool," Glenys said. "Sir Anton knows that I will not cease in exposing him for the deceiver he is, and for that alone he would gladly have me dead. And he would care nothing for any other deaths that might occur for the sake of being rid of me, yours included."

It was clear by the look on Kieran FitzAllen's face that he didn't believe a word she said. He merely sighed aloud and stated, "Sir Anton would find it difficult to kill me, I vow, and you as well, while you are beneath my care. I am not a knight of the realm, but I've matched a goodly share of them in singular battle before now and come away the winner. I have no fear of any man, and most assuredly not of one the likes of Sir Anton Lagasse."

Though she wished it were not so, Glenys had to admit that the man sitting opposite her looked fully capable of besting any number of skilled fighting men; he was well-muscled and moved with a certain ease and grace that might give him an advantage over lesser men.

"Perhaps not of Sir Anton," she said, "but you would be foolish not to consider that among my relatives are those who would fill you with fear. My brother being foremost. He is Sir Daman Seymour, and I think it unlikely that you have not heard of him, or of his skills. But if you have not, I tell you now that he is a famed knight of the realm who is well able to mete out justice to such a one as you.''

The charming smile was back on Kieran FitzAllen's face. Glenys longed to wipe it away.

''I am aware of who your brother is, Mistress Glenys.''

''Then you must likewise be aware that he and his men will come after me the moment he hears of what you have done. No matter how secret your hiding place may be, Daman will find me, and he will deal out a punishment to you and your friend that will have you praying for salvation.''

Kieran FitzAllen uttered a bark of laughter. ''You speak out of love and honor, mistress,'' he said, ''but surely such words sound as foolish to your ears as they do to mine. In truth, 'tis my prayer that Sir Daman Seymour follows our track and finds us. Soon. I cherish the thought of meeting him face-to-face.''

Glenys's mouth dropped open again.

''You cannot mean what you say,'' she murmured. ''My brother will kill you when he finds you. I do not speak falsely. He *will* kill you.''

''He may try.''

Glenys shook her head. ''This has naught to do with Sir Anton, then, just as you said. 'Tis because of Daman that you have done this thing. But why? Have you some quarrel with my brother? But, nay, you cannot. Daman has no enemies, save those that are also the enemies of my family, such as Sir Anton and Caswallan. But you are not in league with them, or so you have said. Why, then, should you wish to draw Daman's certain wrath down upon yourself?''

"My reasons are my own, mistress, and will remain so. Now you understand at least in part why I will not let you go, and 'twould be best if you accept and reconcile yourself to it. My servant, Jean-Marc, who drives the coach, and I will bring you no harm, nor your maid. 'Tis only our intention to hold you until either Sir Anton or your brother—or perhaps both—have come to fetch you. Until that time, be pleased to give me no trouble, I pray, for you'll not escape me. As it may be that we shall be in company for some few weeks, I believe that we should all try to be as merry and comfortable as possible.''

"Sir," said Glenys, sitting back with complete exasperation, "you are a lackwit if you believe that my maid or I shall do any like thing. You have taken us as prisoners, and as such we cannot be merry and comfortable.''

He gave her a certain look out of his blue eyes, so filled with blatant sensuality that it made her skin tingle. 'Twas clearly well practiced, and she wasn't sure whether he answered out of truth or simply out of habit when he replied, in a low, seductive tone, "Even the most unpleasant situation can be made merry and comfortable, Mistress Glenys. I have had the experience many times, I vow.''

His meaning was so clear that Glenys's face flamed hot. If she hadn't already known full well that he was merely teasing—for such a man would never truly be attracted to a woman like her—she had no doubt that she would have melted into a puddle at his feet. God's mercy, he was most clearly a practiced seducer as well as a thief and blackguard. She had no fears for herself, but her maid was another matter. Dina was young and pretty, with the kind of blond hair and blue eyes that men favored among women. She would very likely be a target for Kieran FitzAllen, though he'd yet to look at her more than twice. Glenys would have to take extra care that no harm came to the girl, who was as dear as a sister to her.

For her part, Dina seemed not yet to have taken much note of their captor, much to Glenys's relief. The very last thing she needed was for Dina to fall in love with the man, which was doubtless what most other females did upon setting sight on him. Dina merely sniffled and wiped her nose and murmured, with her head lowered, "Master Aonghus and Master Culain, and your aunts. What will become of them when you don't return to Metolius? There's no one there to watch over them."

Glenys had been thinking much the same thing, now that it was clear her captor could not be reasoned with. She looked him fully in the face, asking, "Aye, what of my elderly relatives? They are not used to being alone, without someone to care for them."

He gave a thoughtful frown. "But were you not going to leave them soon, when you went on your quest to search out the Greth Stone?"

"Nay, I should never do so. I had already arranged that my cousin, Helen, would come and stay with them while I was gone, but she'll not be arriving for three weeks more, at the very least. Now they will be alone, with little idea of how to go on."

"Hmm." He placed a long, beautifully shaped finger against his chin and was silent for a moment, clearly thinking this through. Glenys was surprised that he even cared enough to consider the matter. At last, he lowered his hand and said, "If I can devise a way to send this cousin of yours a missive so that you can ask her to come to Metolius at once, will you give me your vow not to secret some message into it about who has taken you and in what direction we are journeying?"

"Nay," Glenys said before she could think, too angry to do otherwise, "I make you no promises."

"But, mistress!" Dina cried. "You must do so, lest some harm come to your aunts and uncles. There is no other way."

Glenys knew it was so, and felt unfathomably foolish. "Very well, aye," she said tightly, flinging off the comforting hand Dina attempted to set upon her arm. "I give you my vow. If you can arrange such a missive, though I doubt you can do so."

His handsome face held that infuriatingly amused look once more. "I have many friends, mistress," he said, "as you will soon discover."

Glenys looked at him sharply. "So faithful that they would lower themselves to lend you their aid in this heinous crime?"

He nodded. "Aye."

"Very fine," she replied angrily, crossing her arms over her chest and looking out the window. It was dark now, and a soft rain had begun to fall, splattering lightly through the arched opening. If it fell much harder, they would be forced to use the window coverings, and would be shut in together in darkness. That was an unhappy thought. But it couldn't be helped. None of this could be helped. She could only do as he had suggested and accept what had befallen her, and pray that the small white stone in her pocket didn't begin glowing. After all that had just passed, Glenys was in no mood to explain it, or anything about her family, to her wretched captor.

Chapter Four

Kieran knew that he shouldn't have used his well-honed wiles on his captive, especially after he'd vowed not to seduce her. He'd done so more out of habit than anything else, but that gave him little excuse. He shouldn't have spoken to her in so dallying a manner, and would strive not to do so again.

But Mistress Glenys made it hard.

Her face was, indeed, just as he'd thought earlier, quite angular. Perhaps not as square as he'd believed, but possessed of the same intriguing angles and fine lines that a perfectly cut diamond might possess. Not beautiful, nay, but utterly fascinating. He couldn't stop looking at her. Emotions played themselves out along her long, straight cheekbones and in her intelligent, wide-set gray eyes and high, arching eyebrows. And such emotions they were! Anger, frustration, rage—even outright dislike, which Kieran wasn't used to seeing directed at himself. Aye, Mistress Glenys Seymour was a woman worth looking at. Far more interesting in expression and manner, and most certainly in speech, than most women he met. It was a pity that the maid, Dina, was so commonly pretty in her looks, else he might have been able to set his interest upon her. But she looked very like the hundreds of other blond, blue-eyed maidens he'd flirted with in the past dozen years, so much so that Kieran doubted he could pick one from the other if they'd all been lined up in a row.

A man would never have that problem with Mistress Glenys. Even now, as she was gazing out the window, aggravation stamped on every feature, the dwindling light, being rapidly swallowed by the imminent storm, teased the curves and angles of her face, bringing ephemeral shadows to life and causing her gray eyes to appear almost black. Her generous mouth—perhaps her only soft feature—was pressed together in a tight line, and a few strands of her sunset-colored hair had come loose from the braids atop her head, feathering lightly against her cheeks.

"'Twill not be long now before we stop," he said, wishing that he might be able to tell her something else. The rain, which had begun to fall softly now, would make their journey far more unpleasant this night than he'd hoped. In a more positive light, it would also help to cover their trail.

"Good," she replied tightly, not looking at him. "It appears that we will be obliged to lower the window covers soon. That will give us opportunity to do so."

"Aye," he agreed. "'Twould be wisest to do so before returning the carriage to London. I should hate to see such finery ruined by wet." He ran one hand appreciatively over the red velvet covering the heavily cushioned seat. For a town carriage that wasn't meant for travel of any great distance, 'twas both fine and comfortable. True, there wasn't any glass in the windows, but the heavily waxed window coverings would do just as well for keeping occupants dry in a storm.

"Return the carriage?" Mistress Glenys asked, looking at him in the singular manner she'd displayed over the past half hour, which said, quite clearly, that she thought him mad. "What can you mean?"

Even as she spoke, Jean-Marc began to draw the carriage to one side of the road, bouncing them over small rocks and bumps as he drove into a copse of trees. Leaning toward the window, Kieran whistled in greeting to a man who appeared there, already leading a pair of horses from their hiding place.

Jean-Marc brought the carriage to an unsteady halt. Even before it had fully stopped Kieran opened the door and alighted, looking up first to where Jean-Marc sat to make certain all was well.

"No one followed," Jean-Marc called down to him, tying the leads to the carriage post. "Had a bit of company, but that's what comes from being on a main road." He lightly hopped down from the driver's seat. "Better hurry if we want to reach Bostwick's before many more hours."

"Aye, and without being found out," Kieran agreed. Overhead, a loud rumble of thunder rolled across the sky, and the next moment the rain began to fall harder. It wasn't a deluge yet, but that would happen soon enough. He stretched a hand into the carriage and said, "Hurry, now. We must be on our way."

Mistress Glenys gave him a look filled with furious disbelief. "You can't mean to…to ride on horseback in this *rain?*"

"'Tis just what I mean," he told her, impatiently holding his hand more firmly out to her. "Come, mistress. We've a distance to cover before we're safe away. Set your headcover about you, if you have one, and your maid as well."

"We have none!" she cried angrily. "We had no plan to travel far beyond Metolius this day."

"Then you must brave the rain as best you can. Thank a merciful God you had the sense to bring your heavy cloaks." Behind him, he could hear Jean-Marc and Tom Postleheth readying the steeds for riding. Kieran cast one glance at them, saying, "Give Tom his gold, Jean-Marc, and let him be on his way." Turning back to Glenys, he stated, "Come of your own will, mistress, or I will drag you from this carriage. I vow it before God."

Suiting action to word, he leaned in to grasp her arm. She shoved him violently away before he could make his grip firm.

"Do not touch me *or* my maid," she commanded in a tone so regal that Kieran could not countermand it, not even with one of his famous smiles. *"Ever,"* she added stiffly. Gathering her skirts, she spoke with equal sharpness to her maid, who had begun to weep again. "Come, Dina. I suppose we must make the best of this wretchedness, even if we take chill from the rain and die of it." She descended from the carriage, head held high, refusing to accept Kieran's steadying hand, right into the rain. Kieran didn't realize that he was staring at her as she stepped away until the maid, Dina, cleared her throat and set her tiny hand upon his arm. Coming to himself, Kieran helped her descend.

It took but a few brief moments to fix the window coverings on the carriage and settle matters with Tom—good, proper thief that he was. Kieran made certain that he knew where to leave the carriage along the road, near London, hopefully before being discovered. The two menservants, John and Willem, would have been found in the alley where they'd been left and safely delivered back to Metolius by now, and the Seymour family would have alerted the London sheriff. An entire party of rescuers might already be on their trail, but Kieran believed they'd be able to evade them, and once they made Bostwick's, they'd be well and safe.

"There are only two horses," Mistress Glenys stated amid the rumblings of more thunder, pulling her heavy cape more closely about her. She had no hood, and the rain had begun to soak her hair, so that the wayward tendrils he'd admired earlier clung to her cheeks. The maid was faring somewhat better, for Jean-Marc had lifted his own cloak to cover her. Kieran would have done the same for Mistress Glenys—knowing full well that she wouldn't have allowed it—but she was a tall female, coming up past his shoulders, and the attempt would have proved fruitless.

"Aye, just two," he told her, taking her shoulder in a firm grasp that she couldn't shake off. "You will ride with me, mistress. Come."

She gave no fight, clearly realizing that it would do her no good now, but let him lead her to where his great destrier stood waiting.

"'Tis a very large, fine horse for so sorry a knave," she stated, setting her hand upon the wet pommel as if she could possibly lift herself up into the saddle without aid.

"Aye, but he is mine, nonetheless." Kieran bent, folding his hands together to give her a boost up. "His name is Nimrod," he said, easily tossing Mistress Glenys upward and moving so that she could swing her legs about to sit in the saddle. As he wiped his wet hands against his leggings, he added, "My father named him that apurpose before giving him to me, which you will doubtless believe wise." He swung up into the saddle behind her, reaching forward at once to take hold of the reins. He was glad that she hadn't attempted an escape. It would have been fruitless, of course, but also unpleasant and a waste of time.

"Your father recognizes you, then?" she asked, her tone more one of disdain than curiosity. She had taken note of the "Fitz" in his name, knowing that it branded him as either bastard-born or descended of a bastard, and was purposefully stating the fact out loud in order to give him insult. Or so it seemed to Kieran, but the matter of his birth and family had ever been his sorest spot. She could hardly have aimed any arrow more accurately.

"I am well recognized," he told her tautly, waiting for Dina and Jean-Marc to mount their steed before setting Nimrod into motion, "by *all* my family. It can be more of a burden, at times, than a blessing."

She gave a mirthless laugh and muttered, "Aye, 'tis so."

Kieran set one arm firmly about her, holding the reins with the other, and gently prodded Nimrod forward, away from the road and farther into the trees. Water dripped from the leaves, soaking them, and the wind began to blow even more coldly.

"Where do we go?" Mistress Glenys asked, holding herself as stiffly as a statue within the circle of his arm. Despite that, and despite the heavy cloak and clothing she wore, she was unmistakably female, warm against the front of him and clean-scented and far more soft—delightfully so—than he'd initially believed. He tightened his hold with gentle pressure, and felt her draw in a breath.

"To a place some miles away."

A low, wet branch brushed against her face, and with a sound of aggravation she thrust it aside.

"Are there no decent roads leading to it, or must you take us only to such dens of iniquity as exist far out of the reach of civil establishment?"

That tone of hers, so proper and rigid and filled with disapproval, made him smile. It reminded him greatly of his mother during one of the many lectures she'd given Kieran over the past years.

"'Tis warm and dry, and that is what will concern us most once we reach it. And, nay, we will take no roads for some while. The rain will cover our tracks well enough, but I'll take no chances till we're well away."

Another branch slapped at them, and another clap of thunder sounded overhead. The rain began to pour heavily, and the late afternoon grew dark as night. It was altogether a miserable time to be out in the elements, and Kieran couldn't help but feel a twinge of guilt at dragging two innocent females far from shelter. When Mistress Glenys pushed her wet, straggly hair off her even wetter face, that guilt increased.

"We're going to a tavern where the innkeeper, a fellow by the name of Bostwick, is a friend of mine," he said, not certain why he offered the information. "'Tis not a particularly fine place, but there will be a fire to keep you warm and a roof to keep you dry. If fortune favors us, there may even be a private chamber where you and your maid can find a few hours of peace in which to sleep, though I will admit..."

She turned her head slightly toward him. "What?" she asked, her voice filled with suspicion.

"Well, 'tis merely that Bostwick's is often filled with much merrymakng. 'Tis far more likely to be loud and cheerful rather than given to any peace, though we must pray 'tis not so this night.''

"Merciful God," she said dismally, rubbing a hand over her eyes. "It could not become worse than it already is. Please God. It cannot."

It was worse. Much, much worse. Glenys stood in the midst of the hovel that Kieran FitzAllen had brought them to and stared about her with utter dismay. It was a filthy, crude, poorly built dwelling that looked as if it might collapse beneath the weight of the ongoing storm at any moment. The large chamber they stood in was filled with heavy smoke, foul odors and so many loud, coarse, drunken people that there was scarce room to move, and certainly nowhere among the many tables to sit. Glenys had never seen—or smelled—anything to compare. In the farthest, dimly lit corner she could make out, beyond the thick, stale smoke, the figures of two people engaging in an act of intimacy that Glenys knew full well the church demanded should be undertaken only in private and by a lawfully wedded man and wife. That the pair drew very little attention made it quite clear that this particular crowd was well used to such public displays. In truth, the sudden arrival of Kieran FitzAllen and his accomplice drew far more attention and reaction.

They had but just arrived, and the tavern came to life with shouts of greeting and drunken, earsplitting cheers of glad tidings. A sea of arms and smiling faces surged upon them, sweeping Glenys and Dina aside in order to embrace the two knaves who stood just behind them. The body smells and fumes of ale and bitter wine that followed nearly made Glenys swoon. She looked down at Dina, who had gripped her hand, and saw that the girl was deathly white. Glenys set an arm about her shoulders and drew her closer, striving to protect her from the jostling crowd.

In the midst of it all, she could hear Kieran Fitz-Allen's voice booming merrily, returning each greeting as if these filthy creatures were his dearest friends, each and every one. Women, especially, were rushing at him—crude, ill-dressed females with unbound hair and the look of harlots, which was, Glenys knew, most likely what they were. She didn't have to watch to know how happily he received their particular greetings.

"Now," a great, loud voice boomed over the din, causing the entire dwelling to shake, "here are my lads, come at last! Make way! Make way!"

"God save us," Dina murmured, her voice quavering. "'Tis a giant."

"Nay," Glenys said, but it was a lie. The man coming toward them *was* a giant. A great, black-headed, swarthy giant, whose substantial girth was almost equal to his tremendous height. His arms were so long and heavily muscled that he looked as if he could squeeze a great tree and split it into tiny, crumbling bits.

"Bostwick!" Kieran FitzAllen greeted in return, pushing his way through the swarm of dirty bodies surrounding him and embracing the giant just as warmly and heartily as the giant embraced him. "Well met! God above, 'tis good to see you again!"

"Aye, and ye, ye great rogue!" Bostwick pounded him on the shoulder until Kieran nearly doubled over from the force. "And Jean-Marc, as well, ye damned rascal!" He picked the smaller, towheaded man up off the floor and shook him playfully. Jean-Marc flopped like a child's doll. "How are ye, lad?" He set Jean-

Marc down so suddenly that he collapsed upon the rushes. "And here are the lovely captives, brought to me for safekeeping, eh?" He turned to grin down at Glenys and Dina.

"Oh, m-m-mistress!" Dina sputtered, shrinking against Glenys and trembling mightily.

"Hush, Dina." Glenys held her more closely and glared up at the giant. "I'll not let him so much as set a finger to you, I vow." She meant it, too, though she was just as afeard of the huge man. He was approaching them with open arms, as if he intended to scoop the both of them up into a ferocious embrace.

"Gently, Bostwick," Kieran FitzAllen said, stepping forward to stop the giant before he reached them. "These are indeed the prisoners I sent word of, and I pray you've readied a suitable chamber for them. They are ladies of good family, as you can see, and not used to such rough peasants as we are. If you greet them too closely, they are like to swoon, merely from the foul smell of you, by the rood." He laughed aloud at his own jest, and all those surrounding him laughed, too, Bostwick louder than the rest.

"Aye, ye speak well, Kieran, ye great rogue. And what good would these pretty prisoners be to us if they faint away, eh?" All present laughed again.

It was a fine jest, Glenys thought bitterly, knowing full well just what she and Dina looked like. They were sopping wet from crown to sole, their hair and clothing limp and bedraggled after more than three hours riding upon horseback through a raging storm. They were weary and hungry and chilled to the bone. All in all, they probably looked as uncomely and unappealing as two wet mongrels. If not Dina, then certainly herself.

"Well, they do look as if a tiny breath might knock

them down, wet and weary as they're like to be," Bostwick said thoughtfully, surveying Glenys and Dina with a knowing gaze. "'Tis a pity they must be fine ladies, for they will give ye much trouble on your journey, my friend."

"Doubtless, this is so," Kieran agreed with a sigh.

"But naught can be done about it, I suppose," said Bostwick. "We must all take what fortune falls our way, is that not so, my friends?"

The surrounding crowd cheered the words drunkenly. Two of the more attractive women among them had attached themselves to either side of Kieran FitzAllen, Glenys noted, and another had draped herself lovingly about Jean-Marc's smaller person. Neither man appeared to be distressed by such brazen possession. In truth, they appeared well pleased.

"Bring them over to the fire, then, and let us have a better look at such fine, rich prisoners," Bostwick commanded in his booming voice. "Mayhap they'll be more seemly once their color has returned, and they have some ale and bread in their bellies. Gently now, lads," he instructed sharply as Glenys and Dina were poked and pushed and prodded toward the huge, heavily smoking hearth. "They don't want such rough handling as you'll give them. Margie, girl, leave Kieran aside a moment and fetch our guests some ale and victuals."

Despite Bostwick's words, rough hands grabbed at them, and Glenys felt a sharp tug at the small leather pouch Uncle Aonghus had given her, which was yet tied on her girdle. Without thinking, she turned about and soundly slapped the man who'd dared to touch her. He reeled back, a hand held to his reddened cheek, and stared at her in momentary shock. Then he growled in fury and charged forward. Glenys scarce had time to blink before Kieran FitzAllen was in front of her, shoving the man back.

"Calm yourself, Hiram, and give me no trouble," he said in a warning tone as the noise of the tavern began to die away. "These women have no gold upon them, nor anything of value. All of you, listen to me well." He lifted his voice and looked about. "They're not to be touched, nor robbed. They are in my care and I'll not suffer them to be harmed in any way. If I should hear aught—even the smallest complaint—I vow I will deal with the culprit myself." He turned abruptly and pointed to another man, shorter and stouter than the first, who had begun to move to the back of the crowd. "Coll of Chester, come you back. Now."

The smaller man shuffled slowly back, already putting his hand in the pocket of the coarse tunic he wore. When Kieran FitzAllen held out his hand, the man placed what he'd stolen into it—the small white, glowing stone. Seeing it, Glenys gasped and pressed her hand into her inner pocket, feeling, with intense relief, that the valuable chess piece was yet safely within.

"'Twas only a rock," the man said sullenly. "Naught more."

"A rock, by the rood!" Bostwick exclaimed, laughing as he gazed down at the small, smooth white stone in Kieran's palm. "'Tis the truth you speak, Kieran, my friend. They've naught of value upon them if the flame-haired wench carries rocks about. A tiny little rock, by God!" He laughed again, and the crowd laughed, as well, regaining their loud merriment.

Kieran turned to Glenys and set the stone in her trembling hand. She was faint with gladness that it hadn't begun to glow, and quickly shoved it back into her pocket to join the druid queen. God help her, but what would have happened if anyone had seen the stone glowing, or the ancient chess piece, with its lively eyes? How could she ever have explained to these thieves—aye, most especially to Kieran FitzAllen—what they were and why they seemed to possess such magic?

The touch of Kieran FitzAllen's warm hand upon her cheek caused her to look back up at him. He was gazing down at her, his blue eyes possessing a measure of concern.

"You tremble," he stated. She could scarce deny it. "There is naught to be afraid of. I'll let no one bring harm to either you or your maid."

"No one save you," she muttered, then was sorry for it. He was a knave and a fiend, but he was their only protection in this hellish den, and he had meant to reassure her. "We are cold and weary," she said more calmly. "The fire here smokes far more than it gives heat, and these people...these friends of yours..."

"Aye?" His eyebrows rose. All about them the noisy crowd chattered and laughed and jostled one another.

"Is there no place where Dina and I can be left in peace?" she asked more softly, lest one of them should overhear and become angered. Already she could see Bostwick striving to get close enough to listen to what they said. "You mentioned that a room may have been readied. Can we not go there now, Dina and me?" She would plead with him, if she must.

"You should sit by the fire for a while first," Kieran told her, "and dry yourselves. And eat."

Glenys shook her head. "'Twould do us far more

good to lie down, if we could but have some blankets to warm us. And cannot some food and drink be brought to us there? Please," she said, searching his face for some measure of softening, "I beg this of you. You cannot think we would be comfortable here."

He glanced about at his comrades, clearly unable to understand such a sentiment. It occurred to Glenys that Kieran FitzAllen and his servant, Jean-Marc, were looking forward to spending the coming hours drinking and eating and making merry with these people.

"You need not come with us," she said quickly, touching his arm. He looked down to where her fingers rested upon his sleeve. "Dina and I will be content with our own company. You and Jean-Marc must stay here and be as merry as you please with your...your good fellows."

His eyes were fixed upon her hand for a long moment, then he at last lifted his gaze to hers.

"But I do not know if I can trust you, Mistress Glenys, not to try for an escape while Jean-Marc and I take our ease. Though 'twould be foolish indeed for you to make such an attempt, for 'tis wet and muddy without and you know not where you are. But I do not doubt you would try to rid yourselves of us even by such means."

He was right, of course. Glenys did plan to escape as soon as she might, but even she wasn't so foolish as to try such a thing in the dead of night and in the midst of a storm.

"If I give you my oath that we'll make no attempt to escape this night, will you allow us to retire?"

He looked at her consideringly. "You would make such a vow?"

"Aye, and readily."

Nearby, Bostwick boomed, "What keeps ye there in conversation, Kieran, lad? Ye have many a day to speak to yer lady prisoners. The ale has been brought. Come to the fire!"

Kieran was obliged to shout above the din in answer. "A moment, Bostwick!"

"What's amiss?" Jean-Marc's blond head suddenly appeared, at about the same height as his master's shoulder. The younger man held a tankard of ale, which he offered to Dina, but the maid silently shook her head and turned away.

"Naught," Kieran replied to him, holding Glenys's gaze. "Go and tell Bostwick that our prisoners wish to retire now, and that we will take them to the chamber that has been readied for them if he'll but lead the way."

Glenys released an unsteady breath. "I am grateful, Master FitzAllen."

He smiled and gave a shake of his head. "Wait until you see the chamber that has been prepared for you before saying such as that, Mistress Glenys," he advised. "If I know Bostwick, he has cleared away the small room that his whores use to be private with whoever pays for their skills. 'Tis like to be such a place that you may pray to be here beside the smoking hearth, instead."

"It could not be worse than this," Glenys said, then grew hot with embarrassment to think that she had spoken the same words earlier.

Kieran laughed as Bostwick arrived at his side to escort them to the chamber.

"We will pray it is so, mistress. Come." Kieran set a hand beneath her elbow. "Let us see for ourselves."

Chapter Five

It was far better than Kieran ever would have expected. He'd never realized that Bostwick had such a clean, fine chamber hidden away. It was on the other side of the main tavern, so that the noise of the place could yet be heard, but otherwise it seemed as distant as the moon.

'Twas a small room, Kieran granted as he walked the course of it, but swept clean of all filth and made ready for their arrival with pallets, a table, two chairs and three candles, which Bostwick promptly lit. The small hearth, which was set near the chamber's equally small window, glowed warmly, chasing away the dark night's chill.

"''Twill never dry ye as well as the larger fire in the tavern," Bostwick told the two shivering women, waving a hand at the hearth, "but there are blankets there on the beds, and ye may undress yourselves and be warmed as ye please." He ignored Dina's moan of utter dismay. "Set yer clothes by the fire and they'll be a bit drier by morn, mayhap. 'Twould be best if ye'd let us set them by the larger fire."

Kieran looked to see what Mistress Glenys's opinion of this would be, and wasn't disappointed.

Her face, white with exhaustion, cold and hunger, brightened with two spots of anger. She lifted her strong chin and said, in a tone worthy of a queen, "We would far rather throw ourselves *into* the fire, sir, than give our only clothing into the hands of such disreputable villains, most especially in this unsavory establishment. *Your* establishment, Master Bostwick, which 'tis clear suits you full well but suits us *not at all*." She spit out the last three words so precisely that there could be no misunderstanding of her complete disapproval of both Bostwick and his tavern. "Aside from that truth, Master Bostwick, our garments would reek of smoke come morn, and would be unbearable to wear in the presence of honest folk. I have no doubt that you and your kind welcome it readily enough, smelling very much the like at all times." She finished this speech by gifting him with a look of utter disdain.

Kieran had to smother a laugh at his comrade's astonished expression. God's teeth, what a tongue-lashing! Poor old Bostwick had doubtless never heard the like.

"God's blessed feet," Bostwick murmured, staring at Glenys with awe, as if she were, in truth, a queen. "Ye have brought real ladies to me, Kie, my lad. True and proper ladies. We've never seen their kind in my humble tavern, and that I vow before God. Well." He set a massive hand to his chin and rubbed thoughtfully. "Ye must be content then, m'lady, to wear damp clothes come the morn, if that is how ye'll have it."

"It is," was Mistress Glenys's frosty reply.

This only impressed Bostwick the more. He flushed and made an awkward half bow. "We'll leave ye in peace, then, m'lady. I'll have one of the girls bring food and drink to ye here. 'Twill be the best we have, and of that ye may be certain.'' He seemed eager now to somehow gain her good opinion. ''And none of the rogues within—save Kie and Jean-Marc—will enter this chamber without yer leave. I'll have no one molest such fine ladies in my humble tavern, by God. Ye may rest easy about that, m'lady.''

Having given these promises, Bostwick bowed his way out of the room, bumping into the wall before finding the open door.

''Now see how you've frightened poor Bostwick, Mistress Glenys,'' Kieran mockingly chided. ''For shame.''

She was clearly of no like mind to make jest, for she replied, sighing, ''Please leave, Master FitzAllen, and take your manservant with you. We are most weary, and you will be eager to be in company with your friends.''

Kieran nodded, knowing that she spoke the truth. She and the maid were worn to the bone.

''You'll be safe, just as Bostwick promised. I'll let no man enter here during the night—save us. You and Mistress Dina may rest easily.''

Her brow furrowed. ''There will be no need for you to enter,'' she said, releasing Dina, who moved to the nearest pallet to collapse upon it with a low groan. Jean-Marc unlaced his cloak and moved to set it over the shivering girl. Dina shook her head and pushed it back to him, clearly not willing to accept such kindness from one of their captors. ''I have given you my vow that we will not attempt to escape this night.''

Kieran gave his attention to inspecting one of the

two chairs in the room, placing a hand upon the back of it and determining how sound it was.

"We must sleep, as well, mistress," he said. "You would not deny us the comfort of these pallets, which have been made ready for us."

With exact timing and skill, he slowly lifted his gaze just as he spoke the last word, making his expression perfect. He'd practiced for many years how best to melt the hearts of women. Mistress Glenys might prove to be one of the most difficult subjects he'd had, but surely even she couldn't withstand this particular blue-eyed onslaught. He spoke in his most pleading tone, with a certain look—half innocent, half naughty—that had slain the most determined females in both England and France. Even his mother, a woman as formidable as his high-born prisoner, hadn't been able to withstand it.

But Mistress Glenys Seymour did.

Much to Kieran's consternation, she wrinkled her nose at him as if he were purely distasteful and said, "I see no reason why you cannot share the tavern with your friends, either in pleasure or in slumber. Surely they will give way within some hours, and either faint from too much drink or be driven off for lack of money to gamble with." Her gray eyes narrowed. "And I doubt that the women to be had here will allow you to depart their company so easily, most especially for mere sleep. You and your manservant will be far too busy this night to return to this simple chamber, Kieran FitzAllen. There will be naught to offer here save dull slumber."

For the first time in many a year, Kieran knew a much hated sensation in the presence of a female. It went beyond anger or aggravation or mere defeat. He felt...ugly. Unattractive. Unwanted. Such emotions weren't foreign to him. Far from it. From his birth he'd known how truly undesirable he was, the lone bastard amongst a gaggle of lawfully recognized siblings, fully set apart, despite the love they bore him. Even in his name he was branded as being different from them— FitzAllen, rather than Allen, and cursed ever to remain so. It was beyond his power to change or control what he was. But with women...by God, if he'd never been able to control anything else in his life, he'd at least been able to control women.

"You've a clever tongue, Mistress Glenys," he said almost before he knew his mouth was open, so angry that he hardly knew what he was saying. "But you use it far too much. 'Tis hardly to be wondered that you're yet a maiden. I have little doubt that you'll remain so."

They were the cruelest words he could have ever spoken to such a woman. Crueler by far than any dagger might be; he might almost have killed her less painfully. The moment the words were gone he regretted them wholly.

Kieran held his gaze on Mistress Glenys, whose eyes had grown wide and whose face paled once more, but from the edges of his vision he saw Jean-Marc turn from his ministrations to Mistress Dina to stare at him.

"My lord," Jean-Marc said in a voice that made Kieran cringe, one that too clearly told of the younger man's open distress. Jean-Marc was a gutter-born orphan who'd been raised by the most evil, murderous thieves who existed on God's earth; he didn't *have* feelings save in those rare moments when Kieran upended his hard-won faith and entirely made a mess of things.

As he had just done by making so open an attack on

a vulnerable woman within their care. No matter that the woman was a quarrelsome wench with a tongue as sharp as a finely honed blade.

"Forgive me," Kieran muttered, not able to look at her. "I should not have spoken in such a…" He cursed under his breath, knowing there was no fitting apology he could make. He stalked toward the door, saying only, "Good eve," and quit the room.

Jean-Marc was fast on his heels, grabbing Kieran by the arm and swinging him about before he could reach the stairs that led back to the tavern. "By the rood! What was that about?" he demanded.

"Naught," Kieran replied testily, pulling his arm free. "She goaded me. You heard what she said."

"I heard what *you* said," Jean-Marc retorted.

"What of it? She goaded me, just as I said."

"Women don't goad you," Jean-Marc told him. "Never. You're beyond being bothered by the lot of them, except for your mother and sisters. But one day in company with Mistress Glenys Seymour and you've come all undone. I don't like it. Nay." He shook his blond head. "I don't like a moment of it."

Kieran ran a hand through his hair, fully exasperated. "Neither do I," he said. "God save me from quick-witted females." He shook his head and turned for the stairs. "I want a drink."

With a sigh, Jean-Marc followed. "I *need* one," he murmured in agreement.

In the chamber they had left, Dina watched her mistress with troubled eyes.

"He did not mean what he said, mistress," she said softly. "'Tis clear he's not used to being turned aside from dallying."

"Nay, I have no doubt of that," Glenys agreed,

swallowing down the pain his words had given her. It was foolish to be hurt. She knew full well how unattractive she was. And she didn't care what Kieran FitzAllen thought of her, anywise. He was a rogue and a knave and a scoundrel. No one of true worth would care for what such a man either said or thought.

Dina's shivering brought Glenys back to the situation at hand, and she began to unlace her own wet cloak.

"Hurry and undress yourself," she told the maid. "This door has no latch to it, but I'll stand guard until you've wrapped yourself in one of the blankets." With a quick movement, she tossed her cloak over the back of one chair, then went to close the chamber's heavy wooden door.

Dina obediently stood and began to unlace her own cloak, which she set over the back of the other chair.

"This small fire will never have them dry come morn," she said dismally, tugging at her surcoat with frozen fingers. "Master Bostwick spoke the truth of that. Ah, God above, I cannot get this off." She groaned aloud as she strove to pull one arm out of the surcoat's long sleeve. "'Tis too wet and heavy."

"Come here, then, and let me give you aid," Glenys instructed. "We must hurry before the promised food and drink are brought. I vow I'll not partake of sustenance until we're both dry and halfway warmed." She tugged at Dina's surcoat until the maid was able to slip her arms free. The heavy, wet garment slid to the floor, leaving Dina clothed only in her chemise, leggings and shoes.

"God's mercy, 'tis so cold!" she cried, shivering and hugging her arms about herself. "How will we ever get warm?"

Glenys pushed her toward one of the pallets. "Take everything off, quickly, and wrap yourself in a blanket. We'll dry your things first and then, once you've dressed again, you'll stand guard whilst I care for my own things."

"But how will we get them dry, mistress?" Dina inquired, hurriedly removing her remaining garments and tossing them aside in order to wrap herself in the warmth of the blanket.

"I believe this will work," Glenys murmured, untying the small leather pouch at her girdle. "I've seen my uncle use this powder for a like purpose before, though now I wish I had watched him more closely. I'm most uncertain about how much to use, or if 'twill do more harm than good, but we must try it. Bring everything to me here and spread it out. Quickly, Dina!"

"Just a small sprinkling, I think," she said a few moments later as she dug into the now opened bag, pinching up a small amount of the fine, glittering grains. Drawing in a calming breath, she held her hand out over the garments and shoes that lay before her and carefully released the powder bit by bit, lightly dusting them all. They grains fell, sparkling, as if alive—though Glenys knew full well it was only an illusion—and once fallen, sent out a tiny puff of purple smoke that briefly filled the air. Coughing, Glenys waved it away and then bent to touch Dina's surcoat. She felt all about the heavy green cloth to make certain that she was correct, at last lifting her head and smiling at her waiting maid.

"'Tis dry!"

Dina was beside her in a moment, feeling for herself. "Why, it is!" She set a hand to her chemise, then to her shoes. "They're all dry! It worked! May God and your uncle be praised. I always knew his sorcery was powerful, but this is more than I'd ever believed.''

'''Tis no sorcery, Dina,'' Glenys told her. '''Tis alchemy, a beneficial blending of natural elements. There is no magic in it.''

"So you say, mistress," Dina said, gathering up her belongings in order to dress once more, "but you are the only one who thinks so."

Glenys didn't bother arguing. She was too cold and wet to care at the moment whether the entire world believed in such foolishness as magic.

"By the Blessed Virgin," she murmured with relief ten minutes later as she donned her own dried clothing. "I will never again chide Uncle Aonghus for spending so much time in his working chamber."

A knock fell on the door, announcing the arrival of the food and drink Master Bostwick had promised. It was simple fare, but warm and well prepared, and Glenys thought that she had never tasted anything so wonderful in all her life. There was warm bread sprinkled with caraway, a thin but welcome soup of vegetables and a few bits of beef, several slices of good, sharp cheese, and, most surprising of all, especially in such a crude tavern as Bostwick's, two small, thoroughly delicious almond cakes. The wine that accompanied the meal was, admittedly, far too sour to drink, but the girl who'd brought the goods had also delivered ale and, though they weren't used to drinking anything so common, Glenys and Dina found it flavorsome and quite refreshing. Indeed, by the time they'd finished two tankards each, they were well pleased and in a much merrier frame of being.

So much merrier, in fact, that by the time they decided to find their pallets and seek their rest, they were no longer bothered by the din emanating from the main tavern, and so well pleased that Glenys forgot entirely that the glowing stone and queen chess piece were yet in the pocket within her cloak—which she had left, now dry, hanging over the back of a chair. Having fallen deeply asleep almost as soon as she lay down, Glenys didn't even stir when Kieran, sometime just after midnight, slipped silently into the room.

Her captor grew still almost at once and stared at the amazing sight of something glowing brightly within the folds of Glenys's cloak. "Heaven's holy mercy," he whispered. "I've drunk more than I thought."

He closed his eyes and shook his head, but it did no good. When he opened his eyes, the cloak was yet glowing—softly, but glowing all the same.

"What a-God's name...?" He moved toward it slowly, then, reaching it, touched the garment with care. "'Tis dry!" He patted the cloth in disbelief. "But that's impossible!" And yet it was so.

Casting a brief glance to where Glenys lay sleeping, one arm draped over her face, Kieran tossed the cloak over one arm and began to search the pockets. It didn't take long; he was an excellent thief and knew how to rifle through pockets without detection, swiftly and silently. Within seconds he'd discovered the two pockets within the cloak and pulled out the contents.

"Holy Mother," he whispered, staring at what lay in the palm of his hand. The cloak dropped to the floor untended. The small stone that had earlier been stolen from Mistress Glenys by Coll of Chester—that small, insignificant, ordinary little rock—was glowing as brightly as the moon. So brightly that it filled the entire room with light. Yet as it lay in his palm it felt just as cool as before, glowing without heat.

Sorcery.

It had to be sorcery.

Sir Anton had told him the rumors about the Seymour family were false, and Glenys herself had said much the same, but this surely must be part of their magic. Gingerly, he touched the delicate chess figure that lay beside the stone, wondering what kind of evil it possessed. Mayhap the wooden lady spoke, or meted out good fortune or bad. God's teeth, just thinking of it made him shiver.

"Knave!"

A hand flashed out and snatched both the stone and wooden figure away, and the next moment Kieran found himself being struck upon his shoulder with a fist. It didn't hurt him, but clearly pained Glenys, for she hopped about for a moment, holding her hand to her mouth. This only infuriated her the more.

"How dare you go through my things!" she shouted at him, almost loudly enough to be heard over the noise of the tavern.

Kieran set a finger to his lips. "Hush, lest you wake your maid."

"I care not if she wakes!" she said furiously, holding up the glowing rock and the chess piece. "What do you mean by stealing my things? You gave me your word of honor that we'd be safe in this chamber, that we'd have naught to fear."

"And so it is," Kieran said, growing angered as well at having his honor questioned. He was a knave and a thief, i'faith, but he held his vows as dearly as any knight of the realm might do. "I've stolen nothing of yours, and I merely came to make certain that all was well, that you and your maid had every comfort." He moved closer, meeting her angry glare from his superior height. "And what do I find but that your cloak is awash with light—because of that small stone that was nearly stolen from you earlier. When I think back on it now, 'tis no great mystery that you trembled so fiercely once it was returned to you. 'Twas not weariness that weakened you, but the fear of having so precious and strange an object taken."

"Nay," she said tartly, "'twas the gladness of having it back." She held her open palm out toward him, holding the objects almost beneath his nose. "Would you wish anyone to find such as these upon you? A glowing stone, most especially? Would you?"

No, he wouldn't, Kieran admitted silently, but he wasn't related to a family rife with sorcerers.

"'Tis some kind of magic," he said. "You can't deny the truth of that."

She frowned at him darkly, drawing her hand away. "I do deny it. This stone glows merely because it possesses the elements to do so. 'Tis no different than coal that burns with fire, or a diamond that gives back colored light."

Kieran shook his head. "There is more. Look." He reached out to pinch a bit of her surcoat between two fingers. "Your clothes are dry. Your cloak is dry. Yet two hours past you were wet through to your skin." He reached up to touch a rope of her braided hair. Your locks are *still* wet." He grabbed one of her hands—the empty one—and pressed it against his tunic. "*I'm* still wet, even though I've been sitting before a hot fire. But your clothes are dry, and I'd wager any amount you please that your maid's are dry as well. If this is not sorcery, Mistress Glenys, then I pray you'll tell me what it is."

Her expressive face, so clearly lit by the glowing

stone, filled with that same measure of disdain that had earlier made him so maddened.

"I am your prisoner, Kieran FitzAllen. Unless you mean to beat me, I will tell you naught."

She turned away and picked up her fallen cloak, finding the inner pockets and pushing the stone and lady chess piece deeply into one of them. The light in the chamber dimmed with the absence of the stone, while the cloak took up its eerie illumination once more.

Carrying the cloak with her, Glenys returned to her pallet, saying nothing more to Kieran as she lay down with the garment safe in her arms.

He stood for a few moments in the dimly lit chamber, listening to the noise of the tavern beyond, the shouts and laughter. Mistress Glenys lay turned away from him, her face to the wall, her form and features brightly lined by the luminous cloak. Her face was set, angry, as hard and immovable as stone. The next few months, Kieran thought with a sigh, would be long indeed. He remembered with fleeting humor how only hours before Jean-Marc had predicted that Mistress Glenys would fall in love with him, and Kieran himself had agreed. How very wrong they had been. But they had far more to worry over now than simply whether their captives liked them. Now there was a strange, glowing stone, and an odd chess piece, and all manner of unexplained sorcery. These things they hadn't planned on, and the fact of them left Kieran fully discomfited. He could ready himself for Mistress Glenys's angry brother, but how could he defend himself against magic?

Chapter Six

"Shh." Glenys set a finger to her lips and gave Dina a warning look. "We must be as quiet as possible. Do you have all your things?"

Dina nodded, looking longingly at the window. "Can we not go that way? I'm sure 'tis not too far to the ground, and then none would see us."

Glenys gave a shake of her head as she set her cloak about her shoulders, deftly tying it.

"There's no need to trouble ourselves so. They're all soundly sleeping in the tavern. No one is sensible enough to either see or hear us pass by—*if* we are quiet. Come now, let us gird our loins and proceed without fear." She patted Dina reassuringly on the shoulder. "The worst that can happen is that we'll be caught, and the best is that we'll get safe away." She straightened and drew in a deep breath, setting a hand in her cloak pocket to find the stone and chess piece safely there. The bag with Uncle Aonghus's powder in it was tied securely to her girdle. With a nod of determination, Glenys moved toward the chamber door. "I only pray we'll find where the horses are kept without any difficulty. If not, we must walk all the way back to London.''

She opened the door slowly, thankful that it made no noise as it swung upon its giant hinges. Sticking her head out into the short passageway beyond, she looked in all directions before stepping out and waving for Dina to follow. Three footsteps brought them to the top of the short stairway that led to the farthest corner of the tavern. The entrance to the stairway was hidden by a well-worn tapestry, and it was at this that Glenys paused again, carefully moving the tapestry an inch to peer into the tavern beyond.

The sights and smells that greeted her went far beyond what she had expected, but she managed to keep any sound of disgust at bay. A great celebration had clearly taken place during the hours of the night and early morn, and now all those who'd participated paid the price. Bodies were strewn all about the large room, lying here and there on the tables, in chairs, even upon the filthy rushes, in drunken slumber. Several lay with their mouths agape, snoring loudly, but clearly waking none. Some were partly or wholly unclothed, both men and women, their bare flesh pale and chilled in the cold early morn. Empty and half-filled tankards and goblets were littered everywhere, and the smells of the stale, sour libations and sooty smoke were strong enough to make one unused to them swoon. Glenys's stomach clenched uneasily, and she longed to be outdoors in the fresh, cold air.

Pushing down the fear that threatened to turn her back, she stepped past the tapestry and into the tavern itself and gazed about, looking for signs of movement from any corner. There were none, and she took two more steps farther into the room. Behind her, she could hear Dina quietly following.

"Where's Kieran FitzAllen?" the maid whispered near Glenys's shoulder.

"I don't see him," Glenys murmured, looking everywhere for a head of golden-brown hair. Kieran FitzAllen was far too distinctive a man to be missed, even amongst such a tumble of bodies. He wasn't in the tavern, and neither, that she could see, was his manservant, Jean-Marc, or even Bostwick, whose large size certainly made him unmistakable.

"Perhaps they've left without us," Dina said in hushed tones.

Glenys shook her head. "Nay. They're with the whores, mostlike, in the other chamber. Come."

They said nothing more as they slowly and carefully picked their way through the litter of bodies, being very certain not to step on a stray hand or foot. Once or twice someone grumbled in his sleep and rolled over, nearly causing Glenys's heart to stop, but each time the sleeper only continued in his slumbers, while Glenys and Dina continued on their course to freedom.

They came to the large wooden door that served as the entryway to the tavern, and Glenys stopped.

"This isn't right," she murmured, touching the latch, which wasn't thrown. "Surely they were not so drunk that they failed to latch the door. God's mercy." She turned and looked about the disorderly room again. "He must be awake and aware that we seek to escape. The door would not be open if he was not already outside, waiting for us. 'Tis a trap he's set, curse the man!"

"But, mistress," Dina whispered, touching Glenys's sleeve, "mayhap 'twas only left unlatched because all within were too drunk to care. Why should thieves care for such as that, anywise?''

Glenys made a snorting sound, uncaring now who heard her, though none stirred. ''Why should they not?'' She set her hand to the door handle. ''Well, if Master FitzAllen waits without, we must not keep him. Let us by all means greet him good morn.''

She flung the door wide and stomped outside, fully expecting to find Kieran FitzAllen and Jean-Marc awaiting them with those knowing, foolish grins upon their faces.

But no one was there. Anywhere.

The tavern yard was empty, and she was greeted by nothing more sinister than the cold, crisp early morn, only just now being touched by the light of the dawning sun. The surrounding trees were yet damp with rain, but the day itself would be clear, once the sun rose high.

The air was clean and fresh, and Glenys drew in a long, welcome breath, striving to banish the smells of the tavern behind her. Dina made matters even more final by shutting the door softly upon all inside—people, foul smells and smoky darkness.

''Mayhap there is still a chance,'' Glenys murmured, grasping Dina's arm and pulling her across the muddy yard toward what must be the animal shed. ''Please, God, let it be so.''

It was all so incredibly simple that Glenys could scarce believe they'd actually done it. The two horses, among other cattle, were indeed in the shed, and Glenys saddled and made them ready as quickly as possible. Jean-Marc's mare, a steely tempered gray, made her displeasure at being handled by a stranger well known, but the satiny black destrier, Nimrod, stood quietly beneath Glenys's ministrations. He was as handsome as his master, but so large of frame that she was forced to use a stool to get the reins over his ears.

It took longer to mount the horses, especially when Jean-Marc's mare was so stubborn about accepting Dina as a rider, but at last the two women guided their mounts out of the shed and into the tavern yard itself. Here, Glenys ran into trouble.

"Come, you wretched beast!" She set the heels of her soft boots into Nimrod's flanks, but he gave no response. She pulled on his reins to lead him toward the yard gate, but he refused to obey. Instead, with Jean-Marc's horse following, he began to walk calmly and slowly toward the side of the tavern...exactly to the place where his master, Kieran FitzAllen, stood waiting beneath the same window that belonged to the chamber Glenys and Dina had shared. Jean-Marc stood with him, and both men, who had been in the midst of deep conversation, looked satisfyingly astonished at the sudden appearance of their horses, being ridden by their prisoners, coming directly toward them.

Kieran gave a shout of surprise, while Jean-Marc started forward in the direction of his surly mare. Glenys, not thinking upon what she did, pushed herself from the saddle and promptly fell gracelessly onto her backside in the mud. Nimrod, foolish horse, didn't even pause, but continued plodding placidly toward his master.

The great animal was like a wall between Glenys and her captor. All she could see of Kieran FitzAllen from where she sat were his legs. When those legs began to stride in her direction, Glenys pushed aside the momentary shock that had held her still and set herself into motion, leaping to her feet, lifting her skirts and running with every ounce of strength she possessed.

Kieran FitzAllen shouted out again, running after her, while from the far corner of the tavern yard Dina uttered a soft cry as Jean-Marc, cursing, sought to grab the reins of his unhappy mare.

Even as she ran, Glenys knew how foolish it was. She would be fortunate if she managed to reach the yard gate before Kieran FitzAllen caught her, but the sound of his booted feet drawing nearer only seemed to spur her on. Her skirts were heavy in her hands, and the cold morning air caused her lungs to ache and burn with each frantic breath she drew.

"Mistress!" he shouted out, right behind her. She could feel his hand on her shoulder, his fingers closing on the wool of her cloak.

"Nay!" she cried as he finally grasped it tightly, bringing her to a halt, but not managing to stop the weight of his own body as he hurtled forward. They collided and fell together in a tangle upon the cold, muddy ground, Glenys on the bottom, Kieran on top.

She was nearly smothered in the wet dirt, and screamed furiously as the heavy brute squashed the breath out of her.

"Off! *Off!*" she shouted, kicking and flinging her arms back in an attempt to elbow him away. He gasped as she at last struck him, already striving to lift himself off.

The moment she felt the relief of his removed weight, Glenys flung herself over full force, grabbed the unsuspecting villain by his muscular shoulders and shoved him into the mud beside her.

"Brute!" She shoved him down again when he tried

to sit up, his handsome face filled with utter shock. Flinging herself atop him, she pinned him down. "Knave! Fiend! Wretch!"

He tried to lift his mud-smeared head from the ground, but Glenys furiously pushed him down again.

"How did you get out of the tavern?" he demanded, shouting just as loudly.

She brought her face close to yell, "Through the front door!"

"Through the...!" He set his hands on her shoulders to bring her even closer, until they were glaring eye to eye. "'Tis impossible!"

"'Twas not impossible! I only wish to God above that we'd walked out of the yard rather than tried to take your lackwitted mounts! We'd be well on our way by now if we'd done so!" She wrenched herself free of his grip and sat up, wiping mud from her face.

Kieran lay where he was and stared at her, shaking his head. "You walked through the door...when I was so certain you'd try to climb out the window. What kind of woman are you, walking out a front door as if you'd not be caught?"

Glenys flung bits of mud from her fingertips, then gave him a look filled with disdain. "A woman who knows better than to climb out of a window where she would be expected to escape. I'm not so foolish to be so easily tricked."

"Nor am I," he told her hotly. "I was mistaken in the manner in which you would make the attempt, but I knew you'd make it, despite the vow you made."

"I vowed that we'd not escape during the night," she replied. "'Tis now morn."

"I understood full well what you meant when you made your promise. But I've just wasted the past three hours standing in the bitter cold, waiting for you to escape *from the window.*''

He made it sound as if she'd deliberately striven to annoy him by not escaping as he'd thought she would and, heaven help her, Glenys began to feel amused. He lay before her, splayed out in the mud, looking so foolishly disgruntled at being deprived of the little victory he'd planned that it was all she could do not to laugh.

''Don't grin at me, Mistress Glenys Seymour,'' he warned, pointing a finger at her. ''I'll not be made jest of, *not* after I've been nearly frozen to death because of you. And Jean-Marc with me.''

It was impossible. She began to giggle, just thinking of them standing beneath that window for so long, waiting and planning and anticipating how amusing it would be to catch their two captives as they flung themselves from above. And then to be denied because those same captives had merely walked out the front door... Nay, 'twas far too silly. She began to laugh aloud.

''There is no cause to make merry,'' he said sternly. ''You unfeeling, unnatural female. I've treated you well, and *this* is how you repay my kindness.''

Glenys could scarcely breathe for laughing now. She leaned forward to place a hand in the mud, supporting herself as she gave way to her mirth.

''Th-the window!'' she said between gusts of laughter. ''Y-you s-stood beneath the w-window! Waiting for us!'' She laughed so hard that tears began to roll from her eyes.

Kieran looked at her reproachfully. ''You're cruel,'' he stated. ''Cruel and heartless.''

That only made Glenys laugh harder. Jean-Marc and Dina approached them from behind, and their mur-

mured questions caused her to laugh all the more. And
then, when she might have begun to calm, Kieran at
last began to laugh. He chuckled at first, in a manner
so low and constrained that it was obvious he was trying hard to stop. But then he gave way to the clear
humor of the moment and began to laugh out loud, and
all was lost. Glenys found herself lying flat against his
chest, laughing as if she'd never stop, and Kieran set
his arms about her to keep her from falling off, laughing just as uncontrollably.

"God's mercy," Dina said to Jean-Marc. "They've
gone mad."

Hearing that set Glenys and Kieran off into new
gales of jollity, laughing so hard that Glenys thought
she might be ill.

It all came to an end at last, until they lay there in
the mud, chuckling and sighing. Glenys felt weak as a
newborn kitten when she finally pushed upward, and
suddenly realized that she was sitting astride Kieran
FitzAllen in a very unladylike manner.

She looked down at herself in sudden horror, discovered that she was directly atop that most private
area of his person, and leaped aside as if he were made
of hot, glowing coals. Both she and Kieran stopped
laughing, looked into each other's faces for a long, silent moment...and started laughing all over again.
Glenys had always held a perfect dread of even thinking upon a man's body, yet now, having been in the
closest sort of contact with such a body, she thought it
the most humorous thing imaginable.

Gads, she thought as she dragged herself to her
feet—with a little help from both Dina and Jean-Marc.
She must have lost all her senses. Beside her, Kieran
lumbered to his feet as well, still chuckling.

"We need a bath," he said, looking first down at himself, then at Glenys.

"Yes," she agreed, grinning at him stupidly, "we do."

They began to laugh once more, to be interrupted with loud impatience by Dina, who took Glenys by the arm, and Jean-Marc, who took a firm grip upon his master.

"Let us get them back to the inn before they do themselves a great injury," Jean-Marc said above the grating humor. "God's pity, look what they've done. The whole tavern's come awake."

It was true. Glenys and Kieran glanced about as they awkwardly made their way toward the tavern. Many of the formerly sleeping occupants were now standing just outside the front door, gazing at them in amazement. Bostwick, easy to find among the rest, looked especially dumbfounded. Kieran gave a loud snort, which set Glenys off once more. They made their way—with a great deal of help—past the onlookers and back indoors.

"Bostwick!" Jean-Marc shouted as he shoved his large, unhelpful master into the large room. "We want two baths, at once."

"But I've nothing ready!"

"I care not! Rouse some of your strumpets and set them to fetching water. These two will bathe cold, by God, but they'll bathe." He shoved Kieran, laughing merrily, into the nearest chair, then stared at him with anger. "Anyone seeing you would think you full drunk," he told him. "'Twill serve you justly to journey this day in wet clothes...far wetter than they are now, I should say."

"Nay, I will travel dry," his master replied with a wide grin.

Jean-Marc shook his head. "You're filthy with mud. They'll have to be washed. All of them. And your boots into the bargain."

"Wash them, please," Kieran said happily, reaching up to unlace his cloak. "They'll be dry before we leave. Mistress Glenys will see to that, will you not, mistress?"

He looked to where Dina had seated Glenys, his expression smiling, but cunning. She understood him perfectly. She had little choice but to use her uncle's powders if she didn't wish to have him reveal her "sorcery." Not that she blamed him for such trickery. She certainly didn't plan on wearing wet clothes throughout the day, and he'd not wish for such discomfort, either. He was her captor, true, and she owed him naught, but for the mere pleasure that he'd just given her—waiting by the window, indeed—she would repay him.

"Aye, Master FitzAllen," she said with a nod, already savoring the bath to come. "I will see to it."

Chapter Seven

"'Tis truly a most wondrous magic."

Kieran rubbed a hand over his sleeve, amazed anew at how dry it was. She'd not wanted to perform her sorcery, but Mistress Glenys had taken his freshly washed clothing into the private chamber she'd shared with Mistress Dina and returned but a few minutes later with those same garments—perfectly dry. All in the tavern had been astounded, and a little afraid, and Kieran had realized with sudden understanding why Glenys had earlier denied her powers and kept them so secret.

"'Tis *not* magic," she said even now, shifting restlessly in the saddle before him. "No such thing as magic exists—leastwise, nothing that is considered good, most especially in the eyes of the church. If you believe me not, then you need only ask the archbishop. Or better still, all those who've been accused of such evil things and burned at the stake or hanged by the rope."

"There is nothing evil in the magic you possess," he replied easily. "This ability to make wet garments dry, and the little glowing stone...surely no one would declare them evil.'' He had readily forgotten his own initial dismay at the thought of such sorcery.

She gave a loud, unladylike snort. ''You've little idea what would be said of them, or of me or my family. You've no idea what 'tis like to grow up amongst so many odd relatives, or to try to make others understand that those same relatives are harmless.''

''I see. This is why Mistress Dina spoke as she did about your cousin Helen? Is she not, in truth, a witch?''

Glenys turned her head to give him a brief, speaking look. ''Of a certainty she is no witch! By the love of the Holy Mother, how can you speak in such a manner now, when you seemed so clearly to understand the matter earlier? Surely you do not truly believe in such creatures as witches?''

''And surely you do,'' he replied just as quickly. ''You are the one related to so many strange and magical beings, not me. And you possess such magic yourself, for you dried my garments, and I saw the stone with my own eyes. What does the little witch piece do?''

''*Queen* piece,'' Glenys replied between set teeth. ''She is the lone surviving piece to a matching chess set, naught more. She doesn't *do* anything.''

Kieran didn't believe that for a moment. ''She must do something, else you'd not have hidden her away so carefully with the stone. I may have been mistaken, but last eve, as I gazed upon both her and the stone, it almost seemed as if her eyes glowed with light.''

Though Glenys strove hard not to lean too closely against him upon the saddle, Kieran could feel his captive's body tighten at his words, and he knew that he was right. The chess piece was magical, too, but it would do him little good to press her on the matter.

'Twas clear that she wished to deny all that was so plain, and he had well learned that women, when pressed, only became more difficult to draw information from. Being a man well versed in getting what he wanted out of the finer sex, Kieran smoothly changed the subject to one that would far more likely make his way with Mistress Glenys both simpler and more pleasant.

"'Tis clear you do not wish to speak of her," he said, adjusting the hand that was about her waist in a firmer grip. Having her thus distracted, he continued pleasantly, saying, "Tell me of your family, then. Tell me about your cousin, Helen, who is not a witch, even though Mistress Dina says most sincerely that she is."

It had been an interesting moment in the tavern when, as Glenys had sat down to write the promised missive to her cousin, her maid had muttered that she wished there was some better, less questionable relative to take up the task, instead. There had been no other onlookers present at that moment apart from Kieran and Jean-Marc, the latter being the person to whom the comment was directed, but Glenys had immediately grown tense and wary.

"Hush, Dina!" she'd commanded, the inked quill frozen in her hand. "Say no more."

"I mean nothing against her," Dina had disobediently replied, "and I'm glad if she can hurry to London to care for your dear aunts and uncles, but 'tis well known that she's believed to be a witch, and there's been naught but the worst kind of trouble when she and Master Aonghus are together."

"A *witch!*" This unhelpful and disbelieving utterance had come from Jean-Marc, just before Kieran sharply elbowed him into silence.

"Aye, aye," Kieran had said calmly in an effort to smooth the ruffled waters. "She's merely of Mistress Glenys's family, and must be expected to possess some measure of magic. 'Tis clear that such dearly held skills have been misunderstood, and thus she has been proclaimed a witch. There can be nothing more to it."

Glenys had lowered the pen and turned to gaze upon him with a look of such gratitude that Kieran had been momentarily stunned—just as he'd been earlier, in the tavern yard when she'd first smiled, then laughed so fully. Her intriguing face was transformed by smiles into something almost beyond beauty. He had been transfixed by it then, and was now, as well.

"Aye, that is closely what has happened," she said. "You understand the matter perfectly, Master Fitz-Allen. 'Twas naught but a misunderstanding that saw my cousin labeled thusly. A dreadful misunderstanding."

He'd been nearly undone by the words, spoken so openly and with such thankfulness and relief. That he'd not believed anything of what he'd said suddenly made no difference. She had believed it, and had been glad of it, and therefore was smiling at him. Smiles from Mistress Glenys Seymour, he was fast discovering, were as rare and precious as gold.

"You said earlier that you understood how it was that she came to be called a witch," Glenys said now, crossing her arms over her chest.

"And so I do," he assured her, thinking of just how lush and full that feminine chest had been when pressed against him early in the morn, as they'd tussled in the mud. Kieran couldn't yet think of how intimately they'd been pressed together, joined hip to hip, without hardening with unaccountable desire. Even now, simply remembering it, he had to adjust more comfortably in the saddle. "But I wish to know how she came to be called such, and why your family has so great a reputation for sorcery."

Glenys was silent for a long moment, but began to relax by degrees and at last unfolded her arms. Kieran thought that he even felt her leaning—just slightly—against him. She cast a brief glance to where Mistress Dina rode with Jean-Marc, consumed by their own conversation, and then she began to speak.

"My cousin Helen is far more intelligent and witty than most men find acceptable in a female. She is also very comely." This Glenys said with such open longing that Kieran felt a wave of sorrow. She clearly believed herself to be not merely unattractive, but overwhelmingly so.

"She was born to my father's cousin in a small village near the Scottish border," Glenys continued, "which was an unfortunate thing, for if she'd been more properly born in Wales, as most Seymours are, she'd never have been named a witch." She looked at him over her shoulder, saying in confiding tones, "The Welsh are far more sensible about unusual people than most. Of a certainty, they'd not try to burn a young woman at the stake simply because she likes to go out walking at night without escort."

Kieran blinked in surprise. "They tried to burn your cousin at the stake?"

Glenys nodded. "And only because she takes such pleasure in walking out of doors in the dead of night. I'faith, I do not find it so difficult a thing to understand, even if I'd never undertake such a foolishness myself. But Helen has ever preferred the night to the day. 'Tis simply her way."

"A way that is like to bring her harm," Kieran said, "especially if she is as comely as you declare her to be. A great many men would not hesitate to take their pleasure of such a woman, especially if 'tis her habit to go out walking alone."

"No man would dare to bring harm to Helen," Glenys said, turning her gaze forward once more. "No man could, I think."

"How so?"

She sighed. "I do not know if I can explain why. 'Tis simply the way of so many of my family. There is no magic in it, but they—some of them—ever manage to escape harm and danger."

"Yet your cousin was almost killed."

"Aye, but that was because she was taken during the daylight, and also because both her father and mother were away at another of their estates. Helen and the household servants could not fend off the scoundrels who came to take her. She was then but thirteen years of age."

"God's pity," Kieran said in disgust, thinking of how utterly terrified so young a girl must have been, being taken by force by a maddened mob and tied to a stake. "How did she come away alive?"

Glenys hesitated before answering. "She...disappeared," she said, then added, in an even less convincing tone, "I mean to say that she escaped."

"Escaped?" Kieran repeated.

"Aye," Glenys replied weakly. "They had waited to take her, most fortunately, until late in the day. As they prepared the wood for the fire the sun began to sink, and by the time they finally lit the flame the daylight had nearly gone away altogether...and Helen managed to escape. They could not find her."

A shiver ran the length of Kieran's spine. "I see. She must not have been very well tied, and those watching must not have watched very closely—even though they had gone to a great deal of trouble to first take hold of her and then tie her to a stake."

"Yes, exactly so," Glenys agreed with a nod of her head.

"Aye," Kieran continued, "I can see how easily she might escape. Indeed, it must have been a very simple thing. And you say that the rest of your family is much like her?"

"You do not believe me!" Glenys charged angrily, and quite rightly. "You think Helen used some manner of magic, then?"

"I think it a fortunate thing that a young woman who favors walking in the dark of night happened to be nearly set aflame at that time," Kieran replied honestly, "else she might no longer walk the earth at all."

Glenys straightened, crossed her arms over her chest again and made a huffing sound. "You think Helen a witch, just as Dina does. S'truth, you probably didn't even send her the missive I wrote out. I doubt that you mean anything of what you say or promise."

"Of a certainty the missive will reach her." Kieran laughed, and with the hand that held her, he pulled her arms down and apart, having to tug to accomplish the feat. "If you find it impossible to believe that I'm a man of honor, you may at least believe that Bostwick is. And he watched you write that missive with such confounded awe—for he never saw a woman who could write more than her name before—that he will treat it as carefully as if 'twere made of pure gold. Now come, don't be angry," Kieran said soothingly, unable to keep the humor completely out of his voice. "Tell

me of your aunts and uncles, and then I must hear of
the lady chess piece.''

"There is little to say of my family," Glenys said.
"They are like other families, save that they are very
wise and skilled in the old ways."

"The old ways?"

"The ways of the people who lived in Wales long
ago, from whom the Seymours are descended. My uncles know much about the elements of both earth and
water, and my aunts are knowledgeable about healing
and medicines. There is a full explanation and reasoning for all that they do, but few will understand the
truth of it. The glowing stone serves as proof of what
I say. You think it magic, just as others would, merely
because you do not understand the elements that cause
it to glow. Elements from the earth, Master FitzAllen,
created by God and having naught to do with any kind
of sorcery.''

"You are weary of fighting such misunderstand-
ings." It wasn't a question he asked; he could hear the
truth of it in her words.

"Aye," she answered with a sigh. "Most weary.
I've been doing so since I was a child. For almost as
long as I can remember, but more so since my father
died.''

"He was nephew to your aunts and uncles?"

"Nay, he was their half brother, but much younger,
being born of my grandfather's second wife. Among
all my grandfather's children, my father was the only
one to wed. And a good thing it was that he did, else
my brother Daman and I would not have been born,
and there would have been no one to care for my aunts
and uncles.''

"As you do," Kieran murmured. He gently pulled

her more closely against him and felt, gladly, that she gave no resistance. "What happened to your mother and father?"

"Mother died in childbirth when I was but eight years of age, and the child with her. My father followed them four years later, felled by a chill that even my aunts couldn't save him from. 'Twas a time of great darkness in my family."

Kieran had ever striven to keep from speaking so intimately, and of such sorrowful things, with most of the women he knew. It made him uncomfortable and, worse, guilty, for not only could he do nothing to ease such sorrows, he seldom felt any desire to do so. But it was not so with Mistress Glenys. Kieran felt a disturbing desire to comfort her—though he hardly knew how, at least not in any manner that would be welcome to her.

"Aye," he murmured, "I can see that it must have been so. And this is when you began to care for your aunts and uncles, because your father and mother were no longer there to do so?"

"Yes. And Daman could not help, for he was away from home, being fostered in Wales. But you must not think that my aunts and uncles are a heavy burden to me, for 'tis not so. 'Tis merely the rumors—and the many falsehoods that others believe of them—that makes the task difficult. I'll not see any in my family named evil, or called sorcerer or conjurer. Assuredly I will not have them brought before a court of inquiry, or seized by a maddened mob, as my cousin was."

"Your brother, Sir Daman…does he feel as you do? That there is no such thing as magic, and that your family must be kept safe from being tainted by rumors of it?"

"Of course they must be kept safe," she said tautly. "Daman knows that, just as any sane man would. As to the magic…" She lowered her head. "I wish he did not believe in it," she said sadly. "The foolishness has ruined his life."

Kieran gave a snort. "Has it, i'faith? This is not the Daman Seymour I know."

Her head snapped toward him, though her keen gaze didn't meet his own.

"How is it that you know my brother? And why do you seek to gain his wrath? There must be some enmity between you, yet I cannot remember that he has ever spoken your name to me."

"Nay, he would not," Kieran said with disdain. "'Twould not be the way for a noble knight of the realm to mention a lowly bastard thief. Why should he do so?"

"Because you bear a certain hatred for him?" she suggested, so guilelessly that Kieran was instantly on his guard. Glenys Seymour might have warmed to him a small measure, and unbent enough to speak openly of her family, but she was far too intelligent and cunning a female to take lightly.

"Mayhap 'tis only because he has given me some manner of insult, and even one basely born may take such as that without pleasure."

"But to plan revenge, and to throw in your lot with a fool the likes of Sir Anton," she said, "is to act without care. Indeed, 'tis full reckless."

"'Twould be reckless to let such a chance slide by," he countered. "Who can say when I might again have the opportunity to draw Sir Daman Seymour into my net. And how better than to take that man's sister as prisoner? He will come for you, if he would come for no other.''

She gave a single shake of her head. ''And what of it? Daman will kill you, though you sound so pleased. My brother is counted among the most skilled fighters in England. No man has ever bested him with a sword.''

Kieran knew that perfectly well, but he wasn't distressed by the knowledge. ''I am not a knight,'' he said lightly, ''yet neither am I a helpless babe. My own skill with the sword has been well matched...and, like your brother, never bested.''

''Daman will best it,'' she promised. ''You will find your death should you face him. But if this is your wish, I will not strive to sway you. I am far more concerned with the pact that you have made with Sir Anton. To go against Daman is one matter...but how could you have bargained with a man who has but used you to his own purpose?''

Kieran shrugged. ''I also used him to mine. In this way we are equal in our sins.''

''But his is the greater evil,'' she said insistently. ''You do not know him well, as I do. I tell you, Sir Anton will see you dead if it serves his purpose, and most likely it does. If we do not find ourselves in some manner of danger once we reach York, I vow I will shave my head until 'tis full bald.''

Kieran laughed aloud. ''Now that would be a great pity, mistress. Your hair is a thing of true beauty, as well you must know. 'Twould be a grievous sin to destroy a single strand.''

Even sitting behind her, he could see her cheeks darken with pleasure, and Kieran, being a man who liked to please women, was glad for it.

"That is all foolishness," she said, striving to sound stern and not succeeding at all.

"Nay, 'tis the merest truth." Kieran took up a lock of her now loosely bound hair. She'd left it unbraided following her bath that morn so that it might dry more easily. The welcome warmth of the day had nearly completed that task, and now the glorious red-gold strands were only a bit damp, as cool and smooth as fine silk. "I do not think I have ever seen any more beautiful, nay, not once during all my travels. Many women I know would sell their very souls to possess the like." He let the soft strands fall from his fingers, shaking away his fixed contemplation and pulling his mind back to the duty of guiding Nimrod. "Do you have it from your father?"

"My mother," she answered, feminine pleasure yet heavy in her voice. "Her hair was the same. She was from the north, very different from the rest of my family. Daman has his dark looks from our father."

"And a good thing it is, for 'twould be a waste should a man be blessed with such hair. From the north, you said. Do you mean Scotland? Your mother was Scottish?"

She nodded. "Aye."

"Ah," Kieran said. "Now I understand."

She turned her head to look at him. "What do you understand?"

"A great many things," he replied. "Now, tell me about the chess piece. She looks like a small carving of Boadicea. Is that who she was meant to be?"

Glenys hesitated a long moment, holding his gaze, before turning her face forward once more and beginning to speak, answering his questions in a calm, if not perfectly willing, manner.

The afternoon was warm, a pleasant change from the cold, damp day before, and Kieran led them along at a comfortable, steady pace. They kept away from the main roads, riding mainly through oak forests and still muddy fields. In time, Glenys began to yawn. Without knowing what she did, she also began to rest more fully against Kieran, her body relaxing into the curve of his arm. And finally, when Kieran noted how weary she was, and ceased his endless questioning, she fell asleep, her cheek against his chest, her long, unbound hair falling in a curtain over her eyes. So soundly did she slumber, and so carefully did Kieran make certain of her comfort in his arms, that Glenys only came awake when he at last brought Nimrod to a stop two hours later, in the place that was their destination for the night.

Chapter Eight

Glenys never would have believed it possible, but Kieran FitzAllen had managed to find an inn that was even worse than Bostwick's had been.

In truth, Glenys wasn't certain that the dwelling she woke to find herself blearily gazing at could even be called an inn. It looked far more like a poorly built barn meant to provide shelter for animals. There was no actual door to the dwelling, only a wide opening at the front, with so much darkness beyond that Glenys couldn't tell what lay within.

It was a dark, heavily wooded place they had come to, so strange and remote that she couldn't imagine anyone living within it—at least, no one who was normal. It could only be some kind of thieves' den, which, considering who and what Kieran FitzAllen and his servant were, seemed likely.

"See if you can find Xander, Jean-Marc," Kieran said as he swung down from Nimrod. "He and his men must be lying in wait, else they would have made themselves known by now."

Jean-Marc had already dismounted and was pulling Dina down to the ground. Setting her on her feet, he said, "I'd rather stick my hand down a snake hole, but it must be as you say, my lord." Glenys noticed that he withdrew the dagger at his waist before approaching the opening to the dwelling.

Two warm hands settling at her waist caused Glenys to look down, to find Kieran FitzAllen ready to pull her from his steed. His handsome face was etched with lines of weariness, and his blue eyes were grim.

"Please tell me that we'll be sleeping elsewhere tonight," she said.

"There is nowhere else." He tugged her forward, until she set her hands on his shoulders. "Though I assuredly wish there were."

"In the forest?" she suggested as she slid downward, her feet coming to rest on the ground. "Dina and I would not mind it."

He shook his head. "The ground is too wet from yesterday's rain. I had hoped to go some miles farther before nightfall, but 'twill be dark within the hour, and your maid looks as if she can scarce keep her eyes open. I beg your pardon, mistress." He reached past her and slid his sword from its scabbard, which hung on Nimrod's saddle. "I believe our hosts have come to greet us."

He wielded the heavy weapon gracefully, swinging about and lifting it to the ready just as a rustling from the tree above produced a number of men leaping to the ground with their knives drawn. There were five of them, Glenys saw, dark, swarthy and rough looking. The man who was their leader stood taller than the rest, handsome and cunning, though his garments and boots were beyond shabby. He was smiling at Kieran, and lifted a hand to indicate the long sword that was pointed at him.

"This is how you greet old friends, Kie?" He spoke smoothly and pleasantly, just as if he weren't pointing an equally deadly blade at his visitor.

Glenys dared to glance at her captor's face. It was set as if made of stone. In the past two days she had seen a number of expressions on Kieran FitzAllen's countenance, but this one made her shiver. He might be a knave and a dallying rogue, but 'twas clear that he was not a liar. He had told her that he knew how to fight, and as he stood before her now, powerful and intent, clearly skilled at handling his sword, she knew it was the truth.

"This is how I greet enemies, Xander. I name a number of thieves and liars among my friends, but I'm not such a fool as to count murderers with them."

The man named Xander grinned unpleasantly, baring his teeth, which were starkly white against his dark skin.

"A pity you're so particular, Kie. 'Tis strange in a bastard, but you always have been thus. I might have kept Jean-Marc if it had been otherwise. You've brought the little traitor with you, I suppose?" His dark eyes shifted toward Glenys, who nervously moved closer to Kieran. "And someone else, I see." He took a step toward her, to find the tip of Kieran's sword lifted to his throat.

"The woman and her maid are in my care. Touch either of them and you're a dead man, Xander. And your men along with you."

Slowly, Xander stepped back, still gazing at Glenys, his eyes glittering. "And you speak with contempt of murderers? Is she your whore? Not as pretty as your last one, but her body is...perfect." He looked as if he'd devour Glenys whole, given the chance. She began to tremble. "We have gold aplenty if you wish to take some of it," he added. "We've had no women here for nigh over a month. We'll pay well for her time and skill."

"Nay," Kieran said tightly. "We only require shelter for the night. Nothing more."

"You can have it," Xander said, "and gold, as well. Let us have your whore for an hour and you may ask what you wish. We'll bring her no harm. Once each only, eh?" He glanced back at his men, who all nodded and murmured in agreement. Glenys discovered, to her terror, that they were *all* staring at her now. She moved right up against Kieran and set a hand at his waist, pressing herself into the strength of his body.

"She is not a whore," Kieran stated slowly, "and I mean what I say. Touch her and I slit your throat."

"Give us the other one, then." He nodded toward Dina, who stood beside Jean-Marc's mare, her face white with fear. "She is smaller than this one, but if we act with care she might be able to pleasure us all without harm."

"Xander!"

The cry came from one of his men, who suddenly found Jean-Marc's knife at his throat. Somehow Jean-Marc had managed to sneak up behind all of them without being seen, but perhaps, Glenys thought, that was because he had some measure of experience in dealing with them.

"How good it is to see you again, Roald," Jean-Marc said, pressing the sharp blade even more tightly against the frozen man's throat. "As ugly as you ever were. I broke your nose when last we saw each other. What shall I do to you this time? Eh?"

"Call your little hound to heel, Kie," Xander said. "We'll not touch the women."

"On your honor, Xander," Kieran insisted. "'Tis all you possess that's of value. And I'll hear your men make their oaths as well. Their honor is not as certain as yours, but you'll make sure of them, I have no doubt. All our acquaintances will hear of it, if not, and you'll be forever shunned even by the worst of them."

"He *is* the worst of them," Jean-Marc muttered, tightening his grip on his captive so that the man sputtered and squeaked. *"Xander!"*

Xander made a sound of disgust, then sheathed his dagger in one abrupt, swift movement. "Very well. You have my word of honor, and that of my men. Speak aloud!" he commanded, and his men obediently murmured their agreement. Roald was released and shoved to the ground, and Jean-Marc strode away toward Dina, who readily let him set an arm about her in comfort.

Slowly, Kieran lowered his sword and relaxed his ready stance. "We'll stay the night and share your roof, and in the morn we'll be on our way. Give us no trouble, and we'll give you none in turn. If the women hadn't been weary from travel, you may believe that Jean-Marc and I never would have come within a mile of here."

"But you have come," Xander noted, "and now will be our welcome guests. All of you." He looked pointedly at Jean-Marc. "Even the traitor."

"Do you have food?" Kieran asked.

"Food and drink," Xander replied. "We've just now returned from the hunt. There are only rabbits, but enough for all."

"We'll pay you well."

"That," said Xander, motioning for them to enter the dwelling with the sweep of one hand, "we will discuss in the morn. For now, come and be warmed. The fire has died down, but we'll soon have it burning bright again. Come in and have some wine."

He walked in ahead of them, followed by two of his men, clearly expecting them to follow.

Glenys set a hand to Kieran's arm, drawing his attention.

"How can you trust him? They'll murder us in our sleep!"

He gave her a weary smile. "Nay, for I'll remain awake and guard you well, Mistress Glenys. You have naught to fear."

She shook her head. "You're as tired as Dina and Jean-Marc. I'll stay awake and keep guard."

He looked fully shocked for the length of two seconds, and then he laughed. "Mistress, I pray you, this is not the time for jests."

"I mean what I say!" she insisted. "I've slept for hours, and 'tis only right that I should be the one to remain awake and keep a watch on...on Master Xander," she said, not certain what to call the man.

"'Tis not Xander I fear," he told her, moving to slide his sword into its scabbard. "There is a certain honor among thieves, little though you may believe it. If Xander should go back upon his word and attack us, all who are common to us would know of it and disdain him. That is as bad as death among my people. Nay, 'tis not Xander I worry o'er, though he or one of his men may strive to outwit us without breaking their word. 'Tis you and Mistress Dina sneaking off again that holds me afeard."

Glenys looked at him with disgust. "Can you think

us such fools as to try to leave you now? We have no protection, no way to get back to London. I don't even know where we are, and less how to find a decent road.''

Taking Nimrod's reins, he led him toward a small, three-sided shed. ''I can't take the chance of losing you,'' he said. Then, looking over his shoulder to where Jean-Marc yet stood with his arms about Dina, he added, ''Take her inside, Jean-Marc. She's nigh on fainting with weariness. Find the cleanest corner in the dwelling and try to make her comfortable. I'll take care of Strumpet.''

''Strumpet?'' Glenys repeated, watching Dina disappear into the dwelling beneath Jean-Marc's guiding arm. ''God's mercy, is that what he calls his horse?''

Kieran chuckled as he led Nimrod toward the feeding trough. ''Wouldn't you, seeing how she behaves?'' He began to loosen Nimrod's saddle.

''Kieran.'' The word felt strange on Glenys's tongue, and clearly sounded just as strange to him, for he turned to look at her. ''Master FitzAllen,'' she corrected at once, feeling foolish. ''I will give you proof that I speak the truth, that Dina and I will not strive to escape you this night, or in the morn. If a time should come in future when 'tis safe, then of a certainty we will make the attempt…I would be a liar if I told you otherwise. But we will do nothing until that moment comes.'' She looked about at the small yard and poor dwelling. The sun was fast going away, and lengthening shadows made everything before her eyes seem even more eerie and frightening. ''We both know it will not come tonight in this horrible place. I'm afraid even to sleep within the dwelling, let alone try to walk through these strange woods. But if that is not enough to make you certain, then you must take this.''

She dug a hand into her inner pocket and, looking about to make certain that none of Xander's men were watching, withdrew the queen piece.

''Here,'' she murmured, taking Kieran's hand and setting the chess piece in his open palm. ''I have told you that my uncle gave me this and what it means to him, also that it is meant for Caswallan, as a way to regain the Greth Stone. You know that I will not leave without it.''

He stared at the delicately carved lady. ''Glenys,'' he said softly, shaking his head, '''tis not necessary.''

''Aye, but it is, for you do not accept my word as true.'' She hated giving the piece into anyone's care, but set her hand over his own and folded his fingers about it. ''Give her back to me come morn. I will trust you to do so, if you will trust me, as well.''

He tried to press the piece back toward her. ''I accept your word, Glenys. Take it back.''

''Nay, I will not.'' She felt foolish, and could feel her skin heat in consequence. If he gave it back she feared she would burst into tears, and knew not why. ''Only in the morn, when we have left this place.''

His fingers tightened about the piece, and he drew nearer to her to say, ''I will keep it safe. Upon my life, I will.''

She couldn't find the strength to look at him, but fixed her gaze on the ground. ''And I will keep watch?''

He sighed. ''You will keep watch. And if Xander or his men should do so much as gaze upon you while you do, you will wake me. At once. Give me your word upon it.''

"I give you my word." She looked at him at last, to find him gazing at her with a troubled expression. "Do you not trust me to do so?"

"I trust you, Glenys," he said, carefully placing the queen piece in some inner pocket within his tunic, "but Xander and his men are clever. They've given their word of honor to leave us in peace, but they will spend the night striving to find a way to keep that promise and still make mischief. I fear you do not know what you ask when you offer to keep watch. But it will be as you desire. The matter is settled."

The food that Xander and his men provided was, as promised, simple and somewhat crude, but they were grateful for it. Kieran and Jean-Marc took the two roasted rabbits Xander offered them on the end of a sword and deftly cut them into several pieces, giving the best parts to Dina and Glenys. The wine they drank out of coarsely carved wooden cups was bitter and sour and wretchedly old, but it soothed their dry throats and warmed their stomachs.

The decrepit dwelling had two parts—one main room, with a heavily smoking fire pit in the middle of it, and one area that was separated by heavy velvet bed curtains that Glenys suspected had been taken from some wealthy victim rather than bought and paid for out of Xander's ill-gotten riches. Xander grandly offered them this small, private area to sleep in, and Kieran accepted.

The tiny room was very dark, as the heavy curtains kept out most of the fire's light, as well as its warmth, but it was somewhat cleaner than the rest of the dwelling. The packed dirt floor had recently been swept free of the filth that filled the rest of the building, and with their cloaks laid out they were able to fashion places upon it to sleep. Dina and Jean-Marc fell into slumber almost at once, but Kieran, despite his evident exhaustion, sat beside Glenys.

"Are you certain that you wish to do this?" he asked. "I'm of a mind to bear you company in the watch."

She might have accepted the welcome offer if he hadn't looked so weary. His face was pale and heavily lined, and his blue eyes were rimmed with red. If he would but lie down, Glenys suspected he would be asleep almost before he could think of it.

"Nay, you must rest if we're to leave this place in the morn. 'Tis in truth most self-serving, for I confess I wish to be away from here."

"I'm flattered," he said with a laugh, "that you prefer my company to that of Xander's. 'Tis not much of a compliment, but 'twill do. Look, the stone glows." He touched her cloak, beneath which the small stone put out its gentle glow, illuminating their faces but not penetrating the curtains. "May I see it?"

"If I bring it out into the light, Xander and his men will see it."

"Mayhap, but 'tis better that we have some manner of light. Xander gave us this dark privacy in hopes we will all fall into slumber, and thereby give him the upper hand."

"But if he comes in—"

"He will not," Kieran assured her. "He'll want to, if he should see the glow behind the curtains, but he'd never expose such curiosity to others. At least, not until he was certain we slept. Here, will you not let me see the stone?"

Glenys hesitated, wishing that the horrid thing would stop glowing. "It's naught but a great nuisance. I wish

beyond heaven that my aunts had never pressed it upon
me.''

The glowing stopped at once, setting them back into
darkness.

"Oh," Glenys said foolishly, then gave a start as
she felt Kieran's hand searching about in her cloak.

"For shame, mistress. You've hurt its feelings." His
hands moved skillfully, finding her pocket and sliding
within. His face was so close to hers that she could feel
his breath warm upon her cheek, so close that she could
tell when his lips turned upward in a smile as he found
the stone. Only when he had taken the object and
moved away did Glenys realize that she'd been holding
her breath. Releasing it slowly, and wondering why her
heart should be beating so rapidly, she said, in an em-
barrassingly shaky manner, "You'll not get it to work.
Only my aunts know the secrets of making the lack-
witted things behave."

He ignored her, but she could hear him murmuring
to the stone just as if it could understand what he said.

"There, now, little creature. Pretty little creature."

"'Tis not a creature," Glenys told him. "'Tis a
mindless stone."

"Never listen to her, my sweet. Come now. Let us
see your pretty light."

Glenys opened her mouth to repeat what she'd just
told him, but stopped, her mouth gaping—for the stone
had begun to glow. Not brightly, but with its distinctive, soft light.

Kieran's hand was illuminated first—the flat of his
palm, upon which the smooth white stone rested, and
his long, shapely fingers. She could faintly see the out-
line of his face, and his lips as they moved, crooning
gently to the stone.

"Aye, my sweet. Pretty little creature. Just like that. Show me how sweetly you make your lovely light. A little more now…a little more."

As if in answer to him, the light grew brighter, bit by bit, as Kieran requested it, illuminating his face and then beyond, until the curtained area was awash in a gentle glow.

"There, 'tis plenty. No more now, little one, lest we be found out. What a pretty, clever stone you are. You'll not mind keeping us safe throughout the night, in spite of what your mistress tells you?"

As if in answer to his question, the stone dimmed.

"Very fine!" Glenys said, fully insulted until she remembered that it was only a rock.

"Nay, she does not mean what she says," Kieran told the stone soothingly.

"It is *not* alive!" Glenys whispered furiously. The stone dimmed even more, nearly going out altogether.

"Glenys, be silent and let me take care of this."

Huffing, Glenys folded her arms over her chest and sat without speaking, watching Kieran charm the little stone all over again until it glowed more brightly.

"There." He looked at her with clear satisfaction. "It only wanted a bit of coddling. All creatures do."

"If it is a creature," Glenys said, "then 'tis clearly a *female*."

Kieran chuckled and carefully set the stone in the middle of the small room. It put out a pure but gentle glow, as soft as a single candle.

"The trouble, Glenys Seymour," he said, leaning back with contentment and smiling at her, "is that you are surrounded by magic, but don't believe in it."

"This is not magic," she retorted, pointing at the stone.

He was unperturbed. "Of a certainty it is."

"I explained to you how it comes to put out light. 'Tis but natural elements, of the earth...."

He shook his head and yawned. "You seek to make all things practical, but 'tis impossible. Do you find the thought of magic so unsettling, then? 'Tis a wonder that your relatives haven't been able to convince you in all these years. Will you let me see this wondrous powder that your uncle gave you?"

She shook her head. "You are too weary. Mayhap on the morrow. 'Tis good for putting out fires and ridding a dwelling of smoke, as well. But it is not magic."

He chuckled. "As you say, mistress."

They were distracted by Jean-Marc, who, fast asleep, turned over to one side and threw an arm about Dina, who slept beside him. Dina gave a slight sigh, but neither woke nor moved.

Kieran spoke before Glenys could. "I'll have a word with him come morn. Don't worry o'er the matter. Jean-Marc falls in love as readily as rain falls from the sky. A more romantic fool you'll never find. His heart is broken once each fortnight."

"You surprise me, Master FitzAllen," Glenys said honestly. "He does not seem capable of such soft emotions. Most especially since I have seen him with Xander and his men. He was among them once, I gather?"

Kieran sat forward, rolling his head from side to side as if to ease sore muscles, his weariness growing more evident as each moment passed.

"Jean-Marc was born and raised in London, living like a rat in the streets, knowing neither father nor mother. When I came upon him he was but eleven years of age, and 'tis no small thing that he had lived that long beneath such daunting circumstance. He survived because he was far too witty and skilled to die, and because he had been taken in amongst a family of thieves.''

"Xander and his men?''

"Xander was among them, but he was yet an underling himself then. Nay, the man who kept Jean-Marc alive went by the name of Trigere. Japhet Trigere. God's pity, but he was a soulless knave. Ten times over what Xander is. But he knew what a treasure he had in Jean-Marc, and taught him well, treating him as much like a son as he ever had anyone. He even named Jean-Marc, choosing something French, as Trigere was.'' Kieran grinned and uttered a laugh. "And Jean-Marc has ever thought himself French-born since, and quite knowledgeable on all things Gallic, though he's as English as you or I. 'Twas but mere fortune that brought him to me one day, to pick my pocket.'' Kieran looked wistful at the memory. "He might have succeeded, if I'd not been as skilled as he.'' He glanced at Glenys with glittering eyes. "My parents have ever despaired of my peculiar talents, but they've served me well over the years, I vow. And if not for having them, I might never have caught Jean-Marc in his act of stealing from me.''

"How so?''

Kieran stretched, lifting his arms high over his head, before answering. "The only reason Jean-Marc went with me, rather than returning to his thieving family, was because he recognized me as a superior thief. And 'tis truth that I emptied a great many pockets in those days so that I might keep my belly filled and my…well, to speak kindly of it, my bed well warmed.''

"I'm surprised that you needed funds for that,'' Glenys said without thinking, then immediately flushed and set a hand to her mouth. "Forgive me. I should not have said that."

He laughed, but so wearily that she could not but feel pity. "'Nay, you speak well, though I am aware of what vanity I appear to possess. But I am near thirty years of age, and beyond telling lies to that purpose." He shrugged. "I have been blessed in my ways with women, and will not deny it. But the women whose company I have oft sought require sustenance just as needily as any do, and that is what I have paid for. But you did not wish to know of that. You wished to be reassured about Jean-Marc, and I give you my word that I'll speak to him about your maid. 'Tis not our intent to act as seducers while we hold you captive."

Glenys frowned and looked away, thinking silently that he'd have no desire to seduce her for any reason, not even if Sir Anton had paid him for it.

"We could do so, if we wished, of course," he said, and she lifted her head to find him gazing at her very directly. "Seduce you, I mean. Have no doubt of that. You'd be helpless to resist."

Glenys's eyes widened. She hardly knew what to think of such words. Was he making sport of her ugliness? A man so handsome, who could have any female he desired with but a glance, would never waste his considerable charms upon one such as her.

Her silence seemed to exasperate him. He lifted a hand and pointed to the great, filthy room beyond the curtain.

"Xander and his men were willing to pay me *gold* just to have you for a single night. *You,* and not your maid."

"They were afraid of harming her," Glenys whispered.

He rolled his eyes. "They didn't give a holy damn about hurting anyone, least of all Dina. They're murdering swine, Glenys. They only respect those who are faster and more able with a weapon than they are. Nay, Xander wanted you. You've little experience with such things, being used to weak men like Sir Anton, but that was lust in Xander's gaze. For *you*."

Glenys blinked at the sudden tears that sprang to her eyes. Why had he suddenly become so cruel?

"I understand what it is you say," she managed to reply, her voice quavering. "A man—a murderer— who has been without a woman for many weeks may be driven to want…one such as I am."

Kieran tilted his head back and gazed up at the meager roof above, almost as if he was praying for patience. "That is not what I mean," he said at last, finally lowering his gaze to meet her own. "If I were not so weary, and if I had not already vowed to leave you in peace, I would *show* you what I mean, and then you would have no doubt of it. Here." He took his sword, which he had unsheathed before he'd sat down, and placed it between them. "I pray you'll not need this, but 'twill be here if you do. Remember, wake me if one of them dares to pass through the curtains."

Mute, Glenys nodded, and watched as Kieran muttered something beneath his breath and then lay down. He closed his eyes, but kept muttering…something about women and foolishness and not knowing anything at all. At last, however, he yawned and grew silent, and then fell fast asleep.

If he hadn't been so weary, Kieran told himself later, he would have waked the very moment that Glenys started saying his name. And most certainly when she started kicking him. And most definitely, beyond a doubt, when he at last smelled smoke.

As it was, he finally came awake to find Glenys standing almost on top of him, holding his sword in her hands, fending off a very unhappy Roald.

"Master FitzAllen!" Glenys shouted furiously, the heavy sword wobbling back and forth. "Jean-Marc!"

From somewhere behind him, Kieran heard Jean-Marc's reply along with a great deal of movement, followed by one of Dina's unhelpful shrieks. Kieran himself lay as if frozen in his place, staring up with groggy amazement at the sight of Glenys fending off Roald as boldly as an Amazon. She looked as if she'd kill the man if she had to—and if she could keep the sword aloft. There were no tears upon her face, nothing of terror...only fierce determination.

A pair of hands grabbed Kieran by the collar and dragged him up into a sitting position, and then Jean-Marc's angry face appeared. "God's toes, you're getting old, blind and deaf!" he shouted, heartily shaking him. *"Get up!"*

The lethargy that had held him spellbound lifted away at once, and Kieran leaped to his feet. The entire dwelling was rapidly filling with smoke, and he understood at once what was happening. Xander had promised not to touch them—physically. But filling the room with smoke and confusion and trying to steal their belongings wasn't part of his vow. And unless Kieran got them all out of the dwelling soon, they'd be overcome by the smoke and possibly die from it. Already he could see that Glenys was coughing, her grip on the sword faltering.

"Let me deal with this fool," he muttered, taking the sword from her hands and reaching out to grab

Roald by the collar, setting the blade against his neck. "Glenys!" he shouted above the noise and confusion, ignoring Roald's struggles to escape his steely grip, "Stay close by Jean-Marc, and he'll lead you... Glenys?" He looked about in the smoke, just in time to see her disappearing beyond the curtains and into the greater room beyond—where Xander and his men were busy causing the fire to smoke.

"Glenys! Do not!"

But she was gone. All he could hear was her cough, desperate due to the ever increasing smoke.

Kieran spared only a brief moment to shout out to Jean-Marc, "Keep the maid down! I'll see to Xander!" Then he thumped the still-struggling Roald with the hilt of his sword, tossing the insensible body aside, and holding the weapon at the ready, parted the curtains and stepped into the thick smoke of the room beyond.

He heard a brief, feminine scream to his left and surged in that direction, uselessly waving the smoke aside with one hand. "Xander, leave her be! I swear by heaven that I'll have your manhood on a platter if you so much as—"

A bright explosion of sparkling lights filled the room, turning purple as they fell, and suddenly, unbelievably, the smoke was gone. Just...gone. Not blown away by wind, not escaped bit by bit through a window or the many cracks and holes in the poorly built dwelling. Gone. The sparkles fell to the ground, glittering like hundreds of tiny white and purple stars before dying away altogether, leaving all those in the room staring at each other with but the lingering glow of the fire's embers to give light. But it was enough for Kieran to see that Xander and his remaining men were standing near Glenys, their knives drawn and their faces filled with a mixture of awe and fear. Glenys herself stood staring at Kieran, one hand holding the small leather pouch, the other still palm-out in the air. Her face was pale, and he took a step toward her.

"A w-witch!" Xander stammered. "You've brought a witch among us!"

"She's not a witch," Kieran said, knowing they'd not believe him. Glenys did look very much like a magical sorceress standing thus, with her long, auburn hair unbound and flowing down to her hips and her hand stretched out as if casting a spell. She had also banished the smoke in a manner that seemed magical— and despite what she'd said about her uncle's powders, Kieran wasn't yet convinced that they *weren't* possessed of some measure of sorcery.

"Leave us!" Xander implored, huddling with his men against the farther wall. "Leave now! Kieran, I beg it of you. Take your witch and be on your way."

The curtains parted and Jean-Marc and Dina walked into the greater area, carrying the glowing stone with them. Jean-Marc stretched it out upon the palm of his hand, illuminating one and all.

"God's mercy!" Xander crossed himself. "'Tis the devil's own sorcery."

"Aye," Kieran said, losing his temper, "and this is my sword, sharp and ready and of greater threat to you in this moment than a tiny rock." He strode forward and set the blade to Xander's throat for the second time. "Tell me now, Xander, why I shouldn't send your Gypsy soul to hell for breaking your word of honor to me."

"We did not break our word! We've given you no harm!"

"You nearly choked us to death with the smoke you

made from the fire, and sent Roald in to steal our belongings.''

"But we set no hand upon you," Xander argued, then clasped his hands together in a pleading manner. "Kieran, I beg of you, either take your witch and go or let us leave. You'll see naught of us again, I vow, for we'll not return until you're well away come morn."

"Do you think I'd be fool enough to trust you again? Nay, Xander, I have a much better idea, and you'll do as I say, else I'll turn my woman upon you. You've seen little of her powers as yet, but I'll gladly give her leave to send the vilest of curses down on your head if you give us any more trouble. Jean-Marc," he said, not taking his eyes off Xander, who had actually begun to tremble, "find some rope. We'll have a decent night of rest yet, I vow."

Half an hour later they lay down once more, this time around the freshly relit fire.

Kieran had at last convinced Glenys to lie down as well, but she seemed unwilling to close her eyes.

"Are you certain they'll not be able to get free? Xander is so clever...."

Kieran yawned aloud and stretched. "If I'd done the tying, we might have cause to fear. But Jean-Marc tied them. They'll not be free until we set them free. *If* we set them free."

From the other side of the fire, where he lay with his eyes closed, Jean-Marc uttered an amused snort.

Glenys sat on the blanket Kieran had laid out for her, her hands holding her cloak fast about her, looking troubled.

"They think me a witch," she said. "I told you how it is."

"Aye, but 'twas a good thing, at least tonight. Here." He reached into his tunic and withdrew the queen piece, holding it out to her. She leaned forward to take it, looking at him questioningly. "You'll rest easier having it in your possession," he told her, yawning again and closing his eyes, settling more comfortably into the bed he'd made for himself. "Go to sleep, Glenys. We've a long journey come morn."

She was silent and still. Kieran lay where he was, his eyes shut, listening. It was a long time before he heard her lie down and, sighing, make herself comfortable, and longer still before he was certain that she had at last allowed herself to fall asleep.

Chapter Nine

By the time they reached York a few days later, Glenys had lost all patience with her captors. Kieran refused to listen to reason; Jean-Marc ignored her altogether. Dina wasn't much better. She'd given up trying to help Glenys convince the two men that theirs was a fool's errand, and instead seemed content to spend much of her time following Jean-Marc about. Glenys had long since realized that Jean-Marc was attracted to her maid, and it was becoming increasingly clear that Dina was likewise affected. Glenys had spoken to her twice about not allowing her heart to become involved with such a scoundrel, and Dina had assured her, sighing, that she'd take every care. In the next breath, however, she went on to sing Jean-Marc's praises, telling Glenys how kind he was, how gentle, how considerate and how handsome. That he was a baseborn thief seemed not to matter at all.

It was enough, on top of everything else, to make Glenys want to pluck her eyelashes out. She was filthy after so many days of travel. Her hair was a great, awful, tangled mass. Her clothes and boots were spotted with dirt and mud, and she smelled heavily of horse sweat. She was tired, hungry, and every bone in her body ached from long hours of constant journeying. Her only consolation was that her companions were as miserable as she was.

But now they had reached Sir Anton's keep in York. It was just as Glenys had prophesied it would be, a great, hulking, crumbling relic that no sane human would make a home of. Animals, aye, could be housed perfectly well inside the round tower, despite the gaping hole in the front of it where the walls on either side sagged together. Another wall, which had once created an inner bailey and provided an extra measure of protection, had nearly fallen down entirely.

"You see, 'tis just as I told you. Sir Anton never sent you here in order to keep Dina and me captive many weeks." Sitting atop Nimrod with Kieran's arm lashed about her waist, she looked at all the trees surrounding them. "Even now his henchmen may be watching us, waiting for us to come closer so that they may attack and kill us."

Behind her, Kieran gave a weary sigh. "I've told you time and again that 'tis impossible. Why should Sir Anton wish to have you—or any of us—dead? If he wants you out of his way, then 'twould best serve his purpose to keep us all alive, you most especially. Your family will be searching you out even now, and if you're found dead, they might well suspect Sir Anton. Only an utter fool wouldn't know the trouble that would bring into his life."

"Sir Anton *is* an utter fool," Glenys told him.

"But not that great a fool, I vow," said Kieran. He looked to Jean-Marc for confirmation. "How does it seem to you, Jean-Marc?"

"Well enough," the younger man replied with a

nod. "'Tis clear the keep is not occupied. It should be safe to enter, leastwise."

"Aye, and despite the gape, we'll have a warm fire and a good dinner," Kieran said with pleasure, the arm he held about Glenys tightening. "There must be rabbits aplenty in these fields, and we've a fresh loaf of bread from the baker we passed this morn."

"And a full wineskin," Jean-Marc added, leaning to pat the bag that hung from his saddle. "With any fortune we'll find enough soft branches to make our beds, at least for the night. Tomorrow one of us might venture into the city beyond and buy supplies."

"It's a trap," Glenys said, shaking her head. "You refuse to listen to me, but 'tis the truth I speak."

Ignoring her, Kieran set Nimrod into motion, moving forward, down the hill they'd been standing upon and into the valley that led to the crumbling keep.

"Sir Anton gave us enough gold that we may live comfortably," he said, clearly eager to embrace the rest and ease that he envisioned. "We'll have fresh cheese and ale, and extra blankets for all. And oats for the horses. God above knows they deserve it after riding so many miles these past—"

An arrow whizzed past his ear, shot from close behind them, the feather brushing Glenys's cheek as it went. Glenys stared after it with widening eyes, while behind her Kieran first stiffened, then dug his heels into Nimrod's sides.

"Go!" he shouted as the great horse leaped forward, but Jean-Marc had already had the same thought. The two horses ran side by side down the hill, racing headlong toward the keep, while more arrows flew toward them from behind.

"I t-t-told you!" Glenys shouted, fiercely clinging to Kieran's arm and the saddle.

He leaned over her as another arrow shot past. "Aye, aye, gloat all you please," he shouted over her head, steering Nimrod directly toward the gaping hole in the keep, "but be good enough to wait until we're safe!"

A short wall stood at the bottom of the hole, but both Nimrod and Strumpet easily leaped over it and into the keep. It was just as it had seemed from outside—a single empty tower with stairs circling up the walls, leading to floors above.

Kieran and Jean-Marc brought both horses to an abrupt halt, leaping down to the ground and pulling Glenys and Dina down as well. Kieran shoved Glenys toward the stairs with one hand, while unsheathing his sword with the other. Outside, the sound of fast approaching horses grew louder and more imminent.

"Get upstairs!" Kieran shouted. "Take Dina! Hurry!"

He turned away to greet the first of the intruding riders with a thrust of his sword. The man, who never knew what had struck him, fell from his horse, a gaping slash across his chest already filling with blood.

Glenys stumbled back as more riders charged over the wall and into the confusion, meeting Kieran and Jean-Marc head-on as the two men strove to beat them back. Nimrod and Strumpet whinnied nervously and trotted to the far side of the keep, nearly trampling Dina, who had fallen to the ground and covered her head when the attack first came. Glenys hurried to her, shoving Nimrod aside with all her strength, and grasped Dina by an arm to pull her to her feet.

"Stay with the horses!" she cried above the din,

pushing the younger girl toward the wall where Nimrod and Strumpet huddled.

Kieran shouted her name, and Glenys whirled about to find a rider bearing down on her, sword in hand. She stood paralyzed with fear, unable to move or even cry out, her eyes fixed on the gleaming blade that surely meant her death. Suddenly she was struck by a flying body—Jean-Marc's—and tumbled heavily to the ground. The horse passed by, its hooves clattering next to her head. The moment it was gone Jean-Marc rolled away and came to his feet, ready as the rider turned about and charged again. Jean-Marc twirled the dagger in his hand with astonishing skill, his face so fiercely set that he looked like a demon warrior. Almost as if begging for death, he stood directly in front of the horse as it rushed toward him, but the moment the great beast came within an arm's distance, Jean-Marc leaped aside with agile grace, lifted the dagger high and brought the hilt smashing down on the horse's muzzle. The beast fell sideways, crumpling with a scream of protest and trapping its rider nearly beneath him. Glenys scrambled aside, watching with unutterable horror as Jean-Marc pounced upon the flailing man and slit his throat. It was over in but moments. The horse clumsily regained its feet and ran off, dragging its dead rider along.

Glenys stared, certain that she was either going to faint or be ill, until Jean-Marc grabbed her by the arm and shouted at her. "Get out of here! Go!"

He pushed her toward the wall where Dina stood between Nimrod and Strumpet, protected for the moment by the two beasts. Glenys obediently stumbled in that direction, but the sound of the madness and fury behind made her stop and turn about. There were at

least four more men on horseback, and though Kieran
and Jean-Marc fought valiantly and with great skill, she
could see that they would be overwhelmed. Jean-Marc
had just saved her life, risking his own to do so. Could
she simply stand by and watch both him and Kieran
die without doing anything?

But what?

She looked about for some kind of weapon, drawing
in a sharp breath when her gaze fell upon a pile of
charred wood where someone had once attempted to
start a fire. Without letting herself think on what she
did, Glenys ran to the discarded pile, grabbed up the
biggest log that she could easily lift, and entered the
fray.

Swords, daggers, booted feet all came at her, along
with the frightening press of powerful, nervous, confused steeds. From somewhere to one side of her she
heard Kieran's angry voice shouting her name, but she
didn't stop to think upon that. Lifting the piece of wood
high, she brought it down with all her strength upon
the head of the nearest horse, just as Jean-Marc had
done, hearing with dismay its unhappy response and
watching with even greater distress as it stumbled to
its knees, sending its rider tumbling. Kieran was on the
man in a moment, his sword high. Glenys turned away
and lifted the piece of wood again to bring it down
upon the next unfortunate horse.

The next several minutes seemed to last an eter-
nity—one filled with confusion and dread—until the
last two attackers left alive turned their horses about
and fled.

A moment passed. Kieran, Jean-Marc and Glenys all
stared at each other, their various weapons lowered,
breathing harshly. Riderless horses tramped about in

nervous agitation, and at least four bodies lay bloodied upon the ground. Pressed against the wall, Dina stood clutching Nimrod's and Strumpet's reins, wide-eyed with terror.

Kieran stumbled to the keep's opening, watching the two riders fleeing in the distance.

"They've gone," he said, his voice harsh with the exertion he'd undergone. "But they'll come back, if not for us, then for their comrades." He surveyed the bodies on the bare dirt floor. "Let's get them out of here, outside the bailey. Glenys, tend to Dina while Jean-Marc and I calm these horses." He swiped an arm across his sweating forehead. "Don't try to help. They're half-maddened."

Glenys nodded and gratefully dropped the piece of wood, retreating to where Dina stood, shaking and weeping. Glenys put an arm about the younger girl, closing her eyes and leaning against the wall.

Kieran and Jean-Marc somehow managed to get the horses out of the keep and tethered in the empty bailey. Then they dragged the bodies out, one by one, and placed them in a row in the field just outside the keep.

"Glenys." Kieran beckoned to her from outside. "Come out of there. Bring Mistress Dina with you."

Holding out his hand, he helped them over the short wall and led them into the welcome sunlight. It seemed incredible to Glenys that only a quarter of an hour earlier they'd been sitting upon the nearby hill with this same sun shining down upon them. She'd been unhappy then, despite the beauty of the day; now, mere minutes later, she was so thankful to be alive, so thankful simply to feel the warmth of the sun, that she could have wept.

"Sit here," he said, leading them to where several

blocks of the bailey wall had fallen to the ground. "Jean-Marc and I must tend to Strumpet and Nimrod, and then we'll do what we can to sweep the blood aside. Stay here. There's nothing to worry about. They'll not come back until dark."

Glenys and Dina gratefully sat; Glenys leaned forward to rest her head in her hands, striving mightily not to join Dina in her weeping. She felt Kieran's hand fall briefly on her shoulder, a warm, understanding touch that lasted but a moment before it was gone.

Kieran and Jean-Marc disappeared into the keep, emerging from time to time in search of things they needed. Branches to sweep the blood away—if it could be swept away. Grass to feed the horses, and a cloak taken from one of the dead men to wipe them down with once they were unsaddled.

Everything seemed to calm by degrees, slowly, moment by moment, until Glenys felt almost herself once more.

Kieran came out of the keep and, following the curve of it, disappeared. It was several minutes before he reappeared, first calling to Jean-Marc and then approaching Glenys and Dina.

"I've found the keep's well. The water is stale, but clean enough that we may wash ourselves and water the animals. Come and refresh yourselves."

Glenys rose, saying, "Should you not water the horses first? Their need is greater than our own."

His expression was grim, but his voice gentle when he replied, "You will want to wash your garment, Glenys."

She looked down at herself for the first time since the fighting had ended, and saw that her skirt was both badly torn and splattered with blood.

"God's mercy," she murmured, unable to keep the horror from her voice. She began to tremble, thinking of what had passed and the part she had played in it—the death of four men. "God's sweet mercy."

Two strong hands closed over her shoulders.

"When I first set sight upon you," Kieran said, "I could not see how it was that you and Daman Seymour were sister and brother, save perhaps in height, for otherwise you look not alike at all. But now I see full well how it is. You are the bravest woman I have ever known, Glenys Seymour, and your brother, were he here, would be proud of you." He gave her a little shake. "There is no shame or wrong in what you did to help us, and I will not let you think there was."

"He speaks the truth, mistress," Dina said meekly, standing and drawing near. "If you'd not done as you did, 'tis certain that Master FitzAllen and Jean-Marc would have at last been overcome by our assailants, and our lives, too, would not have been spared. We would all be dead."

Glenys slowly lifted her gaze to look into Kieran's eyes. There was a determination there that she could not fight against.

"Very well," she said, her voice as weak and faint as she felt. "I'll not feel guilt for my part in what happened to those men. But tell me…if I harmed any of the horses."

His eyes widened slightly, as if the question surprised him, and then he smiled and gave a shake of his head. "Nay, Glenys." He uttered a laugh that was pure amusement. "None of them is harmed."

"Are you certain?" She searched his face. "I struck them so sharply, I thought I must surely have done great damage, which I should never wish to do."

He bent forward suddenly and enfolded her in his arms, crushing her in a hard, brief embrace, still laughing. When he pulled away, he smiled into her stunned expression and said, "I will let you see the beasts once I've taken you to the well, if't pleases you, but I promise you, Glenys, that you gave them no harm. But come and be washed and refreshed." He tugged her into motion and nodded for Dina to follow. "The horses will want water soon, and there is much yet to do to make ourselves safe before nightfall."

Chapter Ten

They let the horses go just before the sun began to set. Kieran and Jean-Marc spent half an hour trying to decide whether they shouldn't keep two of the steeds for Glenys and Dina to use, but had at last agreed that the extra care and feed would cause more trouble than good. Apart from that, Dina disliked riding, and Glenys admitted that, though she knew how to ride, she was far from being as skilled at handling horses as her brother.

Kieran had been relieved, though he'd not spoken of it aloud. They'd been busy making the keep ready for nightfall and what dangers that might bring them, and only now did Kieran have the freedom to think of what had happened—and what it meant.

Glenys had been right about everything, and he'd been a blind, stubborn fool not to see it. Nay, worse, he thought bitterly. He'd not *let* himself believe it, because if he'd believed, he would have altered his plans for revenge on Daman Seymour, and Kieran's accursed pride hadn't allowed for that. He'd been the one to lead them here to this trap. He'd been the one who'd nearly brought all of them to their deaths. And Glenys, his

prisoner, who had been so fully in his power and helpless to sway or stop him, had been the one to change
the unfavorable balance between them and their attackers. Dina had been right. If Glenys had not lent her aid
in felling the horses, Kieran knew full well that he and
Jean-Marc could not have held out against so many
armed men on horseback.

Everything was changed now. Kieran still wasn't
certain just how, but this he did know: it made him
unhappy and uncomfortable. He didn't want things to
change. Not between Glenys and himself. He didn't
want her riding another horse. He wanted to keep her
beneath his power, beneath his hand. And in the last
day he'd even had the unsettling and hopeful thought
that perhaps Daman wouldn't find them, and then she
would have to stay with him for far longer than Kieran
had planned. For he'd already decided—just when, he
didn't know—that he'd not give her over to Sir Anton's
care. He would still let her go, of course, at some time
in the future. But he'd had no particular date in mind,
certainly no immediate one.

But now such thoughts had vanished. Everything had
changed.

They had unsaddled the horses and removed all their
headgear, fed and watered them, and now sent them
out of the bailey, free to go where and as they pleased.
Nimrod and Strumpet, kept within the keep itself,
whinnied at the sound of their fellows trotting away.
Jean-Marc, with some help from Dina, knelt on the
ground and began to go through the various bags that
had been tied to the saddles, seeking anything that
might be of use to them in the coming days.

Glenys stood beside Kieran, watching the horses as

they slowed their progress, just outside the bailey walls.

''Will the men who came earlier find and take them again?'' she asked.

''They may try, for the horses are valuable, but 'twill not be easy without reins or saddles. Ah, look how they shy away from the dead. 'Tis clear they were not trained for battle. Nimrod was. He hates the smell of blood, as all horses do, but he'll not shy from death.''

Glenys watched but said nothing. After a few moments the horses began to wander toward the open field, where the grass grew taller.

''They'll probably remain there throughout the night, unless some manner of danger comes,'' Kieran murmured.

''Or those men come back,'' Glenys said, setting her arms about herself as if cold.

Though the keep was partly in ruins, the second floor and roof were far more defensible than the bottom level. There was only one entrance—gained by the keep's lone interior stairway—to each ascending level. It was necessary to leave Nimrod and Strumpet in the lower level, but on the second floor they built a fire and made beds of branches and grass. Two of them would keep watch on the roof, where another fire had been built, while two slept below on the second level. Whoever watched from the roof would be able to rouse those below in case of an attack, and with their defenses already in place, Kieran believed that they would be perfectly safe. With but the one entrance, he and Jean-Marc could easily best any assailants, and he truly doubted that the fools would try anything so lack-witted as scaling the keep from the outside. Nay, the worst they had to worry o'er was that Nimrod and

Strumpet might come to some harm, but as the horses couldn't be taken up the stairs, that was a risk that had to be faced. He had little fear of the animals being stolen; Glenys and Dina had already learned just how difficult a thing that was to accomplish. Nimrod was too well trained to be taken by strangers, and Strumpet too mean.

Just before the sun fully set, they gathered about the fire on the second floor, exhausted and hungry, and shared what food and wine they had. In truth, it wasn't so poor a meal as they had thought it would be. They had the loaf of bread they'd bought that morn, and the saddles Jean-Marc and Dina had searched had yielded a supply of dried meats and sweetcakes that had been carefully wrapped in cloth to keep them moist and fresh. There had also been two large wine flasks, almost full, and several smaller flasks. By the time they had finished their welcome meal, their spirits had risen considerably.

"Glenys and I will take the first watch," Kieran said, rising to his feet and pulling his cloak on. "Try to sleep," he advised, holding out a hand to help Glenys stand. "We'll wake you come midnight."

The night air was crisp and cool, and Glenys pulled her cloak more tightly about her, holding the edges together at her throat. Above, the stars and moon shone brightly in the sky, only occasionally lost behind the few dark clouds that drifted across the sky.

"'Twill rain on the morrow," Kieran said from across the keep, where he stood near the low wall, not keeping watch, as he was supposed to do. Instead, he was leaning against the wall, facing Glenys, holding the carved queen chess piece up for close examination.

"What does she do?" he asked, turning the little piece about. "Save put forth light from her eyes?"

"They only appear to glow," Glenys told him, sighing. "'Tis a trick of some kind."

"But not magic, eh?" He gave her a glancing grin. "But 'tis most odd, for the color changes. At times her eyes are golden, but at others green. Just now they've nearly turned blue. As pretty as any real woman's eyes ever were."

Glenys had never seen the queen's eyes turn blue, and her curiosity drew her across the roof to take a look. She stood beside Kieran and peered at the piece he cradled in his grasp, holding the little wooden woman as carefully as if she were made of flesh and bone.

"I see what it is," Glenys said with a wry smile. "You've simply charmed her, just as you charmed the stone."

He pulled the stone out of his tunic with a swift, smooth movement, holding it up in the palm of his other hand, level with the queen piece. The tiny white rock put off a warm, immediate glow.

"It does seem to like me well enough," he said with pleasure, bringing the object closer to coo at it. "My sweet little creature. You glow so prettily for me, don't you, my tiny one?"

The stone's glow brightened almost like a maiden's blushing cheeks.

"I've ne'er seen such a sinful display of vanity in all my life," Glenys told him with disdain. "I don't know how you talked me into letting you care for the stone. 'Tis shameful how you treat it."

"But she only glows for me now," he said. "Don't you, my darling?"

"'Tis not a she."

"Of course she is," Kieran told her with authority. "Can you doubt my knowledge of such things?"

Glenys sighed. "Nay, that I would never do. You are doubtless without peer in the knowledge of the fairer sex. No other man on God's earth can claim that he's charmed a stone, I vow. And now a chess piece, as well."

Kieran lifted the queen a bit higher, turning her first one way, then the other.

"Nay, she's not so easily won. Her heart has already been taken...mayhap by your uncle? The one who gave her to you?"

Glenys uttered a laugh. "You're crazed. She was dear to my uncle Culain, aye, but she's naught but a bit of wood. There's no life in her to love."

"Ah," said Kieran, turning the wooden piece so that Glenys could see it. "Now her eyes have turned gray. Dark gray. Not silver, as yours are. You've angered her."

Glenys took the piece from him and pushed it back into her inner pocket. "Then she'll be glad to have some peace in which to consider her revenge. I begin to think my uncle must have been mad to give it to me."

"The Greth Stone must be of great import to your family for him to have parted with her."

"Aye," Glenys said. "'Tis difficult to tell you how so. But the queen piece...I cannot imagine my uncle Culain without her."

"Then we must be certain to get her back from Caswallan once the Greth Stone has been secured."

Glenys's mouth dropped open.

"Get her back?" she repeated. "From Caswallan?"

"Aye, for I would not have your uncle deprived of the queen's company. And I do not think she'll be happy until she's with him once more."

Glenys was certain she didn't understand him aright. "Have you decided to take me to Wales? To find Caswallan?" She set her hand upon his arm, almost afraid to hope that it was true. "I'll pay you whatever you ask. Far more than Sir Anton offered, and—"

"Glenys." Kieran laid his fingers lightly over her hand. "You will pay me naught, nor speak of such unless you wish to anger me. I owe you not only my life, but Jean-Marc's, as well."

"In that we are equal," she told him. "You saved my life—and Dina's—just as fully. And I owe Jean-Marc even greater thanks, for he placed himself in the path of what would have been certain death for me."

"If not for Jean-Marc and me, none of us would have been at this wretched place to put our lives in danger." Kieran looked down to where their hands touched. "Nay, Glenys, I was wrong to take you prisoner at Sir Anton's bidding, more wrong to use you to satisfy my desire for confrontation with your brother. You will not repay me. Now I must repay you."

"You're giving up your quest to fight Daman?"

Kieran lifted his gaze, smiling at her in the charming manner that she was fast becoming used to.

"Nay," he said simply, "but even if I were, 'twould be far too late to stop it now. Your brother would come after me even if I took you back to London this very moment. What will come between Daman and me is inevitable."

Releasing a taut, angry breath, Glenys slid her hand free. "There is no sense in that. If you would speak of repayment, then do so by making peace with my brother. I will not have you dead at his hands. 'Twould be the start of great enmity between your family and mine, and that I would not have."

Kieran laughed. "My family would miss me, I think, but they would scarce begin a war for my sake."

"How can I know that?" Glenys charged. "'Tis clear you've been recognized in some measure by both of your parents. You told me yourself that this is so."

His expression softened. "I am fortunate to be recognized by both sides of my family, but naught can change the manner of my birth. Neither love nor ties of blood can wash that sin away, and much as my family loves me, they would not drag either of their esteemed names through such a public humiliation. And I would neither ask nor let them. *If* I am alive to do so. Your brother may dispatch me to another realm, despite my best attempts to stop him." Kieran spoke the words in a light tone and smiled once more, but Glenys could feel no amusement.

"I cannot believe that your family would desert you, simply because of your manner of birth. Many among those basely born have become both titled and powerful. Only look at our late King Henry and his brothers, the Duke of Exeter among them."

"But their father, John of Gaunt, wed his mistress, and petitioned to have all of his bastard children legally recognized by both church and crown. This will never happen to me. My mother is a noblewoman descended from a long and revered family line, married to a great lord, and, except for his one drunken sin in begetting me, my father, Lord Allen, is admirably devoted to his wife and legitimate children." Glenys saw that Kieran struggled to maintain the smile that was his constant companion.

"Among all these happy, well-born, assured people," he murmured, looking away, "I am the lone misstep. The single family mistake." He shrugged as if it didn't really matter, but the action did nothing to dispel the pain that Glenys could both hear in his voice and see on his face. "They are good and kind people," he told her. "I've been loved and treated well, and have no cause for complaint. I doubt any other baseborn child has ever been so fortunate. I was raised with my mother's legitimate children from her first marriage and also with those that she later gave my stepfather, and when I was older I was fostered with my own natural father, who trained me alongside his other sons. I have been given far more than I deserved, and have repaid them by living as reckless and fruitless a life as possible." He let out a tense breath and lifted his gaze to meet her own. "I am not the black stain among my family for naught. They have done enough in saving me from a great many disasters in the past. I would not ask or expect it of them again."

Glenys moved before she thought of what she did, reaching up to touch his cheek.

"I would *make* them," she said angrily, immediately embarrassed at the declaration. She lowered her hand, but he caught it in his own and gazed at her with disturbing intensity.

"Would you, Glenys?"

"Aye," she whispered, tugging her hand free and turning away, her cheeks hot. What would he think of her for speaking in such a manner? But she already knew. He would think that she had fallen in love with him, just as every other woman surely did. She walked a few paces along the length of the wall and gazed out over the bailey, relieved that he didn't follow. There was silence for a few long moments; Glenys's heartbeat was loud in her ears as she waited for him to speak, to say anything, even to tease her for her foolishness. But when he did speak, it was as if he instead answered her unasked questions.

"My mother was married to her first husband when she was but thirteen years of age. She had been betrothed to the man since she was a newborn babe, and had no say in the union. He was a great lord, much older than she, but a good and generous man, or so she has ever told me. He took in many boys for fostering, and among these was my stepfather and his cousin...who is my father."

Glenys's embarrassment was instantly forgotten. Wide-eyed, she turned to stare at Kieran, who was standing near the wall some steps away. His arms were folded over his well-muscled chest in defense of the cold night wind, which whipped the folds of his heavy cloak hither and yon. The smile was gone from his beautiful face, and he spoke in a manner so solemn that it was almost as if he was making a dark, painful confession.

"They are cousins," Glenys murmured, blinking away her astonishment. "But how can this be?"

"'Tis not often done that relatives are fostered together in homes apart from their own," Kieran admitted, "but they were not close save in age and birth, and acted more as friends than relations. My mother was younger than both, and very beautiful. My father befriended her, but my stepfather fell deeply in love with her. Many years passed. My mother dutifully bore her husband three children, my eldest brother and two elder sisters. My father and stepfather completed their training and left the care of their foster lord. My father returned to his home and wed the lady to whom he had been betrothed since his childhood, but my stepfather refused to marry even at his family's pleading, for the love he bore toward his foster lord's wife made it impossible for him to give his affections to another. He took up his duties at his father's estate, which would soon become his own, and then, some years later, being restless, gathered an army and went to France to serve the king. My father, having produced three sons in as many years, soon thereafter followed with his own army.''

"And your mother?" Glenys asked, drawing her own cloak more tightly about her as a gust of wind sent her unbraided hair flying. The fire crackled and leaped.

"She spent the six years following my stepfather's departure nursing her husband, who had grown very ill, and in caring for his estate and their children. She was twenty-four years of age when he died, leaving her a young, wealthy and still very beautiful widow. He was hardly cold in the ground, may God assoil him, before she was beset by suitors begging for her hand. And threatening, as well.''

"Threatening," Glenys repeated, thinking on all that implied. She had heard of women being forced into marriage by men powerful and rich enough to buy the king's favor in the matter. She shivered at the thought of what Kieran's mother must have gone through.

"Aye, and though my mother is a strong woman, she felt in need of support. She tried to send for my stepfather, only to discover that he was yet in France, and so instead she sent a missive to my father, begging him to come and lend her his aid.

"My father had returned from France the year before, having been wounded in battle. He had fully healed and taken on his estate duties once more, and had gotten his wife with child again. As strange as this has ever seemed to me, the child was born—and died— on the very same day that my mother's husband passed away. My father, grieved by the loss of both his only daughter and his former master, was not in the most stable temper as he journeyed to fulfill my mother's bidding. He could not have denied her request, even if he had wished to do so, for she was the wife of his foster lord, to whom he owed a great debt for so many years of training.''

Glenys could almost have said herself what had happened. A woman and man both sick with grief... seeking comfort where they would not have sought it before.

Kieran drew in a deep breath and released it slowly, turning his gaze outward, past Glenys and down toward the bailey.

''My mother and father were but dear friends, but 'twas a grave misstep for them to be together at such a time. My mother was distressed by all that had occurred, and deeply thankful when my father dispatched all of her unwanted suitors. And my father, missing his wife and grieving for his lost child, foolishly spent his nights drinking to assuage his miseries. On one such night, they came together seeking mutual comfort. I know none of the whys and wherefores, save that on the following morn they were both filled with utter dismay and remorse. I'faith, I do not think they ever would have set sight upon each other again if my mother had not taken with child. As it was, my father left as quickly as he could, returning to his wife and home, and only later, upon receiving word from my mother, discovered the awful fact of my existence.''

''Do not speak of it so!'' Glenys cried, unable to stop the tears that filled her eyes. '''Twas not awful! I will not hear you—or anyone—say such a thing.''

''Oh, but it was, Glenys,'' he said somberly, still not looking at her. ''So much so. You cannot know how. Only think upon the matter and you will know what my mother faced in having committed such grave adultery. 'Tis true, she might have claimed the child to be that of her late lord's, but one and all would have thought it most unlikely that a man so ill could have fathered a child.''

''Your father was truly honorable to recognize you as his own,'' Glenys said. ''He might have lost a great deal in doing so.''

Kieran sighed and nodded. ''Aye, he might have, most especially the devotion of his wife, for they were, and are, lovers in every sense. She's an unusually kind and understanding woman, my stepmother.'' He glanced at Glenys with a wry smile. ''I am surrounded by goodness and understanding in my family. There are times when it nearly makes me crazed.''

Glenys knew what it was that he said. She, too, was the odd one among her relatives, but they were all too wonderful and loving for her to set her grievances at their feet.

''What did your father do when he had the missive from your mother?''

''In truth, he was not allowed to do much for her. My stepfather had by then heard of his former master's death and returned to England with the hope of winning my mother's hand.''

''Was he very unhappy to find her with child?''

Kieran gave a mirthless laugh. "He was ready to murder his cousin, my father. But as to my mother, no, he loved her far too deeply to be angered. He pleaded with her to wed him at once, and even offered to give me his name and let the world think me his natural child. But my mother is a proud and stubborn woman. Much like you, I think."

Glenys stared at him. "How so?"

"She would not give her heart easily to any man, just as you would not. Would you, Glenys?"

"Nay, I do not think I would," she murmured, though she knew it wasn't true. She had already given her heart. So foolishly. So recklessly. And so hopelessly.

Kieran sighed and let his arms fall to his sides.

"My mother did not then love my stepfather as he loved her, and 'twas no simple thing for him to convince her to wed him for my sake alone. She was willing to face the wrath of both church and crown, knowing that my father would not let her face that wrath alone. And this was so. My father had assured her that he would recognize me and give me his name. But even so, she might have faced great shame, mayhap even punishment, for conceiving a bastard child so shortly following her husband's death if my stepfather had not at last convinced her to wed him and therefore place herself beneath his protection."

"Did she ever come to love him? Your stepfather?"

"God save us, yes," Kieran replied emphatically. "She had not loved before—truly loved—though she had been fond of her first husband. But once she did love, 'twas wholly and fully. But it did not happen quickly. I was perhaps five years of age before I realized that the change had taken place. I think—nay, I know—that my stepfather would say that all his efforts and patience and waiting were not wasted. 'Tis no small thing to gain the love of such a woman as my mother is. Or as you are.''

Glenys's cheeks flushed hotly once more, and she was thankful for the darkness that hid them. But Kieran was not looking at her. His gaze was fastened beyond her, toward the bailey.

''I am not so fine as your mother must be,'' Glenys said in a low, trembling voice. Kieran's gaze moved slowly back, fixing upon her.

''Far more than you know, Glenys,'' he said. ''And there is proof of it, for I have never told anyone what I have just told you now. Not even Jean-Marc.''

Pushing himself from the wall, he began to move toward her. Glenys tried to move away, but found the stone hard against her back. He stopped just in front of her, not touching, but so close that she could feel the heat of his body and the sides of his cloak as the wind flapped them against her.

''All has changed between us, Glenys,'' he murmured. ''You are no longer my prisoner.''

Slowly, he lifted one hand, stroking her cold cheek with warm fingers, a touch so delicate and soft that Glenys shivered at the pleasure of it. She had never been touched by a man before—not like this. Her heart began to pound violently in her chest and her breath caught in her throat. Kieran gazed at her intently, his fingers stroking so gently, so tenderly.

''I vowed I would not do this...that I would not let myself feel such things for you...but for once in my life, I cannot seem to find the way to stop it.''

Glenys gulped, reaching up to grasp his other hand as he lifted it to touch her hair.

"Please, don't," she whispered, ashamed at how weak and pleading she sounded. "You've merely been away from the company of women for too many days, and even someone as awful as I am appeals to you. Please, Kieran...don't make me the object of your jesting. I know that I am not the kind of woman to attract you. I could never be so." Her voice was shaking badly now, and she knew she was about to cry. She shut her eyes, her humiliation complete.

Kieran's hand stopped its stroking, and he made a harsh, wretched sound.

"Is that what you think of me?" he asked bitterly. "That I would use you in such a way, for naught but my own pleasures?" He abruptly cast himself away and moved to the wall, gripping the cold bricks with both hands. "Aye, of course 'tis what you think. Why should you not? I took you and have held you prisoner for little more than my own folly, after all. Everything about me must tell you the kind of man I am. And even the worst of it would be true. God's mercy." He straightened, running one hand through his long hair. Then he turned to her once more. "But you, Glenys...how can you think of yourself so?" He shook his head. "You are all that is desirable in a woman."

She uttered a feeble, tearful laugh. "Oh, aye. Of a certainty I am." She opened her hands, palms out, and motioned to herself. "Only look at me, how beautiful and dainty and feminine. I have no lack of ardent suitors vying for my hand." Her fingers curled into fists and, with a sob, she pressed them against her stomach, closing her eyes tightly. The next thing she felt were Kieran's arms folding around her, drawing her against the warmth and hardness of his body.

"Ah, Glenys," he murmured, gently rocking her

back and forth, "if only I dared...I vow I would make you know the truth of what I say."

He lifted his head suddenly, and his arms fell away. "They've come."

Glenys sniffled and wiped her eyes, turning to look at the place where Kieran was pointing, just outside the bailey. "Look, do you see?"

She moved to stand beside him. "Where? Oh...aye, I do see."

Their two remaining attackers had indeed returned to collect the bodies of their fellows, just as Kieran had said they would. They had only their two horses remaining, and were laying two bodies over the saddles of each. Within minutes they were leading the horses and their heavy burdens away, and soon disappeared into the trees.

Glenys let out a long breath and strove to settle her nerves.

"Will they come back once they've buried them?"

Kieran gave a shake of his head. "I cannot think so. There are four of us now against the two of them, and they've had enough misery for one day. They'll bury their friends and head for easier roads. And they'll avoid Sir Anton as if he were a leper."

Glenys looked at him worriedly. "If Sir Anton doesn't have word from them, saying that we're dead, he might send someone else. He'll do whatever he must to keep me from regaining the Greth Stone."

"Then he will have to work very hard, for you will regain it, and soon. But have no fears about Sir Anton. I'll deal with him," Kieran vowed darkly, and Glenys shivered at his meaning. "For now, we must set our minds to Wales, and on finding Caswallan. Come dawn, we'll begin our journey."

"I'm so glad," Glenys murmured.

Kieran smiled down at her. "Don't be yet. We'll have a hard ride tomorrow and on every day following. But tomorrow night, at least, we'll have a fine meal and warm beds and a decent roof over our heads."

"Where?" Glenys asked, with a bewildered shake of her head. None of the few taverns they'd stayed in thus far had even approached such luxury.

"I'm taking you to one of my sisters. She and her husband have an estate that is but a day's ride from here. 'Tis not directly on our way to Wales, but close enough. You and Dina will be glad to be in good company once more, and to have, even if briefly, the comforts you're used to."

"Aye," she said, "but what will your sister think to have us descend upon her in such a manner?"

"She'll think what she always does at such times, I would guess. That her brother is a wayward rogue who can't be counted upon to give her any warning of his arrival." He laughed at Glenys's expression. "Never fear, mistress. Eunice will be more than pleased to receive us, and she'll like you very well, just as you will like her. In truth, before our time at Hammersgate is done, you'll be amazed to think that she and I are related at all."

Chapter Eleven

"This is heaven," Glenys murmured contentedly, sliding farther down into the warm, scented bathwater. "Or as close as one might get to it on earth."

"S'truth," Lady Eunice, the mistress of Hammersgate, agreed, testing a bucket of rinse water with a careful finger before nodding to her maid that it was all right. "When my husband and I first married," she continued, settling back into the comfortable, heavily cushioned chair in which she sat, "this was the first boon I asked of him. A private bathing chamber for myself and the other castle ladies. He thought it most foolish, but soon gave way. Now I think he is a bit jealous, realizing how greatly we enjoy our privacy here. Will you have more wine, Glenys? And you, Dina?"

"Please," Glenys replied, watching as one of the maids refilled the crystal goblet that was set upon a low table beside the large, wooden tub. The rich red wine glowed like living rubies, illuminated by both firelight and the numerous candles that filled the luxurious room.

Glenys had never seen anything like this private

bathing chamber of Lady Eunice's. It was located on the second floor of Castle Hammersgate's far western tower, where several tall, diamond-paned windows allowed the late afternoon sun to fill the room with warmth and light. In one corner, surrounded by wooden buckets, was a special pump that magically delivered water from a hidden well below. The chamber's two large hearths had been specially built in order to heat great cauldrons of water over a direct flame and keep that same water warm in a separate waiting area.

The chamber itself was splendidly decorated in red and gold, draped with silk curtains at each tall window and carpeted—except for those places where four large wooden tubs resided—with soft Italian carpets. There were large, cushioned chairs such as the one Lady Eunice was now sitting in placed in comfortable groups before the chamber's hearths, perfect for small gatherings to relax and converse in. On one side of the room was a small closet where several warm robes were hung for anyone to use, and beautifully crafted screens to provide privacy while dressing.

There were several cupboards in the room, though Glenys had yet seen the contents of only two. One contained Lady Eunice's private stock of fine wines, along with fresh goblets, both crystal and pewter. Another contained various delightfully scented lotions, oils and soaps. When Lady Eunice had escorted Glenys and Dina to this wonderful private chamber, the very first thing she'd done was ask each of them to choose the scent that pleased them most. Glenys had decided at once upon a mixture smelling of roses, while Dina had fingered a bottle of lilac oil with obvious delight. Now the two fragrances mingled in the chamber to create an even more lovely, relaxing scent. Surrounded by such comfort as she'd begun to think she'd never know again, Glenys sighed and leaned back against the towel that had been set beneath her freshly washed hair. She was so comfortable and happy that she might have stayed where she was forever.

They had been received joyfully at Hammersgate by both Lady Eunice and her husband, Lord Belvoir, and by all their children, who had greeted their long-absent uncle with undisguised happiness. The youngest ones had leaped with almost equal glee upon Jean-Marc, who seemed more than willing to be treated as a human toy. Glenys and Dina, as weary and ragged as they both appeared, had been accepted by the lord and lady of the castle with perfect delight; even Kieran's forthright explanation of how and why he had brought two strange young women to them without warning was accepted without too much surprise. It was clear that Lady Eunice, especially, was well used to her younger brother and his manservant getting themselves into trouble.

She had raised a disapproving eyebrow at her brother's confession of kidnapping, then pushed him to one side and taken Glenys by the hand, welcoming her to Hammersgate and assuring her that both she and Dina would be perfectly safe there and well taken care of. Lord Belvoir had been more stern, inviting Kieran and Jean-Marc to join him in his private chamber to discuss matters more fully. They reluctantly followed him.

Glenys and Dina were left in Lady Eunice's care, and she, understanding their embarrassment at their appearance as only another woman could, had at once brought them to this wonderful chamber to bathe and rest and revive themselves with several goblets of her delicious wine.

"You must spend a great deal of time here," Glenys murmured contentedly. "I would, if I had such a wonderful chamber."

"You must ask Master Aonghus to make one for you at Metolius," Dina suggested, just before one of the maids poured a bucket of warm water over her hair to rinse it free of soap.

"Mmm," Glenys agreed, opening her eyes and reaching out to pick up her wine goblet. She sipped the dark, rich wine, then said, "This is very kind of you, Lady Eunice. Dina and I are most grateful."

Dina was mopping wet hair out of her eyes. "Oh, indeed we are, m'lady."

Lady Eunice smiled and nodded. "'Tis my great pleasure, and you are both my welcome guests. I'faith, 'tis I who am grateful, for you have brought my brother to Hammersgate for the first time in many years." She uttered a sigh. "I fear Kieran is not given to visiting with our family. Even our mother goes many months with no word of him. That you have brought him here, Mistress Glenys, is a gift of no small measure, and I thank you."

"But I did not bring him," Glenys replied. "'Twas his determination that we should pass this way."

Lady Eunice set her own wine goblet aside with a graceful gesture. She was a delicate, beautiful woman who, just as Kieran had promised, was nothing at all like her younger brother.

"I know Kieran well," she said in a wistful voice. "Though he loves me, he would not have come to Hammersgate if he could have avoided doing so. He feels guilty for having taken you and Mistress Dina against your will—and rightly so—and bringing you here so that I may give you my care is, in some small measure, part of the recompense he now feels honor-bound to make. If not for you, he would have passed Hammersgate by without a glance. Kieran has never been comfortable for long within such confining walls.''

Glenys looked about at the beautiful chamber. It was but a small example of the entire castle, which was wholly comfortable and inviting in every way. She thought of the grand feast that Lady Eunice had ordered to be prepared for the coming evening in honor of her sudden guests, most especially her brother.

''Surely not,'' Glenys said. ''There is nothing at all confining here. 'Tis a wonderful place.''

Lady Eunice smiled with pleasure. ''You are very kind, and I thank you, but I fear that what I say is true. Even when he was a boy our mother had great diffi-culty in keeping Kieran at home. And I understand 'twas much the same when he was fostered with his father, Lord Allen. He was ever disappearing for weeks at a time, willing to face his father's wrath when he at last returned. But that has always been Kieran's way,'' she said. ''He never seems to think of the outcome of all that he does.''

Glenys thought of how Kieran desired a meeting with her brother, of the mysterious enmity he bore for Daman.

''Aye, I believe that must be true,'' she murmured.

''I only wish I might find a way to extract him from what will surely be a just punishment once you have been returned to your family,'' Lady Eunice said un-happily. ''But he is determined to repay his sins by accompanying you to Wales. In truth, I would be saddened if he did not do whatever he can now to lend you his aid, but I wish he'd not been so foolish as to take you prisoner in the first place.''

''As do I,'' Glenys agreed wholeheartedly.

''I pray that your efforts, and Kieran's, will be successful. This ring that you seek must be of great import to your family. Or of very great value.''

Glenys could hear the honest curiosity in Lady Eunice's voice, and could scarce blame her for wondering why anyone would risk her life over a mere ring— unless, of course, the ring was quite special. Kieran, in his explanation to them, had left out all mention of magic, for which Glenys was truly thankful. She'd hate for Lady Eunice to hear any of that foolishness, or, worse, believe it to be true.

'''Tis not that it is of great value,'' she answered carefully, ''but the Greth Stone has been in my family for many generations. 'Tis a much loved heirloom, most special to my aunts and uncles, all of whom are elderly, and I would have them be assured that the ring has been returned to its rightful place while they are yet alive. 'Tis for their sake that I seek to reclaim the ring from the one who stole it.''

Lady Eunice's gaze was at once sympathetic. ''Of course. I understand fully how it must be. But come, the water will be growing cold. Let my maids dry and dress you, and then you must both join me here by the fire. We will speak further once you are comfortable and warmed.''

Fifteen minutes later, Glenys sat across from Lady Eunice in one of the comfortable chairs, her long hair spread out toward the fire, drying. Lady Eunice had kindly provided both her and Dina with clean undergarments, and Glenys now reclined lazily in a linen chemise, covered by one of the warm robes from the closet. Dina had excused herself as soon as she'd been wrapped in similar garments, pleading weariness and a desire to sleep before the evening meal. Lady Eunice had excused her at once, saying that she must certainly rest for as long as she pleased and not to worry over anything at all. Dina had followed a maid out of the delightful chamber, leaving Glenys and Lady Eunice to enjoy the warmth of the fire alone.

Glenys's bare feet were propped up on a cushioned stool and her wine goblet had been refilled. One of the maids had brought a tray of offerings from the kitchen: spiced almonds, lightly sugared sweetcakes, dainty, perfectly cut squares of soft yellow cheese, and honeyed figs. All in all, she felt wickedly lazy and replete. She and Lady Eunice happily attacked the delicious repast, exclaiming over the lightness of the cakes and the delicate flavor of the cheese.

"You are fortunate to have such a skilled cook," Glenys told her with all admiration. "I've had some difficulty keeping good cooks at Metolius. There are too many houses in London and few skilled servants to fill them."

"Aye, we are most fortunate in our cook, but I think we have Kieran and Jean-Marc to thank for these delicious treats. Their presence tends to enliven all those in the castle." She picked up her goblet and sipped from it, looking at Glenys from beneath her lashes as she added, "Especially those who are female."

Glenys felt her cheeks grow warm. "I am certain that must be so," she murmured.

"Aye," Lady Eunice continued, "'tis ever something of a problem when Kieran so suddenly appears. I am fully glad to see him, of a certainty, but all of my ladies and the female servants behave so foolishly around him. His great handsomeness and charm can be a curse, at times. S'truth, I am often amazed that he can bear it.''

''He does not seem to suffer much for it,'' Glenys said quietly, not looking at Lady Eunice. ''I believe he enjoys the attention he receives.''

''Not always,'' Lady Eunice said softly. ''Nay, not always.'' She set her wine goblet aside and sat forward. ''He has ever sought approval from one and all—most especially the kind of approval that he can never have.''

Glenys regarded her with a furrowed brow. ''Do you mean...because he is basely born?''

Lady Eunice nodded. ''Kieran is well loved by all who know him, and has ever been the favorite son of both his parents, and without doubt the favorite brother among his siblings, but 'tis not enough. I understand his feelings, and have naught but sympathy, for I remember how difficult it was for him as a child, ever being left behind. Once, when he was but ten years of age, we journeyed to court to be formally presented to the king. All of my mother's children were brought forward one at a time and grandly presented—save Kieran. He was not allowed, and had to stand and watch as the rest of us bowed to the king. My mother and stepfather strove to explain the matter to Kieran, but he was disconsolate. His father had never even taken him to court, for he could not further shame his wife in so public a way. He had already done as much as he possibly could for Kieran by openly recognizing him as his son and fostering him. But, though Kieran understood the truth of this, 'twas not enough. Not when he was a boy, and not now. I fear it never will be.''

"He loves his family well," Glenys said, deeply saddened at Lady Eunice's words. "He told me that it is so. I'faith, he said that he was the one dark stain set among so many nobler souls." She shook her head. "'Tis a great sorrow that he feels as he does. I think him one of the finest men I've e'er known.''

"Do you, Glenys?"

Glenys had lowered her gaze, and so could not see the interest in Lady Eunice's eyes as she asked the question.

"Oh, aye," she replied almost without thought. "I did not think so at first, for who would not be angered at being taken by force? *Then* I could only think of getting away from him.''

Lady Eunice's eyebrows rose at this, and she leaned farther forward. "Indeed? I have never heard any woman say that she wished to get *away* from Kieran.''

Glenys laughed. "I not only wished it, but made the attempt, though 'twas a terrible disaster." She recounted the event very briefly to Lady Eunice, and they both ended up laughing.

"And you never made the attempt to escape him again?" Lady Eunice asked.

"Nay," Glenys answered, embarrassed but unable to tell Kieran's sister a falsehood. "I was not happy to be taken from my family, but I knew that I was safe with your brother. He is an honorable man, though he insists that he is not. I'faith, I think he wants one and all to believe him a complete rogue. A knave. But though I have not known him long, I know that he is as good and honorable as any knight of the realm might be. A bit of a scoundrel, aye, and given to jesting when 'tis least needed, but otherwise…'' Her voice drifted off and she looked away once more. ''He and Jean-Marc saved my life, and Dina's, twice over. Once from a band of thieves, and again only yesterday, as he told you, from the men whom Sir Anton sent to kill us.'' She lifted her gaze to Lady Eunice's. ''I do not think a man without honor would do such a thing. He has treated us well…despite our circumstances.''

''And he brought you here to me,'' Lady Eunice murmured, gazing at Glenys with an odd expression. ''Aye, Glenys, I think you understand my brother well. Perhaps better than I do.''

Glenys's cheeks flamed with embarrassment. ''I'm sure that's not so, my lady. I have not known Kieran FitzAllen above a few days.''

''I think it must have been enough,'' Lady Eunice told her. ''S'truth, I think 'twas more than enough. But come. Let my maids dress you, and we will go down to the hall to join the others. 'Twill be time for the evening meal soon, and I would make certain that all is as perfect as it can be. If I can have you here at Hammersgate for only one night—for I know Kieran will never agree to staying longer—then we must make each moment as pleasant as possible. I have brought one of my own surcoats for you to wear while your own is being cleaned and repaired, and you will honor me by wearing some of my jewels.''

''Oh, but my lady, I cannot ask that of you,'' Glenys protested.

Lady Eunice's smile widened. ''You do not ask, Glenys. I insist. 'Twill give me great pleasure to see you properly clothed and jeweled, and Kieran will be well pleased in turn. I can see by your expression that you do not believe me, but you will see soon enough that I speak the truth.''

Chapter Twelve

Kieran knew that he shouldn't be here, standing on the balcony of the chamber Glenys had been given, hidden in the darkness and watching through the gauzy, silken curtains as she sat before a polished steel mirror, slowly brushing her long, unbound hair. Two of his sister's maids had earlier removed the beautiful, emerald-green surcoat she'd worn at the evening meal, and the delicate circlet of emeralds and pearls that had crowned the braids attractively piled atop her head. She had looked as regal and beautiful as a queen.

Kieran hadn't been able to draw his gaze from her; he'd scarce even tasted the food placed before him or heard what those around him said. He had only stared at Glenys's fascinating face with all its angles and smooth, perfect skin—and thought of stroking his fingers over every inch of it. Running the tips of his fingers across the bridge of her high cheekbones, over the delicate curves of her ears. Pressing his palms against the sides of her long, lovely neck…and sliding lower to her shoulders…slowly, very lightly, a mere breath of touch to make her shiver. And lower still, until he could see her eyes filling with naught but pleasure, and the same desire that he felt even now....

The cool breeze lifted the curtains inward, parting them so that he could see Glenys more fully for a brief moment. The brush had fallen still in her hand, and she was staring at her reflection, a slight frown on her face. The maids had gone, and she was alone, dressed in naught but her chemise and a silky, dark blue robe that was left untied. The chamber was lit by both candle and firelight, which the increasingly fitful breeze teased moment to moment, sending shadows dancing about the walls.

A storm was coming. Kieran could smell it and feel it. Aye, mayhap a great storm to match the one raging within him.

He had never been so utterly bewitched by a woman. 'Twas a new and fully unpleasant feeling—and shocking, as well, i'faith, that such a thing should happen to a man of his age and vast experience. He was a soulless knave who'd never cared much for anyone apart from his family and Jean-Marc. He had felt great affection for almost every woman he'd ever known, even those he'd not taken to his bed, but love had eluded him.

Until Glenys.

He had been told by any number of other men that love was a dreadful, painful torment. He'd ever scoffed that he was safe from such misery, for love would ne'er find him—'twas impossible that it should be able to make its way past the defenses surrounding his heart.

God's pity, how foolish he had been! And how small his understanding. Love had not needed to come sneaking up upon him, striving to find the way to trick him. Nay, it had needed nothing but his own lackwittedness, for he had stolen it—her—of his own accord and to his own purpose. He had trapped himself.

Kieran knew there were ways to be free again. He could leave Glenys and Dina here and sneak off with Jean-Marc to some dark, quiet hiding place where they'd not be found. His sister Eunice would see Glenys and her maid safely back to the Seymour family. Glenys would not get to Wales as quickly as it suited her, but Daman would take her within another month or so.

Aye, Kieran could slip away now and save himself the misery of what would be their final parting. He didn't let himself consider that there could ever be anything permanent between himself and Glenys, for that would be impossible. She would never be allowed to align herself with a man of his birth, and he could not help but think that she'd not wish to do so. She might want him—i'faith, he already believed she did, for he had seen her look at him in a manner he was well familiar with—but Glenys was far too sensible a female to let her feelings overwhelm what she knew was right and acceptable. How very unlike every other woman he'd known, he thought wryly. But that was part of what lured him. Her assuredness and strength and intelligence—perhaps even her unattainability. And so the time would come, after Wales and Caswallan, after he and Daman had met and fought, when he would be parted from her forever.

He might spare himself the pain of that if he left her now…but he found that he couldn't. For the first time in his life, he couldn't run away. Because love, as he had discovered too late, was a force beyond even his reckoning, and the thought of being parted from Glenys for even a moment before it was necessary was beyond consideration. It couldn't be done. He was caught. Snared by both his need and hers—for she did need him, and very much, though she didn't realize it was so.

Kieran watched as Glenys suddenly set the brush she held aside, then lifted her beautiful, sunset-colored hair in both hands, turning her face one way and then another to see how she appeared. Kieran knew enough of women to understand what her thoughts were, what it was she wished to see. When she dropped her hair and leaned forward, setting her face in her hands, he knew that she had also found her answer.

Kieran had never been good at giving; he'd been far better at taking, especially whatever was offered by a woman's sweet hand. But now he was going to give a gift—to Glenys. And he would give it freely, if he possibly could, without binding her to him. It was the one thing that he could do for her, that he possessed the skill and experience to impart. Before he left her forever, he would make certain that Glenys knew she was most lovely indeed—at least in one man's eyes. It would not be, mayhap, so fine a gift, for he was not a man whose admiration such a woman would particularly care to have, as jaded and unworthy as he was, but he would give it, nevertheless.

A sudden, harsh gust of wind lifted the curtains straight from the floor and put out several of the sputtering candles. Glenys looked toward the balcony's open doors, not seeing Kieran where he stood in the dark shadows, and rose from her chair. As she neared the doors to close them, Kieran took the glowing stone out of his pocket and held it in his palm. It instantly gave off its gentle light, revealing him. Glenys stopped, surprise crossing her features for a brief moment, then she stepped back and took her robe in both hands, folding it over herself to hide her near nakedness.

"Kieran," she murmured, staring at him as if he were a ghost, "what are you doing there? How did you come to be there?" And then, as it occurred to her, she added, with less surprise and greater distress, "How *long* have you been standing there?"

"A few minutes," he lied. He'd been there well over an hour, and had shamelessly watched her being disrobed, but he had no cause to distress her over such matters. "I climbed up from my own balcony, which is directly below this one. 'Twas a simple matter. Will you not come out a moment?" He lifted his other hand toward her, beckoning. "The air is cool. 'Twill rain soon."

She took another step back, her hands tightening on the robe. Shaking her head, she said, "'Tis cold. I wish to close the doors. Why have you come?"

"'Tis not too cold," he countered, his hand held out. "The wind feels good. And only think how pleasant 'twill be to lie down upon warm, soft sheets once the wind has chilled your flesh."

"I don't wish to be chilled."

"Then I will keep you warm. Come."

She hesitated, gazing at him warily, but at last she moved forward, step by step, until she reached him. She did not take Kieran's hand; he bent and took one of hers, prying it away from the cloth of the robe, and tugged her forward. He pocketed the glowing stone and slid that hand about her back, bringing her even closer and enfolding her in his arms. She did not resist, but stood in the embrace stiffly, perhaps even a bit fearfully. He could feel her warm, heightened breath against his neck, a stark contrast to the wind that buffeted them. Kieran rested his cheek against the top of her head and gazed upward at the dark clouds.

"You see? Warmth feels even better when 'tis cold. The wind whips about us, but we are warm and comfortable together. Do you remember the nights as we journeyed to York, when we slept on the ground, and I kept my arms about you to keep you warm?"

She made a sniffing sound against his skin. "To make certain I did not run away, is what you mean. I would have preferred to huddle with Dina, but that you would not allow."

"That is true, in part," he admitted, pressing his hands against her waist and back to hold her more closely, "but we kept each other warm, as well. 'Twas much like this, was it not?"

"Why are you here?" she asked once more, lifting her head slightly so that she might look at him.

Kieran gazed down at her, touching her temple lightly with his fingertips, brushing her hair back as the wind blew the silky strands upward.

"I came to see you," he replied simply.

She tilted her head in confusion.

"To speak to me? Of Wales?"

"No. But if 'tis what you wish, I will oblige."

"But why, then? I thought that you..."

"Aye?" he asked, gently pushing his fingers into the wealth of her soft hair, enjoying the way the strands caressed his skin. "You thought I would be seeking out the company of another woman? Mayhap one of the serving maids?"

Even in the darkness he could see her blush, and knew that he'd struck truth. He could scarce blame her for thinking such a thing. If she'd not been there—and if he'd not been so utterly besotted—he would have done exactly what she'd believed. Several of his sister's serving maids had already made their interest perfectly understood, as they usually did when he made one of his rare visits to Hammersgate. Kieran could have had his pick from the lot of them, or several picks. But going to another woman would do him no good, despite the neediness that plagued him. Only one female could assuage it. He knew enough of physical pleasures to realize how different this was from anything he'd known before.

"Nay, I want none of them," he told her, gazing into her eyes, which were as dark and beautiful now as the stormy gray sky above. "I have told you that matters have changed between us, Glenys, now that you are no longer my prisoner."

She grew rigid in his arms and put her hands up to push him away.

"Go away," she pleaded. "I have already said that I cannot bear to be made a part of your jesting."

Kieran held her fast. "And that is why I have come, Glenys. Nay, stop pushing and listen to me, for I will not let you go until you've done so." He waited until she grew still, her head lowered as if she could not bear to hear him speak. Kieran lowered his own head slightly, speaking softly near her ear. "I could have almost any woman in this castle sharing my bed—you know that I speak the truth. Yet I have come here. Not," he added quickly when she began to squirm once more, "to dishonor you. Only to prove that I would rather be with you than any of them. And knowing full well that it will do naught to assuage my need." He smiled and spoke even more softly. "I admit that 'tis pressing, for I have seldom gone so long without the company of women."

She pushed at him once more. "Go to them, then," she said sulkily. "You need prove naught to me."

"Nay?" he murmured, closing his eyes as a particularly strong and cold gust of wind enveloped them. He loved the feeling of it, being buffeted, standing against it, holding Glenys warm in his arms, though she was shy and afraid and even a little angry. There was much work to do to convince her of his sincerity. Kieran believed he was equal to the task. "Let us go inside, Glenys. I felt a raindrop just now, and the storm will come in earnest soon. We will be safe and warm within."

Her hands burrowed inside his cloak, fisting in his tunic. "Kieran," she whispered in a voice so frightened that it made his heart lurch, "please go. I'm afraid."

"I know, sweeting," he murmured, pressing a kiss against her ear. "I know. But if I go, you will only lie awake and worry and wonder, telling yourself terrible untruths. But you must not be afraid of me, ever, for I'll bring you neither harm nor dishonor. Only pleasure, Glenys, and goodness. This I vow."

Glenys was shaking as he led her inside and closed the heavy wooden doors behind them, dropping the long bar into its place to keep them shut against the wind. The curtains, which had been flying wildly, calmed at once, as did the firelight, which was all that remained of the light in the chamber. All of the candles had fallen prey to the coming storm.

She put her hands up as Kieran approached her, his steps slow and measured. He removed his cloak and let it drop to the floor, then began to unlace his tunic.

"Kieran!" she said with panic as he pulled the garment over his head and tossed it aside, exposing his chest and arms, so smooth and finely muscled. She could scarce continue to look at him, battling between astonishment at his beauty and fright at seeing him so exposed. She dropped her gaze to his booted feet... only to find that they weren't booted at all. His feet were bare. How in God's name had he climbed up the castle walls without boots on?

He kept moving toward her, and Glenys kept moving away.

"What do you fear, Glenys?" he murmured, his voice as gentle and unthreatening as a mild, warm breeze. "Is it me, or yourself? Or mayhap only discovering the truth of what I say?"

What did she fear? Glenys thought. She feared pain. And humiliation. Or that her feelings for him would be exposed so that he might laugh at them. He was so beautiful, so perfect, and she was so ugly in every way. Only minutes earlier she had gazed at her reflection in the steel mirror and seen the truth of that. He had looked at her in such an intense manner during the evening meal, or so she had thought...hoped. But it could only have been a dream, and not the truth. There was nothing in her to attract the least of men, let alone one the likes of Kieran FitzAllen. The mirror was far too honest to let her think otherwise.

And yet...he was here, and his eyes were filled with unmistakable desire. And Glenys loved and wanted him.

What was she afraid of?

She knew so little about men, and had ever wondered what it might be like to be held and caressed and kissed by a man—to become one with him. But she had believed that she would never have the chance to know, for no man had shown any interest in her, not even for her wealth. But Kieran did not find her thus...at least, she did not think so. Even if he did not love her, he did seem to want her. If she turned him aside now, she might lose her one chance to know what it was like to be with a man. To be with Kieran. It would not matter if she gave away her virginity, for she would never marry. But she would gain something wonderful, even apart from knowledge. She would gain memories of Kieran to keep and cherish throughout the remainder of her life. What, then, did she have to be afraid of?

Glenys fell still. Kieran moved to stand in front of her, his smile tender as he lifted his hand to cup her cheek. He searched her eyes and Glenys was proud of herself for holding his gaze.

"You tremble," he murmured. "There is no reason, Glenys. Can you think I would ever bring you harm?"

"Nay," she said weakly, hearing how badly her voice shook, "but I am not...I have no...skills or knowledge. I know nothing."

"And I know everything," he said softly, rubbing his thumb lightly across her lips. "We are not well matched. I vow I wish I could be as you are again, but 'tis impossible." He lifted his other hand, sliding his fingertips slowly down the side of her neck. "Have you ever been kissed, Glenys?"

"Nay," she whispered, filled with both terror and anticipation.

He smiled. "Good. 'Tis most selfish of me, but I confess that I am glad to be the first."

With his thumbs he carefully tilted her face upward, leaning toward her slowly, so slowly...until he was but a breath away. He murmured her name, his lips barely touching hers. Glenys closed her eyes and stood very still, waiting for him to press his mouth fully on her own, but he seemed content to tease her, brushing his lips back and forth, murmuring words she couldn't understand, until Glenys at last lifted up on her toes to close the space between them.

It seemed to be what he'd been waiting for. Kieran's mouth covered her own gently but firmly, not staying still, as hers did, but moving in a slow, sensuous manner that was so pleasurable it drove every remaining bit of fear out of Glenys's body. One of his hands slid down her back to her waist, drawing her even nearer. Glenys hadn't realized she'd lifted her own hands to circle his neck until she felt his warm, smooth skin beneath her fingers. She nearly lifted them away again but Kieran murmured, "Nay, I like it when you touch me," against her lips, and she left them as they were.

After a few moments, she began to copy him, moving her mouth in the same, delicious slow movements, finding that it not only made Kieran murmur in appreciation but also increased her own pleasure. When he parted his lips over hers she didn't hesitate to do likewise; he was so skilled and self-assured that she could do naught but trust him and let him do as he wished.

She had never dreamed that anything could feel so wonderful. His hands moved over her, caressing, petting, stroking. Somehow her robe had fallen to the floor, and his fingers skimmed the most sensitive places along her bare arms, causing her to shudder and press more fully against him. And then he began to touch her lips with his tongue, so warm and moist and sinful, gliding in the lightest of caresses. She hadn't realized that people could kiss in such a way...she was certain it was unutterably wicked...but, God's mercy, it felt so good.

His hands slid slowly to her hips, cupping and drawing her against him. Glenys gasped at the shocking intimacy and what it meant. He wanted *her*. To lie with *her*. She could feel his manhood, hard and fully aroused, against her most delicate place, pressing almost as if he would join them together through their clothing. His mouth yet consuming hers, Kieran held Glenys firmly and began to rock with her, back and forth, in a sensual rhythm, until she felt the measure of her own desire growing to an undeniable, fevered pitch.

Gasping, Kieran pulled his lips away and pressed his forehead against her own, his breath harsh and unsteady, pelting her face.

"Let us lie together," he murmured, his voice shaking with desire. "I would pleasure you, Glenys, but I vow I will not take your maidenhead from you. Do you trust me?"

Unable to speak, she nodded. Kieran bent and picked her up in his arms, striding to the high feather bed that sat in the middle of the chamber. Despite the fire, the air about them was cold, seeping through the closed balcony doors from the storm outside. Thunder rumbled in the distance, and the smell of rain was heavy.

The sheets were cool and soft against Glenys's heated flesh when Kieran gently placed her in the bed. A moment later he climbed in beside her, still wearing his leggings, and reached to pull the covers about them both.

Kieran was half pressed against Glenys, half leaning over her. She could feel the tremendous power of his body, so much greater than her own. He began to kiss her again, touching her face with the fingertips of one hand, stroking lower, down her neck, lightly, barely brushing against her skin, and lower still, until he had reached the laces of her chemise.

Kieran slid one of his legs between hers, coming slightly on top of her. Again Glenys could feel the power of his arousal hard against her thigh. Her chemise had come fully undone, and she felt his hand glide between the parted cloth, his long, beautiful fingers brushing over the tip of one of her breasts. Her nipples were painfully hardened and sensitive, and the delicate touch made her shiver with pleasure. His mouth slid lower, kissing her cheeks, her chin, her neck. Glenys stretched, lifting her chin so that he might have access to all of her. Her body was filled with a wholly new delight, a pleasure so wonderful that she could never have guessed at it. She could no longer think that it was wicked or that she would find herself a fallen, sinful woman come morn—she could only feel, and each new touch of Kieran's hands and mouth was a revelation.

He had parted the front of her chemise so that she lay fully exposed and could feel the warmth of his breath as he hovered above her.

"Beautiful," he murmured, gazing at her in the dim firelight. "So very beautiful, Glenys."

He lowered his head and touched his tongue to one of her nipples, licking it lightly. It was such a shocking pleasure that Glenys nearly came off the bed. Kieran's hand, now stroking up beneath the skirt of her garment, held her down, as did his mouth, which covered her nipple fully.

"Oh," she uttered, almost incoherent at how good it felt. He suckled harder and she twisted beneath him, her fingers finding their way into his long, silky hair and fisting. It must have hurt, but he only chuckled and moved to torment her other breast with the same sweet pleasure.

Later, Glenys would be amazed at how easily she gave way to him. He could have done anything at all that he pleased—taken her virginity and found his own pleasure as well as hers. But he did not. He touched her with his hands, pressed his fingers gently inside of her while Glenys moaned and strove for him to go deeper. He whispered to her as he carefully and skillfully caressed her, telling her that she was beautiful and very dear to him, that he held her far above all women. Such beautiful lies, she knew, but 'twas so sweet to hear the words, especially in that moment as he pressed even nearer and gifted her with shattering pleasure.

Afterward, she lay in his arms, trembling and breathing unevenly, her heartbeat slowing by degrees as his hands slid over her arms, her back. He was breathing harshly, too, and she felt his arousal still hard and unappeased.

Gingerly, she reached down to touch that part of him, only to have him stiffen and groan as if in pain.

"Nay, do not," he said, his arms tightening about her.

"Can I not give you pleasure, as you did to me?" she asked timidly.

He grasped her hand and brought it up to his mouth, kissing it.

"Aye, sweeting, but I have good reason that it not be so—at least not till morn."

"But why?"

"Because I would have you know that I did not come to you this night for that. Tonight was only for your pleasure, not mine. I would always have you remember it thus."

Glenys stared up at him in wonder, thinking of what it cost him to make her this gift. But she could not let him suffer so. His face was taut and filled with misery. She strove to sit up.

"Nay," he insisted, firmly holding her down, "do not argue the matter with me, Glenys. I vow I am too near to giving way to speak of it further. Only let me hold you now, while you slumber. Come morn, I promise, you may do whatever you please to me—and I pray you will. I'faith, I shall gladly show you whatever you wish to know."

Chapter Thirteen

The next few days were among the happiest Kieran had ever known, and that was saying a great deal; he had known many pleasurable days—aye, far more, he supposed, than most men might dream of.

But being with Glenys, especially as he was with her now, gave him a sustenance he'd not known before. He had accepted that he would ever feel a certain lack because of his manner of birth, and that naught would ever change it, but he'd not realized how greatly loving someone and, even more, being loved by that person, would assuage the emptiness inside him.

He'd always tried to end his relationships with women almost as soon as they began, but not this time. Their journey to Wales was meandering at best, creeping at worst, and Jean-Marc was becoming openly aggravated, despite the happy state of his own situation with Dina. Kieran knew of a certainty that they'd shared a bed at Hammersgate, and Glenys, though she refused to speak of it, knew it as well. But there would be no difficulty for Jean-Marc and Dina to embrace a more formal union; she was not of high birth, and Jean-Marc had set aside enough treasure from his years of wandering with Kieran to take a wife and live out his remaining days as comfortably as a rich lord. As well, unlike Glenys, Dina had no family to contest such a match, while Glenys's family... But Kieran didn't let himself think on them, or on the surety that Daman Seymour was fast on their trail.

Kieran was quite familiar with the part of Wales that Glenys directed them toward; he and Jean-Marc had made a habit of visiting the area at least once each year. How strange it was that Glenys's ancestral estate should be so near to one of his favorite brothels, stranger yet to think that at some time or other in the past, they might have been within but miles of each other. Mayhap their paths had even crossed a time or two when Glenys and her family journeyed into the town of Cardigan to purchase supplies.

They had journeyed south from York and followed Offa's Dyke along the border of Wales before turning inward and crossing the mountains toward Aberystwyth. From there they had followed the coast toward their destination, Cardigan, though Glenys called it by its Welsh name, Aberteifi.

She had grown almost immediately easy and relaxed upon crossing into Wales, as if she had arrived at her soul's true home. Kieran had not realized just how fully she embraced her Welsh heritage, not only the language and manners, but a complete belief in all things Welsh. The rest of England might not have existed, or even the rest of the world. Here was what mattered to her, and this was the place where she was at peace.

He had not heard her speak her native tongue until they had reached the Berwyn Mountains and stayed the night in a small village there. Glenys spent more than an hour in conversation with the village elders, asking questions about Caswallan, Sir Anton and the Greth Stone. Kieran stood at a distance, watching, admiring. Her face had become so expressive; her hands fluttered with motion as she made herself clear. Her behavior had been all that was respectful and polite, and the elders responded accordingly, recognizing both her family name and that she had the manner of one well born, despite the condition of her dress and the mode of her travel. Kieran, by previous agreement, posed as her husband, while Jean-Marc and Dina had readily taken on the roles of man- and maidservant.

Kieran thought he had done particularly well, acting out his part as Glenys's haughty English lord. He'd clearly been successful, for the villagers had looked at him with open disdain and at Glenys with pity and understanding. 'Twas not uncommon for fine Welsh ladies to be forced into marriage with English lords, especially a Welsh lady with both property and fortune.

She came away from the encounter satisfied that she had been right about Caswallan's whereabouts, but disappointed to have yet had no word of an Englishman fitting Sir Anton's description. Caswallan clearly troubled her very little, but Sir Anton weighed heavily in her mind, despite Kieran's assurances that he could easily handle the fellow.

"Surely he's in Wales," she told him that night as they sat together, feasting on bowls of a wonderful leek stew that Kieran couldn't seem to get enough of. "He would not have delayed his search for Caswallan once you agreed to take Dina and me from London."

"But mayhap he did," Kieran said, setting his third empty bowl aside, "even if to make certain that I kept my word after I took his gold."

"But even so," Glenys argued, "he would have left

for Wales almost at once. He should have been here for weeks now, but how is it that no word of such a strange Englishman has been heard? He is just the sort of brightly dressed lordling the people would be wary of.''

"If he's remained in south Wales, as you think, then they'd not have heard of him here,'' Kieran told her. ''Certainly in none of these little villages, where they hear little of what has happened about them. Caswallan would be a different matter, for he's not only known to be a Welsh sorcerer, but has held the Greth Stone for many months. Word of him would spread far more quickly than word of a strange Englishman.''

''Aye,'' Glenys had agreed slowly, ''that is so. S'truth, that must be why we've heard nothing of Sir Anton yet. Mayhap when we come closer to Aberteifi, 'twill be different. I cannot be easy until we know where he is. You think him a weak and foolish man, but there is a measure of cunning in him, and you know firsthand that he has no conscience against killing.''

''He has surprised me in that,'' Kieran admitted, ''but whatever cunning he possesses is blunted by desperation. He did not make his plans well in dealing with us, because he acted without care, and 'tis likely that he'll do the same in striving to gain the Greth Stone from Caswallan. He'll trap himself. And then,'' Kieran promised, stroking a finger down her soft cheek, wanting to smooth away the worries he saw on her face, ''I will deal with Sir Anton Lagasse.''

That night, in the small hut they'd been given by the villagers, she paced back and forth, murmuring to herself thoughtfully in Welsh until Kieran was so aroused that he couldn't help but take her in his arms. There was something about it, hearing her speak in the Welsh tongue, which she called *Cymraeg*, that made him feel half-crazed. She seemed to realize quickly just how it was, and began to seduce him not only with touches, but with her words as well. It had been that way every night since, and Kieran, for all his vast experience, had never known anything better.

For a woman who was yet a virgin, Glenys was astonishingly adept at seduction. From the morning they'd come awake at Hammersgate she'd been an ardent student, and Kieran her willing tutor. But she'd surprised him at how very demanding she could be, wanting to know everything all at once—all the secrets and skills that he'd spent years perfecting. Fortunately for Kieran, Glenys learned quickly and well. Unfortunately, she used her newfound skills to turn him into a mindless, helpless slave, ready and willing to do her bidding, whatever it might be.

It was a miracle that she was yet pure for marriage. In years to come Kieran would look back and marvel at how he'd managed to hold himself back from fully possessing her. God alone knew that Glenys didn't help. She was insistent that she would never marry, and did everything she could to make him lose all sense and join with her as he longed to do. The temptation was near overwhelming, but he held fast to his determination not to bring her to ruin. Perhaps it was the memory of Elizabet's shame and misery that gave him such strength of will. He couldn't bear to think of parting with Glenys, mayhap leaving her with his child, and of what she would suffer because of such momentary passion. He had ever been careful not to leave any of his lovers with child, but with Glenys he would take no chances. Nay, it was enough that they were together and that they gave each other such sweet pleasure. It was more than he had hoped he might share with her, and far more than he knew he should.

Cardigan was among the most ancient Welsh cities, as well as one of the most prosperous. Its bustling seaport brought both prominence and a great many foreigners to the town, and wealth to the English, who dominated the entire land. No Welsh man, woman or child was allowed to live within the town's borders, Glenys told Kieran as they made their way along the main road, a lingering punishment for the rebellion of Owain Glyndwr. Her voice rang with unrepentant anger as she spoke of how unjust the English were in their treatment of the Welsh...until Kieran reminded her that her family owned vast properties in England, not just Wales, and Metolius in London one of the brightest jewels among them.

Glenys, sitting before him on Nimrod, drew herself up straight. "There is no choice for us save to live in London throughout much of the year," she told him, "for the many businesses held by my family require it. But Wales is our home—our *true* home. 'Tis where the heart of the Seymours will always be."

"How far is your family's estate from Cardigan?" he asked. "You said it was in Dyfed?"

She nodded. "Just beyond Presili. 'Tis called Glain Tarran—the jewel in the rock. We will pass it when we journey to the hills."

Kieran didn't ask if she wished to stop there on their way; it would be far too dangerous to do so. Yet he needed to know where he might safely leave her once Caswallan had been found and dealt with. He intended to go after Sir Anton on his own, and would settle with Daman privately if he could, as well. If he could possibly put Glenys in Glain Tarran before that, he would. Whether she wanted to go or not.

"You must point it out to me when we journey past it. It is very old, is it not?"

She nodded. "Ages old," she said, sighing, "but I cannot promise that you will be able to see it. Glain Tarran is not always visible to all people."

"Not visible?" Kieran repeated, not certain that he wanted to know what that meant.

Glenys shifted uncomfortably before him. "'Tis not simple to explain. Usually the castle is easily seen from a distance, but at other times...'tis more difficult to find. The weather is, um, strange in that part of the country. Fogs come and go almost without warning."

"Fogs that hide entire castles?"

Glenys cleared her throat. "Aye."

"Mayhap that is why Glain Tarran is so ancient," Kieran suggested dryly. "That would be most convenient during a war, do you not think? To become invisible from time to time?"

"There is no magic to it," Glenys said sternly. "It simply happens."

"Nay, of course there is no magic to it," Kieran agreed at once, smiling at the ire that came into her voice. He heard it each time she realized that he didn't believe her explanations regarding the mysteries surrounding her family. She was so delightfully determined never to believe in what he found perfectly obvious—that magic was real. He wished he could find the way to convince her, but wasn't sure it was possible. If her family couldn't manage the task, how could anyone else? "I'm certain the entire estate disappears just as you say, because of the weather. Have you ever noticed that 'tis often very windy near the

Presili hills? The fog must have a difficult time hiding great castles there.''

Her elbow came back sharply, hitting its mark, and Kieran's laughter spilled out of him. He pulled Glenys against him and hugged her hard, kissing her cheek.

"I'll make you believe in magic,'' he whispered into her ear.

"Never,'' she vowed, but laughed the next moment as his fingers tickled her ribs. "Kieran!''

Her good mood lasted until they reached their destination. Kieran had chosen the safest dwelling he could think of to hide them from both Sir Anton and Sir Daman Seymour, but Glenys, upon seeing it, didn't seem to think it quite as good a choice.

"Oh, no,'' she said, twisting about to give Kieran a sharp-eyed glare. "Not here.''

"Aye,'' Kieran replied, swinging down from Nimrod. "Here. There is no better place.'' He held his hands up to pull her to the ground, steadying her until she gained her feet, then holding on to her when she angrily tried to struggle out of his grasp. Beside them, Jean-Marc and Dina were dismounting from Strumpet. "This is the only place where we'll be fully safe from discovery by Sir Anton. It was all he could do to sit for a quarter of an hour at the Black Raven in London. He'd not last a full minute at Berte's.'' He laughed. "Though I'd like to see him try it, surrounded by Berte's girls.''

"I will *not* set foot inside that dwelling,'' Glenys vowed tautly, jabbing a finger at the brothel, which was very well known in this particular part of Wales. "I refuse. You've taken Dina and me into hovels and thieves' dens and the lowliest dwellings on God's earth, but you'll *not* lodge us in a brothel.''

Kieran had anticipated Glenys's refusal, and ignored it. He began to untie their belongings from Nimrod's saddle.

"There is no other place," he repeated. "And 'tis not so bad as you might think. I've spent many a night at Berte's and know it well. 'Tis clean and dry and the beds are comfortable."

"Aye," she said angrily, setting her hands on her hips, "I imagine you've tried them all and found none lacking."

Kieran smiled at the jealousy in Glenys's voice, finding it rather delightful. He turned to her and slid an arm about her waist, ignoring her struggles and drawing her near. Kissing her soundly right in front of anyone who happened to be passing by, he murmured into her ear, "I don't deny the truth of what you say, but I vow I'll only try one bed this visit, and share it with but one lady, and her as sharp as a dagger and fierce as a warrior." He kissed her again before she could slip away.

"Kieran!"

"And as wicked as any of Berte's girls, I vow," he said before releasing her at last. She was still angry, he could tell, but couldn't hide the smile that strove to tilt her lips upward. Kieran couldn't resist leaning forward to add, in a soft tone, "Mayhap you could teach them a few things, eh?"

She uttered a laugh. "You're the very devil, Kieran FitzAllen. And I'm not going into that brothel."

Kieran hefted a leather bag over his shoulder and winked at her. "We'll see, Mistress Glenys."

Somehow, he got her inside the place. Glenys wasn't quite certain how it was that her resolve had crumbled, though perhaps the fact that he'd stood out in the street, beneath the midday sun and in front of dozens of strangers, kissing her over and over again until she at last agreed, might have been what did it. She'd muttered that people would mistake her for one of the girls at the brothel, so she might as well go inside. Kieran's laughter had followed her all the way to the door.

Inside, his laughter died away, far more out of necessity than desire, she was certain. No sooner had the rogue set foot in the brothel than the entire building erupted with shouts and squeals, and a herd of half-dressed females descended upon both him and Jean-Marc. Glenys and Dina were pushed aside without care, and stood, watching, as the two men were squeezed and kissed and fondled and exclaimed over. Glenys noticed that neither Kieran nor Jean-Marc seemed much inclined to bring such lewd behavior to a halt. S'truth, they seemed to like the attention very much.

The chattering of the herd was overwhelmingly loud and silly. Glenys heard snatches of half-finished sentences, such as, "Oh, Kieran, I'm so glad—!" and "Jean-Marc, I can't wait until—!" and "Oh, it's been so long, Kieran! Why haven't you—"

"Silence!"

This particular female voice was too compelling to ignore. The noise died away and all eyes turned to the woman who stood upon the dwelling's stairs, midway between the spacious lower level and whatever was above. A stunningly beautiful woman, though somewhat older than any among the gaggle of girls surrounding Kieran and Jean-Marc, she had long black hair that fell unbound to her waist, and lips that had been dabbed with red dye. She was dressed in nothing more than a thin chemise, almost as if she'd just come from bed, and her full, curved figure was readily evident beneath it. Her blue eyes, very light in color and somewhat unnerving, surveyed the scene before her, settling at last upon Kieran in a way that made Glenys blink twice. She'd never seen such open lust in her life. The woman looked as if she might pounce on Kieran and devour him whole, uncaring of onlookers.

Heart pounding painfully, Glenys chanced a glance at Kieran. He was gazing at the woman in return, but there was nothing that she could see in his eyes save warmth and friendship, a gladness to see an old acquaintance that matched what he'd shown to his friends at Bostwick's.

But still Glenys felt troubled. Clearly, Kieran and this woman had been lovers. Indeed, Kieran and every woman in the place had most likely been lovers. That had been the way of his life, and ever would be, regardless of what had passed between him and Glenys.

As if sensing her regard, Kieran turned to look at her. He smiled and winked in a reassuring manner, and began to put the women surrounding him gently aside. Before he could be entirely free of them, the beautiful woman had descended the stairs to stand in front of him.

"Kieran, love," she murmured in a deep, rich voice, setting a hand upon his chest and sliding it slowly upward until it rested upon his stubbly cheek. "What a wonderful surprise. I was just thinking that you and Jean-Marc would be coming to visit us soon. 'Tis that time of year, is it not?" She pressed closer, moving her body seductively against his. "We'll have to give you a special welcome this evening. But first, I'll have you to myself. Come upstairs and I'll make you most comfortable after all your travels.''

"Um, Berte," Kieran began, taking her hand and pulling it away, "I fear we've come for a different purpose this time...Glenys!"

Glenys had had enough. She took Dina by the arm and pulled her toward the still open door, striding out of the brothel and into the sunlight once more. Dina walked beside her without resistance, her face pale and her eyes filled with obvious dismay. The poor girl had been submitted to far too much these past many days and nights, and Glenys cursed her own weakness in not striving to protect her innocent maid more fully.

"We'll go to Master Tremayne at once," she said aloud. "He'll be surprised to see us in such a filthy state, but that cannot be helped. And as he's been the Seymours' banker in Aberteifi for nigh on forty years, I cannot but think that he'll lend us his aid. Aye," she said more assuredly, walking down the road without noting her direction, "I don't know why I didn't think of it before. We'll be rid of these heartless, lecherous knaves."

Dina replied with a sob.

"Glenys!"

Kieran wasn't far behind them. Glenys began to walk more quickly, pulling Dina along.

"Dina!"

At the sound of Jean-Marc's unhappy, pleading voice, Dina's steps slowed, but Glenys said, "Don't listen to that scoundrel. He was covered in women." She pulled her on.

"By the saints," said Kieran from closer yet, "you're the most stubborn female God e'er made. Glenys, *stop!*"

His hand closed over her arm, but she yanked free and, head held high, kept walking.

"You're coming back with me, whether you wish it or not," he told her, aggravation heavy in his tone, and his fingers tightened on her arm again, pulling her to a stop.

She jerked free once more and rounded on him furiously, shouting, "By God, I'm not! Do you think I'll stand in the corner, watching as you and Mistress Berte fondle each other?"

For the first time since she'd known him, his cheeks pinked, almost as if he felt some measure of shame. He opened his mouth to answer her, but Dina's weeping voice stopped him.

"Don't you dare to touch me!" Dina cried, slapping Jean-Marc's hands away. "After all you've said to me...after all we've done...and especially last night!" She covered her face with both hands and burst into loud tears.

"Dina," Jean-Marc pleaded miserably, trying to take her in his arms. "I meant everything I said. Dina, please, only listen to me."

She shoved him away, shaking her head and weeping even more loudly.

A crowd had begun to gather around them, murmuring.

"Sir Anton won't need to ask for word of us," Kieran muttered angrily. "The whole of Wales will be talking!" The next moment he bent and picked Glenys up, slinging her over his shoulder.

Glenys uttered a furious shout and began to pound his back with both fists. "Kieran FitzAllen!"

He slapped her bottom with a stinging hand. "Quiet, woman!" he said in a loud voice, turning about to face their onlookers. "Two of Berte's new girls," he told them cheerfully, ignoring Glenys's outraged screams. "They didn't like their chambers." He laughed and the onlookers laughed, too. "But we'll see that they're made happy," Kieran vowed, slapping Glenys's bottom once more to stop her squirming. "Come along, lad, and let's return these strumpets to their good mistress."

Glenys heard Dina's cry as Jean-Marc followed Kieran's example and slung her over his shoulder, though he did so saying, apologetically, "Dina, please don't be angry."

Kieran strode back toward Berte's brothel with long, rapid strides, while Glenys flopped on his shoulder, still trying to push herself free.

"Be still," Kieran commanded in a taut voice, his arms tightening their hold on her as he bounded up the two steps leading to the brothel's entrance. "Make way, my dears," he said aloud, and Glenys could hear, rather than see, the women in the dwelling moving aside to make a path. Still Kieran didn't stop, but headed for the stairway.

"Where are you going?" Berte cried. Glenys lifted her head to see the beautiful woman standing with her hands on her hips, glaring at them angrily. Behind her, Jean-Marc entered the dwelling, carrying a furiously unhappy Dina.

"I'm going to borrow your chamber for a few moments," Kieran called down to the brothel's mistress. "We'll disturb nothing, have no fear."

"Kieran!"

He kept climbing the stairs. "I apologize, Berte, but it can't be helped. I'll be down shortly to explain in full. Until then, leave us in peace, I pray."

They reached the next landing, and the bewildered faces that Glenys, from her unusual position, was gazing at disappeared. Kieran walked the length of a hallway and opened a door, walking into the chamber beyond and shutting the door behind them. He threw the iron bolt before turning about and setting Glenys on her feet.

She was in a murderous fury, and balled up a fist to strike him full across the face, but he grabbed her hand before she could do so and said, "You can scream and shout at me all you like in a moment, but first you will listen to me."

Glenys flung herself away, turned about...and fell suddenly still.

"Sweet Holy Mother," she uttered, wide-eyed and astonished at the sight before her. She'd never been in a whore's bedchamber before, and it was something of a revelation. The walls were covered with tapestries depicting scenes that Glenys had never been exposed to before. Men and women, all nude, in every manner of embrace, from loving to lewd. She stared at each tapestry—four in all, quite large—wondering how anyone could have created them without blushing the whole while. And who on God's earth *would* sew such things?

Behind her, Kieran cleared his throat. "Berte's tastes are rather...unusual," he said.

Glenys moved farther into the chamber, nodding. "Indeed," she murmured, turning about and taking everything in.

It was drowning in red silk, from the bed curtains and coverings to the window coverings and the cloth that covered each piece of furniture in the room. Here and there gold trim drew the eye, but otherwise, it was a sea of gleaming red. In its opulence, it was very much like Lady Eunice's richly decorated bathing chamber. In every other way, it was completely different.

Glenys's gaze fell on the bed, which looked as if it had been recently occupied. It was set in the center of the room, the focus of the entire chamber, and was large enough to comfortably accommodate five people. She could almost see Kieran lying upon it, with the beautiful Berte in his embrace, just as Glenys had lain in that same embrace these many nights past.

His fingers gently touched her arm, and she moved away.

Kieran sighed in a resigned manner. "Everything you're thinking is true," he said, "and far worse, i'faith. I never said that I wasn't a bad man, Glenys, or that I hadn't lain with other women."

"A great many of them," she said.

"Aye." He sighed again. "I probably couldn't set a number to them. And there's naught that can be done to make them disappear. They are all there, along with the rest of my sins and crimes and lacks. And the worst among them is that I let myself love you. This, I think, is a sin that cannot be forgiven, by either you or God." He moved slowly until he stood behind her. "But I couldn't find the way to stop what I felt. 'Tis no excuse, Glenys, yet 'tis all I can say. I knew 'twas wrong to bind you to me in any manner, but I am the worst man on God's earth, and gave way to what I desired. I have only redeemed myself in that I have not taken your maidenhead. If I had loved you less, I would have done so—God alone knows how truly I speak. But this ruin I could not bring to you." He touched her arm again, so uncertainly that Glenys's heart, already softened by his sweet words, could not withstand the gentle pleading behind the gesture. "I love you," he whispered. "I have no other defense or way to ask forgiveness. Glenys...will you not even speak to me?"

"You called me a strumpet in front of all those people," she said. "You m-made them think that Dina and I are w-whores. In *this* brothel."

"What else could I do?" he asked with desperation. "Should I have said your name aloud, or treated you as a grand lady? If Sir Anton is looking for you, what better way than that to have word of you reach him?"

Glenys hid her face in her hands. "What if someone who recognizes me saw and heard? My family is well-known in Aberteifi." She groaned at the thought.

Kieran's hands curled over her shoulders, comforting now. "Nay, Glenys, they would not know you. Not as you are now, with your dress so dirty and worn from travel. Nor with your hair so tangled and undone. I can only pray that none took note of the color, else Sir Anton will surely know 'tis you, and that you're in Cardigan. But you must have no fears, even if he should discover the truth. I have told you that I will keep you safe, and I will do so."

She nodded, lowering her hands and gazing at the tapestry on the nearest wall. It depicted a scene of such astonishing wickedness that Glenys couldn't conceive that 'twas possible for a man and woman to do such a thing. It looked painful, the way the woman's back was bent so far, and the man's legs—nay, surely he'd fall right on his face after but a few moments. Wouldn't he? She titled her head to better observe the position.

"Glenys, you are a naughty, wicked woman, gazing at such things." Kieran actually gave her a shake to break her consideration of the work before them. "I'll tell Daman when I see him, and he'll beat you."

Glenys pulled free, walking a few paces forward to examine an intricately carved wooden box set upon a table. "It matters not. He'll beat the both of us without mercy once he discovers what has happened between us."

"There is no need for him to know the truth," Kieran said, watching her intently. "I will say nothing of it to him, if you wish."

She couldn't look at him, but stared at the box, running a finger over the highly polished top. "Is it what you wish? To pretend that we have never lain together?"

He let out a harsh breath, uttering, "Nay. But I'm a selfish knave, and ever have been. You are the better between us, Glenys. You must say how it shall be— and if you wish there to be nothing more after today."

She was silent for a long while before finding the courage to speak. "'Tis hard for me," she said. "You cannot know how hard. You are very beautiful to gaze upon, and ever have been, I believe. I am not beautiful, and have never been, not even as a child. I have grown used to the truth of that." She swallowed hard. "But I do not think I have ever felt so ugly as I do at this moment. Though mayhap many women would feel lacking in the presence of Mistress Berte and her collection of naked females."

"Partly naked," Kieran corrected, though without humor in his voice, as she might have expected.

"Aye," she admitted, equally dismal. "Just partly."

He stood where he was for a moment, staring at her, then uttered a terrible curse and strode away to the other side of the room, tossing back a red silk panel to reveal a window, out of which he gazed. For a long while they were both quiet, and Glenys stood where she was, her finger moving idly over the wooden box, a feeling of dread in her belly. He would tell her the truth now, she knew, despite the declarations of love he'd made before. He would tell her that she was ugly, and that he wanted nothing more to do with her because she was petulant and childish as well, and no man could want such an ugly, ugly female when he had so many beautiful ones throwing themselves at him. She was a *fool*. She had just pushed away the most wonderful thing that had ever happened to her—something that would never happen to her again once she and Kieran parted ways. God's mercy, she would spend all of her life regretting what she had just done.

"I have often known what it is to feel ugly," he said suddenly, as if forcing the words out. Glenys was stunned at such sentiment, and turned to look at him. His head was bowed; his hands clutched the sides of the windowsill. "I have felt ugly much of my life, compared to the rest of my family. If that is how I've made you feel, then I…" He made a choking sound and was silent again. Glenys knew better than to speak.

"I do not know how to tell you how beautiful you are to me, above every other woman. God have pity upon me, for love is like a very curse from hell! I would happily have gone all my days never knowing what it meant, but it was not to be. For here I have told you that I love you—words that I have never spoken to another—and you can only feel ugly at hearing them."

"But you cannot mean them!" she cried. "You cannot love me! I am not fit for you! "

"Nor am I for you," he said, turning to look at her. "Glenys, I do not know the way to make you know that my words are truth. I thought to make you a gift, to let you know how beautiful you are to me, but it has come to naught, as all else I have set my hand to has done. I *love* you!'' he shouted, growing angry now. ''You have never told me the same, even in lie, though I have waited with hope every moment to hear you so much as whisper the words. What else can I say—or do—to convince you that I mean what I say? I would take you for my wife if I could, but I do not even dare to think of that, knowing how fully unmatched we are. And knowing, too, that you would reject me. Handsome as I am,'' he said bitterly. He turned away again, his face lined with unhappiness.

''You would take me for your wife?'' Glenys repeated in disbelief.

''Aye, with full joy,'' he told her, ''but it matters not. I am no fit husband for you or any woman.''

Glenys took a step toward him. ''Of a certainty you are,'' she murmured. ''I cannot think of a woman who would not give all she had to be the wife of Kieran FitzAllen.''

He uttered a laugh. ''You do not know what you say. You think me handsome, a pretty fellow with a pretty tongue, and even if this is so, it cannot change what I am. Basely born. The bastard son of a great lord. You say that I cannot love you, but 'tis the other way 'round. You are so far above me in every way, Glenys, that I could never hope to reach you.''

Glenys moved closer, touching his arm. ''I thought you must already know that I love you,'' she told him. ''Because surely every woman who sets sight upon you must do so. How could I be any different? I have loved you almost from the first.''

'''Tis not love,'' he told her tightly. '''Tis but lust and wanting, because I have taught you pleasure. 'Tis but my form and face, which you will forget the very moment we part. This is the manner of love that I have known with other women. And I do not want it from you.''

''Oh, Kieran.'' She set her arms about his waist and drew near, hugging him from behind, resting her head against his shoulder. ''We are a wretched pair. You cannot convince me of your love, and I cannot convince you of mine. And yet I love you so fully that I do not know how to tell you. Aye, your face and form are pretty indeed, and your manner as well, but none of this matters to me. Just as your birth does not, nor your lack of standing or wealth or name. I would gladly be your wife—nay, more than that. I would thank God without ceasing for such a joyful honor.''

His hands pressed over her own, so tightly that they almost gave pain.

''Would you, Glenys?'' His voice was urgent, husky.

''I vow it is the truth. If it were not so, would I be so jealous of Mistress Berte and her women? And of every other woman who has lain in your embrace?''

He abruptly turned about, taking her shoulders in a firm grip and staring at her intently. ''I have cared for almost every woman I've known, but I have never loved a one of them as I love you. Can you believe that, Glenys? Despite all you know of me...despite all my sins. *Will* you believe it?''

''And will you believe that I love you, as well?'' she asked. ''Despite my own many faults?''

A slow smile crept over his lips. ''Aye,'' he murmured, ''I will dare to believe it is so.''

''Then so will I.''

''Understand,'' he said more soberly, ''that naught

can come of it. There will only be this time for us. Once Daman arrives—''

Glenys reached up to touch his lips, stopping him. "I understand. But I'll not think of it yet. Neither of us knows what the future will bring."

"Glenys," he said, his tone worried.

She smiled and rose up on her toes, setting her arms about his neck. "I love you," she said, softly kissing his mouth, "and you love me. If these miracles can occur, then anything can happen."

Chapter Fourteen

Berte gave them a private chamber, though not without expressing her complete disbelief that Glenys was Kieran's preferred choice of companion. She openly scoffed when they returned to the lower great chamber, and eyed Glenys up and down with utter disdain.

"Kieran, my love," Berte said, "you jest, striving to make us believe such a silly tale and appear as fools. But I know you too well to be so easily taken in. She is not the kind you would take as your woman, even for a single night."

Kieran held Glenys's hand in his own and squeezed hard, glancing down at her, afraid to find that she'd believe Berte's words. Much to his relief and great pleasure, he saw that she merely looked amused. Glenys had believed what he'd told her—she had placed her *trust* in him. No woman had ever made such a gift to him. Glenys looked up and smiled and squeezed his hand reassuringly in turn. Kieran loved her so much in that moment that it was all he could do not to grab her up in his arms and kiss her until she was breathless.

Berte, seeing the exchange, moved slowly toward

them, giving Glenys a particularly unfriendly glare. "I might believe it of Jean-Marc, with this foolish, weeping female of his," she said, glancing to the corner where Jean-Marc stood with his arms about Dina, who yet looked pale and upset. "But never of you. Now, pay this woman and tell her to go away." She moved close enough to seductively slide a beautifully long-fingered hand from Kieran's belly to his chest. "I've missed you far too much for such games, and we waste moments that could be spent in a far more pleasant manner."

Kieran took her hand in his own and carefully, but firmly, set it aside. "I know you far better than you know me, Berte, which is why Glenys has caught my heart in her delightful snare and you never could. Howbeit," he continued, ignoring her angry gasp, "as we are friends of many years, I'll let your insults to Mistress Glenys go for now—so long as I hear no more of them."

Berte stepped back, gazing at Kieran with a particularly menacing expression that he knew well. She was but moments from losing her temper and making a scene that the whole of Cardigan would be able to hear. But he knew how to assuage her anger even better than her taunts. Before she could open her mouth he had withdrawn a small leather pouch from an inner pocket and held it before her face.

"Gold," he said. The single word worked a miracle on Berte, for though she looked at him with suspicion, her temper calmed.

"You've never had but a few coins to warm your pockets, Kieran FitzAllen."

He loosened the leather strings and let her gaze inside the pouch.

"We will pay you well to house and feed us for a few days, Berte, and to keep quiet about our being here. I was certain, when Jean-Marc and I brought Mistress Glenys and her maid here, that you and your girls would be able to meet our needs perfectly."

Her attitude was fully changed; she even managed a slight smile at Glenys.

"Of course, Kie. Who else should you come to but friends, eh? You'll have the best chambers, and I'll send one of the girls out for fresh wine and bread. You must stay as long as you wish and trust that you will be perfectly safe—from whatever or whoever you want to be safe from."

Within half an hour Kieran and Glenys were ensconced in a chamber that was much smaller than Berte's, but far less cluttered or extravagantly decorated. Kieran was familiar with the room—he supposed he was familiar with all of the private chambers at Berte's—and was pleased to think that he and Glenys would be together here for however long it took to find Caswallan. Or at least until Daman discovered them, which Kieran greatly hoped to avoid. Even if they had but a few days, however, it would be worth the risk.

They were sitting together in one of Berte's many bathing tubs, most of which she'd had specially made to fit two people, and some to fit three. Kieran had asked that one be set in their chamber and filled at once with whatever warm water was at hand. Fortunately, Berte's customers enjoyed her special tubs so greatly that she wisely kept water on the fire. He and Glenys had taken turns washing each other's hair and bodies; he'd been delighted at how quickly she'd mastered the particular pleasures to be had and imparted with the help of mere water and soap. There had been no speaking as they'd stood together, sliding their hands over each other slowly, sometimes lightly, sometimes pressing hard. Only now, when they'd brought each other beyond a pleasure that had left him gasping and her half collapsing, had they settled into the tub to rinse themselves and regain their senses.

Now, with Glenys's fully relaxed body nestled in the curve of his own, her head resting on his shoulder and her eyes closed, Kieran said, "I'm sorry for all Berte said. She must ever have things as she wishes them to be, and if they are not, she makes them so by force. Or attempts to, anyway."

"You need not make apology," Glenys murmured sleepily, moving slightly to make herself more comfortable. Kieran's hands slid up the silky skin of her thighs to rest upon her hips. "She doesn't know you as she thought she did. You spoke truly about that. She should have realized that you are too honorable to lie about love."

Kieran kissed the top of her head. He wondered if he had ever felt such contentment.

"You know me far better," he told her, "even after only a few days. I have waited all my life to find such a woman. I was beginning to think she did not exist."

"She doesn't." Glenys chuckled with gentle amusement. "I do not think 'tis possible to ever fully understand such a man as you are, Kieran FitzAllen, but I will love you regardless of that."

Kieran stroked his hands lazily over the curve of her hips, her flat stomach, and upward to her breasts, to impart pleasure and affection, but not to arouse. She was too weary to be loved yet again, so soon. But he greatly enjoyed touching her wonderful body, and the soapy water made the sensation even more pleasurable.

As to loving her again, he could be patient for a little while longer. His thoughts wandered to what lay before them. A good dinner, the warmth and comfort of the large bed that stood in the center of the chamber, and a very late morn.

"On the morrow, we must begin to look for Caswallan in earnest," he said.

"Aye."

"Nay, I mean what I say, Glenys. I would like nothing better than to keep you here in this comfortable chamber for many days—weeks, i'faith. But your brother is like to find us if we linger too long, and I must have you safe before that. We will journey to the mountains tomorrow, where you think Caswallan resides."

"Nay, not tomorrow," she said, yawning. "Tomorrow we must go to Pentre Ifan, in the Presili hills. 'Twill be a full day's journey there and back, but we will know of a certainty where Caswallan is afterward."

"Then we will go to the sacred burial chamber," he agreed, rather amused at the idea.

"I must go alone into the hills once we're there," she murmured. "Otherwise, I will not know."

Kieran's amusement fled. "Nay, you'll go nowhere alone, even a short distance. How can I know where Sir Anton may be, or if he will have men hidden and watching us, as he did before? Whatever you must discover in the Presili hills you will discover with me at your side."

Slowly, Glenys pushed up, sloshing water and turning to look at him.

"But I must be alone else the answer will not come to me."

"Is this more of your family's magic, then?"

She frowned. "There is no magic," she said firmly. "It is just that...certain things can be sensed in the sacred places, not only in Presili, but elsewhere...if one knows how to listen."

Kieran's eyebrows rose. "And do you possess this gift of listening?"

Glenys looked away. "I suppose that I do. Since I was a child, whenever my family went to any of the sacred places in Wales, I have heard things that others have not. 'Tis but a trick of the wind, I believe, but my family—some of them—would have it that the spirits who abide in such places speak to me." She flushed. "'Tis all foolishness, but I would yet go to the Presili hills and see what good comes of it. I believe Caswallan will be near, but there is more to be learned, as well."

Kieran smiled, running a wet finger down her cheek. "You know more of magic than you would have anyone think," he said. "I wish I knew why you are so determined not to believe in it."

She lifted her gaze to meet his own. "Because magic—and having a family that embraces it—sets me apart from the rest of the world. My brother and me both. But you will understand this more than another."

"Aye, I understand what it means to be set apart," he agreed softly, leaning forward to kiss her warm, damp mouth. "But possessing magic is a fine and good thing, far unlike being basely born. And i'faith, I can't imagine anything making Sir Daman Seymour feel rejected in any manner. He is well received by the crown, the church and his fellow man. But come." Kieran kissed her again. "I can see that you would argue the matter, but both the water and air begin to grow cold."

Taking her hand, he rose from the tub. "We'll lie in bed until we've warmed ourselves, and after you've slept awhile, we'll speak more about Caswallan and our journey to this sacred place you speak of. I can't truly let you go into the hills alone, you know."

"But you must," she protested as he pulled her out of the water and wrapped her in a large sheet of fine linen. "I'll hear nothing if another is with me."

He smiled, swung her up from the floor and cradled her in his arms.

"I must simply find the way to charm the spirits, then," he said as he carried her toward the bed. "Are any of them, perchance, female?"

Pentre Ifan, the ancient Celtic burial chamber in the Presili hills, was an eerie place, but Glenys had never been afraid of it. As a child, she had always enjoyed the days when her family made their yearly visits to the sacred places is Wales, but she had especially liked going to Pentre Ifan. It had always felt very familiar and welcoming, as if it were part of her home. And it was here, in this very place, that she'd first heard the whispering voices. They had been indistinct and she'd not understood what the words were, but she *had* heard them. When she'd told her aunts and uncles, they'd seemed very pleased, as had her father, but Daman and her mother had been far less so. Her mother had forbidden her to tell anyone outside the family of what she'd heard; Daman had insisted that it had only been a mixture of the ever present wind at the burial mound and her imagination. Nothing else.

Glenys had been six years of age, and had then believed in magic. But from that time she began to be wary of it, even to question whether it was real or whether her father and aunts and uncles just pretended it was. But one thing she understood from her mother's and brother's behavior was that magic, whether real or not, was dangerous.

Knowing this, she'd quickly learned not to speak of the voices she heard in the sacred places, or the words they said that she could increasingly understand. The trouble was that they often foretold the future, which was difficult to ignore. That her mother would increase with child was one such prophesy, but not that she would die from childbirth. That her father would be taken from her was another, although Glenys hadn't understood that the voices had meant forever. And here at Pentre Ifan Glenys had stood only months ago, with the winter's snow cold beneath her feet, and been told that the Greth Stone had been stolen from them—by Caswallan.

For once, Glenys had broken her imposed silence and told her aunts and uncles what she'd heard. Their dismay had made her wish she hadn't, but at the same time she'd felt greatly relieved. They had readily believed her, just as they'd done when she was a child, and hadn't questioned the truth of what she'd said at all.

Now Glenys stood beside the sacred place once more, the afternoon windy and cool, with the smell of the sea in the air. Above, clouds raced across the sky, growing increasingly darker as yet another spring storm approached.

The burial chamber was truly no longer what it had once been, for the earth had shifted and been blown away, leaving naught but giant stones standing alone, much like Stonehenge. The Celts had placed them here hundreds of years ago, and they still stood, as important to people like Glenys's family as they had been then.

"Is it not beautiful?" Glenys murmured, turning all about, feeling the cold wind on her face with full pleasure.

"Aye," Kieran replied absently from where he sat not far away, the queen piece in his hand. "Most beautiful. And cold. Boadicea seems pleased," he added, his gaze fixed upon the small wooden piece. "Her eyes burn as with fire. Do you see?"

Glenys moved to stand beside him, looking at the delicately carved lady. "Aye, they do," she agreed. "'Tis strange to see you sitting here, with her in your hand. My uncle Culain was ever given to bringing her up to Pentre Ifan in his pocket, as you have done, and would sit in this very spot, as you are, holding her out in the open air. He said it was good for the faeries to see her." She glanced at Kieran and smiled. "'Tis very foolish, I know, but it did give him such pleasure."

Kieran looked all about him. "Faeries?" he repeated. "Living here? I thought they had better sense than to choose a cold, windswept hillside."

Glenys laughed. "Oh, aye, I'm certain they do—if they exist. 'Tis said that they come together at Pentre Ifan in the depth of night, though I have never seen sign of them."

"I doubt you've ever been here in the depth of night," Kieran replied wisely.

"Nay, not I, but my cousin, Helen, has often done so when she has visited at Glain Tarran. She's never seen faeries, either."

Kieran stood and gave a shake of his head. "The more I hear of your cousin Helen, the odder I think her." He tilted Glenys's chin up with a fingertip, bent to kiss her mouth, then straightened and said, "Shall I leave you for a few moments now?"

"Aye," she said, nodding. "Ten minutes will suffice."

"Five," he told her. "I'll leave you for no longer than that, and will be close enough that I can hear your cry, should you need me."

He strode away, leaving Glenys alone. She watched him go until she could see him no more, her heart filled with the love she bore him and no small measure of admiration for the fine, tall figure he made as he walked. With a sigh, she pulled her cloak more closely about her and moved to stand directly in front of the burial chamber. Closing her eyes, she lifted her face to the sky and listened.

She had no idea how much time passed before she heard Kieran's furious shout. The next moment he came running into sight, yelling, "Stop him! Catch him!"

Glenys looked all about, but saw nothing.

"Grab him! Quick!" Kieran pointed toward Glenys's skirts. "He's right there...accursed knave!"

Glenys turned about wildly, but could see nothing and no one. "What is it?" she cried. "I don't see anything!"

"He's run off again!" Kieran shouted as he raced past her and into a small copse of trees. "He's taken the queen!"

He disappeared from sight once more, and Glenys stood in utter confusion, wondering if she should wait or follow. She could hear Kieran's voice, sounding as if he were struggling with someone else, and wondered if he'd suddenly gone mad.

"You little wretch! I'll knock your head off for that! Arghh!"

"Kieran!" Glenys began to move forward, but hadn't reached the copse before Jean-Marc and Dina, riding Strumpet and leading Nimrod, arrived.

Jean-Marc tossed his leg over Strumpet's head and slid to the ground, unsheathing his dagger and asking, "What's amiss? Where's Kieran?"

"Here." Kieran came striding out of the copse, his face angry and flushed, holding one of his fingers tightly in his hand. "The damned thing bit me," he said furiously. "Look, it's bleeding."

"God's mercy." Glenys pulled a handkerchief out of a pocket and hurried forward. "Let me bind it." She took his hand and gazed with astonishment at the small, sharply dealt wound. It almost looked as if he'd been bitten by a small animal. "How did this happen?"

"That little man did it," Kieran said, grunting as she wrapped the cloth tightly about the wound.

"Is he yet to be found?" Jean-Marc demanded, clearly ready to go in search of his master's assailant. "What did he look like?"

"An elf, he was, with a red cap," Kieran said, adding, "Nay, he's gone now. There's no use looking for him."

"An elf," Jean-Marc repeated, staring at him.

"Aye," Kieran said, ignoring Jean-Marc's look of disbelief, "but he gave me back the queen piece, at least. She told him to, else I think the little brute would've disappeared and taken her with him. Ouch!"

"I'm sorry," Glenys said with sympathy as she tied the cloth tight, then lifted it up and kissed the offended finger. "There. 'Twill stop bleeding in a few moments.

I'm sorry he bit you. Did you say aught to make him angered?''

"Do you believe me?'' Kieran asked. "He *was* an elf. Or one of those faeries.''

"I don't know what to believe anymore,'' she told him, "though I'd not speak aloud of such things to any sane person, were I you. But as none of us seems to be sane, tell us what happened.''

"I scarce know myself,'' he admitted, looking at each of them in turn. "I was leaning against a tree, gazing at the queen piece and keeping count of the time, when a little man wearing a bright red cap appeared as if from the air. I knew at once that he was some sort of elf or faerie.''

"Oh, come,'' Jean-Marc muttered with a shake of his head. "That's foolishness. He was a small man, mayhap, but a huntsman or herder only.''

"Nay, he was not,'' Kieran insisted. "He bowed and addressed me as 'my lord,' in such a manner that I thought him to be making jest of me. I told him that I was not a lord, but he bowed once more and called me 'my lord Eneinoig.'''

"*What?*'' Glenys murmured with astonishment. "Lord Eneinoig? But that is impossible!''

"I told him the same,'' Kieran said, "but he merely smiled and snatched the queen piece from my hand and ran away. I gave chase—as you saw, Glenys—but when I reached him he refused to give her back to me, and when I strove to force him, he bit me! I was sorely tempted to wring his neck, but then the queen spoke and I was too astonished to do anything save stare.''

Glenys looked at him closely. "She spoke? My uncle has ever said that she speaks to him, but I have never heard her do so.''

Kieran paced away from her, running his unbound hand through his hair in exasperation.

"I do not truly know if 'twas her, for the wooden piece moved not at all. But 'twas a woman's voice I heard, and the elf—or whatever he was—looked at the queen piece that he held as if it came from her. She told him to do as I bade him and to beg my pardon, and at once he handed me the piece, bowed in the manner he had done before and made apology...and then he disappeared. I mean what I say!" he insisted when Jean-Marc snorted. "He moved not at all from his place, but was gone nonetheless. And there was more," Kieran added, turning to look at Glenys. "She—the voice—told me something else, if your voices have not already done so."

"What?"

"That Caswallan is at Frenni Fawr, not far from Cardigan, and Sir Anton is with him. They've joined forces, Glenys. If we mean to regain the Greth Stone, we must take it from both of them."

Chapter Fifteen

Jean-Marc preferred blunt force. Kieran advised stealth. Dina didn't want to have anything to do with the matter at all, though she bravely said she'd do as her mistress asked. Glenys refused to be swayed. She had to face Caswallan alone and use the queen piece to strike a bargain for the Greth Stone.

Kieran was equally firm in his determination that she should do no such thing, but Glenys, as he was discovering, could be remarkably stubborn.

"For I must speak to him alone, don't you see?" she said as they ate their evening meal back at Berte's brothel that night. "How can I make a bargain at all if any of you or Sir Anton is present? No. I will speak with Caswallan alone, and you will find the way to stop Sir Anton or anyone else from disturbing us."

"But I have vowed not to let Caswallan have Boadicea," Kieran told her. "Your uncle must have her back."

"That is a fully different matter," she said, "and one I shall leave to you, for surely you and Jean-Marc, with your many skills, can contrive to get it back. Sir Anton's presence worries me more. I can scarce believe that he persuaded Caswallan to join with him in making use of the Greth Stone, but if 'tis what was told to you, then it must be so."

"Your voices told you naught?" Kieran asked, refilling Glenys's goblet with Berte's best wine.

"Nay," she replied stonily, looking at him with a frown. "'Tis not the first time that they have abandoned me, but 'tis surely the first and only time they've done so in favor of someone who is not even of my family. I find that most odd," she said, observing him more closely. "Are there not any in your family, Kieran, who claim to be magic, or at least to have knowledge of it?"

He shook his head. "None. They are all as practical and sensible as you are, sweet. My people are conquerors of the earth—not friends of it."

Glenys seemed unsatisfied with this, and sat back with a sigh. "Yet they spoke to you and not to me. There must be a reason for it."

"Surely you're not jealous, my love," Kieran said lightly, striving to make certain that it was not so. He would not grieve her for any reason, could he avoid it. "'Twas a mistake, most like, or merely because I held the queen and the red-capped fellow wanted her. I'faith, there could be no other reason."

Glenys fingered the rim of her goblet, gazing at Kieran thoughtfully.

"There could be one reason—but I will not speak of it now. Let us make our plans, instead, for the morrow, when we will face our foes and regain what rightfully belongs to my family."

"There may be many of Caswallan's followers with him," Kieran warned. "And they may defend their master with their lives."

"I have no fear of that," Glenys told him. "My uncle Aonghus's name is not unknown among those who embrace the old ways, and my family is even more greatly known. I do not think they would cause us harm for the sake of Caswallan, despite what he has accomplished with the ring—though I doubt he has done aught at all. There is more of mystery than magic to the piece. Its only power is that many *believe* it to have power, and such belief holds great sway over those who bear it."

"Caswallan is not a famed sorcerer?"

She made a scoffing sound. "He is a sorcerer, if a man can be named such, but no man can make a mere ring perform tricks if it hasn't the inclination to do so. Any magic that has come of the Greth Stone of late has come because Caswallan has conjured some illusion, not because the ring itself has done aught."

"Is he a simple magician, then?" asked Jean-Marc, setting his own wine goblet aside. "If so, we truly have naught to fear. You deal with Sir Anton," he said, nodding at Kieran, "and Mistress Glenys will take care of Caswallan. Dina and I," he added, reaching out to take her hand, "will manage the rest."

Caswallan's encampment gave Kieran serious misgivings about his promise to let Glenys find the man and speak to him alone. 'Twas not that there were so many followers, but that the few there were seemed so strange. They dressed mainly in white and said very little, but when Kieran and Glenys rode together toward their small collection of huts and tents, they at once began to gather around her.

The moment Glenys's feet touched the ground, she

turned to the gathered and said, with urgency in her tone, "Where is he?"

Neither young nor old spoke aloud, but turned and pointed to the largest building among the group, which looked to Kieran like some kind of wooden chapel that had either fallen into disuse or been abandoned. Whoever had built it would have done better to fashion the building out of rock. Frenni Fawr was windy and cold, and the nearby villages small. Only the hardiest souls could make a life in these hills.

"And Sir Anton?" she asked next.

The hands swung in a different direction, toward where a large, very fine pavilion had been raised and now stood with its silken sides fluttering in the wind. Yes, Kieran thought, that was the sort of grand dwelling Sir Anton would choose, despite its great impracticality.

"I'm going now to speak to Caswallan," Glenys told the onlookers, speaking slowly and in English for Kieran's benefit. "Alone. I am Glenys Seymour, and my uncle is Aonghus Seymour. The Greth Stone belongs to my family, and though it has been in Caswallan's care for these many months, I have been sent to return the ring to its rightful place."

Kieran noted that Glenys said nothing of Caswallan's stealing the ring—a wise decision, considering that these people thought so well of the man.

"This man is Kieran FitzAllen," she said. "He is a great warrior who has been recognized by those who dwell at Pentre Ifan." At this, a low murmuring began among those surrounding them. Glenys raised her voice to be heard. "He was sent by them to guard me in my quest and lend me his aid. However, he has a grievance against Sir Anton Lagasse—a just grievance, which he will lay before him now. Do not try to stop him or me, lest you anger those who have sent us both, and we will give word that no harm will come to any of you. Is it agreed?''

More murmuring followed this, along with both agreement and dissension. Kieran understood how difficult it was for those who'd devoted themselves to Caswallan to so readily give him up—and even more so the Greth Stone—especially at the word of a mere woman.

Glenys clearly understood the difficulty, as well, for she raised her voice even more loudly and said, ''Do you require a sign?''

''Aye,'' came the reply from several voices. ''A sign!''

''Very well,'' Glenys said calmly. She turned and began to walk toward one of the many small fires that had been set about the camp, sheltered by rocks that had been piled to keep the wind from blowing the flames out.

Kieran followed, with the small crowd at his heels, and whispered in her ear, ''What are you going to do?''

She cast a grin at him. ''Perform magic,'' she replied.

One of her hands had already disappeared beneath her cape, and Kieran at once divined her purpose.

''Won't they realize 'tis merely a powder?'' he asked.

''They'll see what they wish to see. If it goes wrong, then we must think of another plan. But if this isn't very like what Caswallan has been giving them in the way of showing his powers, I'm much mistaken about the man.''

She came to a stop before the first fire, then raised

her fists high in the air, lifted her face to the sky and said in commanding tones, "Spirits of the earth, give truth to all that I have said before these, your servants. Give us a sign that you have sent us to retrieve the Greth Stone and bring it to its rightful home."

With that, she brought her hands down quickly, opening her fists and releasing the powder. It was well done, Kieran thought, watching carefully. If he'd not known that the powder existed, he'd not have realized that she'd thrown it into the fire.

As it had done before, the powder immediately quenched the flames and smoke, sending sparkling lights glittering in the air until they, too, faded, leaving naught at all.

But then, just as those behind her had gasped and Glenys was turning to face them with a satisfied smile, something else happened that had nothing to do with the powder.

Where the now cold embers lay, a new sparkling had begun, very different from that which the powder made. It was brilliantly white, like a thousand tiny stars, but as round and cold as a Gypsy's crystal ball. It rose from the ashes, so achingly bright that all who watched had to either turn aside or shade their eyes.

The crowd stepped back, Kieran put his arm about Glenys and pulled her away, and they all stood there and stared with gaping astonishment.

The ball rose higher, like a blazing moon, and then higher still, right up into the sky. Slowly, over their heads, it began to spin, and they all stood with their eyes lifted upward, watching. Faster and faster the bright ball spun, burning so brilliantly that it appeared to be made of white fire. Of a sudden, it burst into thousands of tiny shards, falling like miniature stars to earth. The people surrounding them shouted and began to run away, fearing that the sparkling pieces would be hot, but Kieran and Glenys stood where they were, showered by the glittering sparks. They were cool to the touch, ticklish and tingling where they landed on the skin, and they brought with them a sweet perfume. Kieran held out a hand to try to capture some, but they disappeared as soon as they landed, like glittering snowflakes. He'd never experienced anything like it.

"What's happened?" he asked Glenys as the others slowly began to rejoin them, reaching out their own hands to touch the tiny stars. "What is this?"

"Our sign," she murmured with wonder. "But we must not linger over it long, for Caswallan and Sir Anton will hear of it almost at once. Come." She took Kieran's arm and tugged him away from the crowd. "They'll not stop us now. Look at them."

Kieran looked. Caswallan's followers were still staring up at the sky, amazement on their faces.

"Let us hurry," Glenys said, pulling him along. "You to Sir Anton and I to Caswallan. If Jean-Marc and Dina play their parts, we'll be safely back at Berte's before dark has fallen."

The decrepit chapel was dark as Glenys stepped inside. She blinked away the brightness of the day and strove to focus on what lay within the small building. Several candles, their flames fluttering as the wind whipped through the open door, made it somewhat easier.

Caswallan was indeed there, dressed in flowing white robes, and sitting upon a ridiculous chair that was clearly meant as some kind of throne. He was a tall, thin man, of an age with her uncle Aonghus, with a tufted white beard that failed to cover his entire chin, leaving bald spots here and there.

He rose when Glenys entered the chapel, a long wooden rod clutched in one hand. She could see the Greth Stone glinting on one of his fingers, reflected by the candlelight. His other hand was shaking slightly, and as she moved closer, step by measured step, to face him, she could also see that his eyes were filled with fear.

"I knew you would come," he told her, his voice quavering. "One of you, though I prayed it would not be Aonghus."

"He did not know where to find you," she replied, speaking in Welsh. "I did."

"You've come to take the ring, but you cannot have it. Nor can you take it from me by force, for it cannot be removed from the hand of he who wears it, save by the wearer himself."

Glenys stopped directly in front of the elderly man, holding his gaze. "You should never have stolen it, Caswallan. 'Twas not only wrong, but you know as well as I what the legend of the Greth Stone says. Only the legitimate heir can claim its power."

"You mistake the matter, girl," he said. "The ring bears no power of its own, but I need none, for I am as skilled a conjurer as your own uncle. But I must have the ring to gather my people about me. Without it, they will leave this place."

Glenys frowned. "Why should you wish to keep them here? This is no powerful army you've brought, but simple people who cling to the old ways. You've naught here save that which strokes your own pride, foolish as that is. 'Tis all but laughable."

"It may seem so to you now, but it will not always

be thus," he countered. "In time, word will spread throughout all of Wales that a true priest has returned to the land, and then one and all will flock to me."

"To what purpose?" Glenys asked. "Do you imagine that you will one day gather enough of a following to make another rebellion? Is it Owain Glyndwr you wish to be? Has Wales not seen enough of blood and revenge? Is this why you've struck a bargain with Sir Anton? Because he has the money you need to arm yourselves and make ready for war?"

"Nay, not for that," Caswallan replied quickly. "Sir Anton is my disciple. He desires to learn all that I know and carry on the old ways, the right ways. And unlike your treacherous family, who have taken lands and wealth for themselves throughout England, he is faithful to Wales alone."

"But that is a lie," Glenys said calmly. "I know Sir Anton well, and he is faithful to no country and no man—save himself. He has sworn to gain the Greth Stone for his own purposes, and this, I believe in all truth, is what he intends to do. I swear it on the name of my family. Ask what you will of me regarding Sir Anton, and I will tell you all I know. Afterward, I pray that we may bargain together regarding the Greth Stone. I have brought with me something which I believe you will gladly exchange for it."

"What is it?"

Glenys shook her head. "First tell me that you believe what I say of Sir Anton, for when I leave this place, I want to know that you are finished with him forever."

Caswallan was thoughtful, and Glenys patient, though she knew she must strike the bargain with him quickly. Still, it would do no good to push too hard or too fast. She wanted Caswallan to feel fearless in the coming exchange.

In Sir Anton's tent, matters were faring in a far different manner.

Kieran had surprised Sir Anton in the midst of breaking his fast when he strode into the large pavilion with his sword drawn, shouting loudly for his foe to show himself. Sir Anton, sitting at a small trestle table and being tended by two of his servants, stood so quickly that he overturned the table and all of its contents onto the floor. Upon seeing Kieran, who was bearing down upon him in a fearful manner, he shrieked and ran for cover, while his servants—there must have been half a dozen, at least—scurried in every direction. There were half a dozen fighting men, as well, sitting about their master's tent, eating and drinking, but these had been taken so much by surprise that they had no time to grab up their weapons and stop Kieran's progress. Two of them made an attempt at throwing themselves in his path, but he readily dealt with them and tossed them aside. He had but a moment, he knew, before the rest gathered both their wits and their swords, but before then he'd wreak as much mayhem as possible and keep Sir Anton away from Caswallan, at least until Glenys could make the trade. After that, he simply needed confusion to break loose in every corner of Caswallan's encampment.

"Dog!" he shouted, chasing Sir Anton from one end of the pavilion to the other. "Knave! Liar! Murderer!"

"Stop him!" Sir Anton pleaded to his fighting men and servants alike. "Kill him! Quickly!"

"What, this sorry lot?" Kieran asked, kicking one of the fighting men in the behind and sending him reeling. Another was elbowed in the shoulder and fell to his knees with a shout of pain. "Kill me? I'd sooner be eaten alive by a herd of pigs than let such wretched louts send me to God. Now come and receive what is justly yours, Anton Lagasse." Kieran advanced upon the cowering man with his sword at the ready. Behind him he heard the remaining fighting men preparing themselves for attack. He'd not be able to hold them off for long, and prayed that Glenys was finishing her business with Caswallan rapidly.

In the darkness of the chapel, Caswallan stood in awe, staring at the queen piece, which Glenys held in her hand.

"I've heard rumors that she existed, but never let myself hope that I would see her." He glanced briefly at Glenys, licking his lips. "You lie, girl. You'd never part with anything so valuable, not even for the Greth Stone. This queen piece, centuries old, possesses powers that neither you nor I can dream of."

"I would not give her to you, nay," Glenys admitted, "but 'tis my uncle Culain who has parted with what he holds most dear in order to regain that which belongs—rightly and fully—to my family."

Caswallan took a step nearer, holding out a reverent hand toward the queen piece. Her eyes, Glenys saw, had gone black, as they had done only once before that she had seen. She felt it growing warm and tingling within her grip, as if the little chess piece were coming to life. Nothing could be more perfect.

"She's so beautiful," Caswallan murmured, his gaze riveted upon the piece. "If I possessed her my power would be endless. She would whisper all her secrets in my ear and give me guidance. There would be naught to stop me from..."

Glenys stepped back, holding the piece away.

"Do you agree?" she demanded. "I would have your promise that you will sever all ties with Sir Anton Lagasse forever, as well as return the Greth Stone."

"Aye," he said, his hand yet held out. "You have my vow. I will send Sir Anton away at once. Give her to me. Only let me hold her."

"The ring," Glenys reminded him. "Remove it first, and then you will have her."

Back in Sir Anton's pavilion, Kieran had been chased into a corner, but not without the satisfaction of felling two servants and another of Sir Anton's fighting men. As to Sir Anton, Kieran had not only left him bruised and battered, but had received the knight's promise never to show his feckless face again, lest Kieran exact a more lasting revenge for Sir Anton's dishonorable behavior. From his corner, Kieran could see Sir Anton at the other end of the pavilion, curled up and weeping like a babe. That was enough for now, he decided. It was past time that he made certain Glenys was well.

The exchange had been made. Glenys wore the Greth Stone safely upon her finger, and Caswallan held the queen piece in his hand.

"Beautiful," he said, as if he'd just been granted the greatest boon on earth. "Beautiful." He looked up at Glenys. "She feels hot to the touch. Almost as if she might burn my fingers. Is this how she always is?"

"Did you not know?" Glenys asked, lifting innocent eyes to his gaze. "She burns when she is at her happiest and most pleased, as she must be now to at last be in the hands of a true believer. Howbeit, you must set her in some pocket until the moment when you wish to reveal her to your followers—then she will be ready to do your bidding. You must take her out to them now, for she would wish to be admired at once, and as I am taking the Greth Stone away, your followers will desire reassurance."

"Oh, aye," Caswallan agreed happily. "I will make the presentation now, and you must stay. 'Twill lend credence to have a member of the Seymour family here, and to know that this gift was made by them."

Glenys bit her tongue to keep from telling him that the Seymours would never make a gift of anything so precious to a man who'd stoop to outright thieving. Instead, seeing that he had already carefully pocketed the queen piece within the folds of his white robes, she said with all graciousness, "I would be pleased."

Kieran waited until the right moment to lift his sword high and slice an opening in the silken roof above his head. Just as two of Sir Anton's fighting men charged at him, he leaped through the slit, causing them to stumble over each other rather than him. Quickly, while confusion reigned within, he circled the pavilion, bringing his sword down upon the ropes that held it in place, watching with satisfaction as the silk began to sag on those remaining within. Sir Anton's increasing shrieks brought a smile to his face.

"Fool," he muttered, looking about the encampment. He saw that Glenys and Caswallan had just left the chapel and that they, along with the crowd surrounding them, were gazing at Kieran and the fallen pavilion with bewilderment.

Perfect.

"They've gone mad!" Kieran shouted, striving to sound as frightened as he could. He began to run toward the crowd. "They're coming to get us! They've all become crazed! Ahh! Get your children! Run for your lives! Ahh!''

He realized that he made a foolish—and rather bizarre—figure, but it didn't help when Glenys covered her mouth with both hands in order to control her laughter. Jean-Marc, fortunately, played his own part to perfection. Dressed in white robes that Kieran suspected he'd stolen, and standing in the midst of the gathered, he began to shout, too. ''They've got their swords! They'll kill us all! Run! *Run!*''

They'd filled an unwitting crowd with groundless terror many a time, and Kieran never failed to be amused at how simple and helpful a thing it could be. Within moments utter confusion had taken hold, panic had filled the air, people were running in all directions and shouts had turned to deafening screams. Glenys and Caswallan stood in the midst of it, swarmed by Caswallan's frightened minions. Caswallan turned in circles, shouting, ''Calm yourselves!'' while Glenys merely waited for Kieran to force his way through the crowd to her.

He took her hand and they easily slipped away, and even before Sir Anton and his men could cut themselves free of their silken confines, they'd disappeared into the trees.

Dina greeted them with obvious relief. ''I thought you would never return, mistress,'' she said, gladly handing the horses' reins to Kieran. ''And when all that noise began...''

'''Tis all right now, Dina,'' Glenys assured her. ''Look, I have the ring.'' She raised her right hand to show it to her.

''Oh, mistress! Your good relatives will be so glad!

May God be praised. But where is Jean-Marc? Why has he not come with you?''

"I'm here, sweeting," came a voice from the other side of the small clearing in which they stood. Jean-Marc appeared the next moment, strolling toward them with a smile upon his handsome face. He was in the midst of removing the white covering he had worn in the encampment, and readily tossed it aside. "Here's what you're wanting," he told Kieran, pulling the queen piece out of a pocket and holding it on his open palm. "She was hot as fire when I took her, but has cooled enough to hold now. Caswallan never knew a thing," he added with a wicked grin. "He was carried off by his people much against his desire, for they wanted to keep him safe." Jean-Marc laughed. "I wish you had stayed to see it," he said. "I vow I've never seen the like, with the old man shrieking like a girl."

They all laughed, a mixture of jollity and relief.

"Jean-Marc, I owe you every thanks," Glenys said, looking at the queen's eyes as Jean-Marc passed her to Kieran's waiting hand. They were golden once more, for which she was thankful. "And my uncle Culain will as well, once he knows that you have regained what was most precious to him."

Jean-Marc made her a sweeping bow. "I am glad to have been of service, mistress. But if you are of a mind to grant me a boon, I'd not hold back from asking it of you."

"Anything," she declared. "You must only tell me what it is."

He cast a glance at Dina. "There is not time now," he said, "but if you will allow it, Dina and I would speak with you this night, when we are safe at Berte's."

Glenys, knowing full well what he meant to ask of her, opened her mouth to say, "Anything but that," but Kieran's arm came about her waist, squeezing so hard that naught but a squeaky breath came out.

"Mistress Glenys will gladly receive you there and hear you out, Jean-Marc. For now, let us away, before Sir Anton, stupid as he is, decides that he must make the attempt of regaining either the Greth Stone or her ladyship, the queen."

Chapter Sixteen

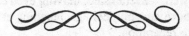

"They're coming to get us!" Glenys cried, laughing as Kieran chased her about the bed. "Run! Ahh!"

"Most...ouch!" He stubbed his toe and began hopping on one foot. She lunged for the bed and Kieran leaped after her, catching Glenys about the waist and tumbling her to her back. "*Most* amusing," he repeated dryly.

Glenys was yet laughing, and Kieran couldn't help but grin, too.

"It was!" she insisted, wiping tears from her eyes. "If only you had seen yourself running about like a lunatic. By the rood, I shall never forget it."

"Just as I shall never forget your terrible behavior," he said chidingly. "Laughing at me as if 'twere all a merry jest. You made it most difficult to be convincing in my effort to terrify."

"Oh, but you *were* convincing," she assured him, smiling. "I was quaking with fear as you shouted for us to run. Never have I been so afraid." This was followed by a telling snort.

Kieran pulled her beneath him, setting his fingers to her sides. "You are the cruelest female I've e'er known," he told her, tickling her until she writhed with laughter. "Aye, cruel—making jest of me after all I've done to regain your precious ring *and* the queen piece."

"Peace!" Glenys begged, grabbing his hands to still them, chuckling with merriment. "Peace, I beg you. I make truce."

"Very well," Kieran said, moving even closer. "But now you have hurt my feelings, laughing at me so, and must make reparation."

"Gladly," she replied at once. "I shall rub your back. Will that do?"

He shook his head. "Nay."

"Hmm," Glenys said more thoughtfully. "Shall I buy you a new cloak, made of the finest wool and dyed scarlet?"

Now *he* snorted. "Nay, mistress. You must think of something better."

"Better?" She wiggled her eyebrows lecherously. "Shall I tie you to this bed for a day and a night and do all that I please to you?"

He uttered a laugh. "God's toes! From cloaks to wickedness with scarce a breath between. You have a wonderful mind, Glenys. I'll choose the latter."

He lowered his mouth to kiss her, and soon all manner of playfulness fled as they became intent upon each other. Kieran's hands found their way beneath the thin, gauzy chemise that Glenys wore, while hers wandered boldly over his bare chest and shoulders, sliding down his back to tunnel beneath the leggings he had donned but an hour earlier when they had risen from bed to partake of their evening meal.

Despite their mood of happiness at both the success and the humor of their earlier undertaking, there was a measure of desperation to their lovemaking, especially for Kieran. They had no sooner returned to Berte's than he'd stolen Glenys away to their private chamber, possessed with an overwhelming urge to spend every possible moment alone with her.

This would be their last night, now that the Greth Stone and the queen piece were safe. He could no longer pretend that they had time, pleasant as that dream was to him. Already Glenys had been parted from her family for too long, and Daman would soon be upon them.

Kieran had decided what must be. In the morn, whether she wished it or not, he would take her to Glain Tarran and there they would part ways. Forever.

The chemise had disappeared, as had his leggings. Kieran touched her everywhere, stroking, kissing, giving her every pleasure he could think of, taking all that she gave him in turn.

"Come inside of me," she whispered, her fingers in his hair as he kissed her breasts. "Please, Kieran."

"Nay," he murmured. "God's mercy, don't tempt me, Glenys."

"Please," she said once more. "Just once. I want to be one with you. I want to feel you inside of me."

With a groan Kieran moved up to silence her with his mouth, kissing her both long and hard.

"There is nothing I want more," he said, his voice harsh with the effort to keep from doing as she asked. "But I will *not* take your maidenhead from you. I love you, Glenys," he said, kissing her again and stroking a hand through her hair. "Do not ask me to bring such ruin upon you."

She reached up to touch his cheek with her fingertips. "Then will you marry me, instead, and take me to wife?" she asked. "Just as I would take you as my husband? Then we could come together without fear."

Kieran stared down at her, searching her eyes. His heart felt as if it had just been clutched in a tight, squeezing grip, and he wasn't certain that he could speak without revealing how painful her words were to him. He opened his mouth—but nothing came out. With a harsh breath, he rolled away and off the bed, standing up. He went to stand by the chamber's small window, setting his hands on the sill and closing his eyes, striving to calm his senses. Behind him, he could hear Glenys sitting up in the bed.

"You no longer wish to wed me?" she asked softly, hesitation in her voice.

"I have already told you that I would take you for my wife if I could, but 'tis impossible. It is a torment to me even to speak of it, knowing that I must leave you on the morrow and never set eyes on you again."

"I did think it impossible," she admitted, "before yesterday. But now I know that 'tis not. We *can* be married, if we both wish it."

"Your family would never allow you to marry a man such as I," he told her, shaking his head. "How can you even begin to think any such miracle could happen?"

"I'm not certain that you will understand," she murmured. "It was what that…that little man at Pentre Ifan called you. Lord Eneinoig. That changes everything."

Kieran uttered a hollow laugh. "It changes naught, Glenys. A strange little man with a quick temper and sharp teeth may call me whatever he pleases, but nothing can change what I am—and what I have been since I was born. If you do not believe that your elderly aunts and uncles would be dismayed at the thought of such a union, you have only to think of how your brother, Daman, would greet such news. I vow he would rather see you dead by his own hand than wed to a man like me.''

Her voice trembled when she spoke again.

''That may be so, Kieran, but I would take the chance of it. I never thought…nay, I *knew* that I would never wed. That no man could ever love me. And I—''

''Glenys,'' he pleaded hoarsely. ''Speak no more, I beg you. Kill me, instead. You know that I love you. I would give all I possess to wed you—aye, even just to keep you, wicked as that is. Don't make me weep for the foolishness you've known, for I vow I cannot bear it. How could I bring you such ruin by grasping at my own happiness? You do not know what it is to be set apart as I have been—as you would be should you wed me.''

''And yet,'' she whispered, ''I would rather be scorned by the world, if scorned we would be, than live out the rest of my life as I have done before. And I do not think you have any choice in the matter, Kieran. I think—knowing what you were named at Pentre Ifan—that we are fated to be together. Despite every argument that may be set before us.''

At last, Kieran turned to look at her, finding Glenys sitting upon the bed, fully naked, her long sunset hair falling about her shoulders as a covering and her hands twined together in her lap. She was gazing at him with shining eyes, and he found that he wasn't proof against that—and certainly not against the overwhelming desire of his heart.

''I…have an estate,'' he said stupidly, making his offering in a manner that he could only find foolish and perhaps even insulting. "Small. Very small. My father gave it to me."

Glenys, rather than appearing shocked, as he'd imagined, gazed at him with what he thought seemed affectionate amusement.

"A small estate?" she repeated, smiling. "Where is it?"

"In Derbyshire," he said, one of his hands clutching the windowsill for support. "There are sheep—well, mainly sheep. I've visited a dozen times, mayhap, not often enough to know much of the place. There are servants caring for the manor house, and vassals who care for the sheep and cattle. My father gave it to me many years past, when I was but eighteen. Greenvale, it is called. But I have never been a true master to it, Glenys. I have left it and the people there to deal as they will, without help from me. I have been as poor a master to them as I have been to my own life."

"Aye," she said thoughtfully, "but that is at an end now, my lord Eneinoig. I will help you to set all right at Greenvale, if you desire it."

"Glenys," he murmured, and said nothing else.

She smiled again. "'Twill be a simple thing. I'll not leave you to face the task alone. Or anything else. I'll stay beside you, Kieran. *If* that is what you wish."

Kieran's heart was beating like a maddened drum. He hadn't felt so hopeful since he'd been a child, when he had learned the foolishness of such an emotion.

"Of course that's what I wish."

"Then that is how it will be," she said simply.

He shook his head once more, but took a step toward her. "Glenys, you're not thinking aright."

She held a hand out to him. "For the very first time, I am."

She made it sound far too easy. Far too possible.

"You would lose all that you have. You would become an outcast, the wife of a bastard, and worse, the wife of a thief and knave."

"The wife of Kieran FitzAllen," she said. "That is what I would become. Far more than I have ever dreamed of being. I do not know the words to tell you how proud I should feel to be named your wife."

"Glenys." He crossed the room and set one knee on the bed, taking her outstretched hand in both of his. "Do you mean this?"

"Aye, with all my heart."

He hardly knew whether to laugh or weep.

"You would wed me," he said with wonder, "knowing all that I have done? The women...all my crimes...my endless sins?"

"Yes, Kieran. I will wed you because I love you, and because I need you, and because you need me, as well."

"God alone knows how so," he whispered, then suddenly pulled her up to her knees and into his arms, crushing her in his embrace. He closed his eyes and pressed his face against her neck, into the softness of her hair. "I pray that He will make me a fit husband for you. If you should ever come to know sadness because of me, or a moment of regret—"

"I'll not," she murmured, stroking his hair with a gentle hand. He heard the deep pleasure in her tone, and could scarce believe that he had been the one to give her that. "All will be well. I promise you this."

"Aye," he said, lifting his head to smile into her beloved face. "Aye, we will make it so. I should never have dared such a thing before, but you make me brave, Glenys, as I have only dreamed of being. Bastards possess a certain measure of boldness, but not that which better men are born with. But now I think that mayhap it no longer matters. You do not seem to care.'' He searched her gaze intently. ''Do you?''

She shook her head. ''No. I never will. You are Kieran FitzAllen, and if you had been born a king or a beggar, it would make no difference to me.''

He smiled and then kissed her.

''Magic does exist,'' he murmured against her lips. ''You have it within your very soul, I vow.''

Her arms began to slide about his shoulders, but a loud knocking at the door made her stop and pull away.

''Who would disturb us at this hour?'' she asked.

''Jean-Marc,'' Kieran replied with a sigh, pulling her chemise from beneath the covers and untangling it. ''Come to ask for Dina's hand in marriage, mostlike. Here, cover yourself quickly before he grows too impatient.'' He put the thin garment over her head and helped her to slide her arms into their places. ''Where is your robe? And my leggings. Ah, here, on the floor.''

More knocking sounded, far more furious this time.

''A moment, Jean-Marc!'' Kieran shouted, as he thrust a foot into his leggings. ''We're not yet dressed to—''

He lifted his head, realizing too late who was at the door. In later years, he would think with a measure of understanding how he, who was so accomplished a knave, could have been so slow to recognize imminent danger, but at the moment he could scarce believe that love had made him so lack-witted.

He had but a moment to shout a warning to Glenys and pull his leggings up to cover himself before the door came crashing open and Sir Daman Seymour and his men rushed into the chamber, their swords at the ready.

Glenys, who stood on the other side of the bed, tying the strings to her robe, let out a cry of both surprise and fear. Her fingers had fallen still and her face, upon seeing her furious brother, had gone white.

"Daman!" she cried. "How did you—?"

But it was all she could say before Sir Daman's outrage erupted.

"Bitch!" he shouted wrathfully. "Slut! I will kill you both!"

In a blur of motion, Kieran leaped across the mattress and set Glenys behind him. He was weaponless, nearly defenseless, and knew full well that he'd have been in a rage to equal Daman's if he'd found his own sister in such a circumstance.

"'Tis not as it seems, Seymour," he said loudly, firmly, though it seemed ridiculous even to his own ears. He stood before the man half-naked, having obviously shared a bed with that same man's sister. "You must hear us out before acting rashly. Glenys is *innocent.*"

"She's a whore!" Daman shouted, his voice filled with pained emotion, as if he might begin to weep at finding his sister in such a state. He advanced upon them with his sword held high, a maddened look in his eyes. "And a traitor! Lying with a baseborn knave without care for our family's name."

Kieran could both hear and see the crazed emotion that pushed Daman onward, truly ready to commit murder. He lunged forward, gripping Daman's sword arm with both hands, desperate to buy enough time to bring him to some sense. They struggled furiously, equal in strength.

"Stop!" Glenys pleaded. "Daman, no!"

"Only listen to us," Kieran growled beneath the punishing force of Daman's fury. "For Elizabet's sake, for Glenys's sake, *listen.*"

The words checked Daman. He pulled his gaze from where his sister stood to look at Kieran.

"Why do you speak of Elizabet now? *How* can you speak of her?"

"You fool!" Kieran said bitterly. "If you kill me you might as well kill Elizabet. If you ever cared for her at all—"

"Don't speak of her!" With a violent thrust, Daman knocked Kieran to the ground.

Glenys cried out his name and ran to him, but Daman's gauntleted hand flew up, striking her full across the face, a sickening blow that sent her reeling into the wall. She slid to the floor, unconscious, and both Kieran and Daman moved toward her at once.

"Leave her be!" Kieran shouted furiously, gripping Daman by the collar of his chain mail and hauling him upward. He didn't think what he did, only knew that he must keep Glenys safe from her brutish brother, and sent his fist into the other man's face with all the strength he possessed.

Daman fell back, his eyes wide with shock, but Kieran had no time to think of him. He turned back to where Glenys lay, kneeling beside her.

"Glenys," he murmured. She was fully unconscious. Her cheek, where Daman had struck her, was already bright red and swelling. "Oh, God, Glenys." He reached out a hand to touch her, only to find himself jerked nearly off his feet by a fist in his hair.

"You'll not touch her!" Daman shouted, swinging Kieran about. The hilt of his sword was in his other fist, and it was the last that Kieran saw or knew as Daman brought it down on his head.

Chapter Seventeen

"Glenys, won't you even speak to me? I've already told you how sorry I am that I struck you. I was maddened—full out of my wits. You know that I'd never have done such a thing otherwise. I've never struck you before, even when we were children. Please, only look at me."

Glenys kept her gaze upon the blazing hearth in Berte's main chamber. She had come awake to find herself lying on the bed, with Daman bending anxiously over her, tearful apologies on his lips. Kieran and Jean-Marc had been taken away and confined in a wagon outside of Berte's, and everyone else within had been sent out into the street, as well, despite Berte's shrill protests, leaving the two of them alone in the entire dwelling.

"Will you let me see Kieran?" she asked.

Daman gripped the back of her chair, behind which he had been standing for the last half hour, pleading with her to forgive him for striking her.

"Nay," he said harshly. "Never. He has shamed you and—"

"*You* have shamed me," she said bitterly, speaking

to him in Welsh. "Before all your men and half the women in this dwelling. Before the townspeople of Aberteifi. You have accused me of that which I have not done—not because I did not wish it, by the rood, but because Kieran refused to subject me to such as this. I am yet a maiden, Daman. You see fit to name me both a whore and a liar, but you're wrong."

"I know Kieran FitzAllen too well to believe that it is so, Glenys," Daman said, striving for gentleness. "He is far too famed for his many conquests for it to be otherwise. But I attach no blame to you," he added quickly. "I know I was maddened at first, but now I realize that you are too innocent to have seen FitzAllen for what he is. And too…inexperienced with men."

"Daman, I swear to you upon my soul, I do not lie! I am yet a maiden. Only fetch a physician to examine me and let him tell you that I speak the truth."

"I should never put you through such a spectacle," he said, affronted. "Nay, listen to me, my dearest. I understand fully how it is. He told you sweet lies, of a certainty, mayhap even that he loved you, and you would not know that they were false. Indeed, I'm sure you found them very sweet, as you have never heard anything like them before. But as you were never thought to wed, mayhap there is no need for lasting shame, unless," he added more dismally, "by some evil chance he has got you with child. If that is so, there is naught to be done but hide you away until the child has come, and then find a place for it somewhere."

Glenys didn't think she'd ever been so angry in all of her life. She loved her brother, but at the moment she would have gladly disowned him for a fool.

"Go away," she said tightly. "Leave me in peace."

"Glenys," he pleaded, "I can't. Not until you've forgiven me for striking you as I did. Even so, I will never forgive myself. I might have killed you in such a temper, may God have mercy on me."

Glenys folded her arms over her breasts and said nothing.

Daman knelt beside her, so tall that their heads were of an equal height.

"Glenys, I beg of you, forgive me. I vow that I will never touch you in anger again."

"I cannot forgive you if you will not believe me, Daman. You have never held me in such contempt as this before. If you believe that I lie to you, then you must surely do as you think best. Drag me to the nearest church. Stand upon the steps and disown me for a whore."

"How can you think I would do such a thing to you? Glenys, you're my sister, and I love you as dearly as my own life. But can you not understand how it was for me? To see you with Kieran FitzAllen, in such a manner? Do you mean to say that you never shared a bed with him?"

She unfolded her arms and looked him full in the face.

"I shared a bed with him, aye, and of my own free accord. But we did not…" She stopped at the look on his face and said, more calmly, "He left me a maiden. I'm certain, Daman, that I need not explain to you how such as that is accomplished. You've bedded any number of women, I have no doubt, and must know something of what a man and woman may do together apart from consummation."

His cheeks flushed hotly, and he rose to his feet,

angered anew. "The bastard! I'll wring his neck for teaching you such lewd things!"

"You'll not," Glenys told him tautly. "For I mean to marry him, and then he will be your brother by marriage. 'Twould be the foulest manner of murder. And such a hypocrite you are, Daman Seymour, for you've done just as he has, and behave as if you'd the right to resent it in another man."

"When my own sister is the one ruined, aye!" he shouted.

She stood at last, facing him with all the fury she felt. "Aye, your own sister, who went to him with all her heart and consent! I love Kieran FitzAllen, and I have chosen him for my husband, whether you will it or not, whether our family wills it or not and, aye," she said more daringly, moving to stand in front of him, "whether you beat me again and again! Do so, Daman," she dared, offering him her already swollen face. "Go on! Beat me into submission, if you think you can."

"Cease!" he begged. "You know that I will not strike you. Never again, please God! But I cannot let you continue in such foolishness. Kieran FitzAllen doesn't love you, Glenys. He took and seduced you only to gain revenge upon me."

Glenys shook her head. "You're wrong. I realize there's some enmity between you, but Kieran took me because Sir Anton Lagasse paid him to get me out of his way while he went in search of the Greth Stone. His desire to anger you was second to that."

"Nay, Glenys," Daman said gently, "'twas not. Kieran FitzAllen had no need to take Sir Anton's money. He's wealthy, as rich as a great lord."

Glenys's eyes widened. "Wealthy?"

Daman nodded. "'Tis well known among his kind that he only accepts the tasks that please him, for he has no need of earning gold. His years of thieving and knavery have served him and his manservant full well."

Glenys stared at her brother, striving to contain her surprise. She supposed it made sense that Kieran should have gained a measure of wealth over the years, but why had he said nothing of this to her?

"It doesn't really matter," she said, more to convince herself than Daman. "I'faith, if it is true, this should make him more acceptable to you. At least you'll not think he wished to wed me for my wealth, as God above knows that my face and form would drive away all but the most ardent fortune seekers."

"You don't look as you did in London," Daman said gruffly. "S'truth, I did not recognize you at first, for you appear almost fetching, and...changed. Though this is but some manner of evil, clearly wrought by Kieran FitzAllen's foul wickedness," he added bitterly. "But it has now come to an end, and you will soon be yourself once more."

"Daman—"

He struck a fist in the palm of his other hand. "*Naught* could make him acceptable! Do you not understand, Glenys, that he decided to take you only for his own purpose? Because he knew that I would come after you and give him a chance to confront me."

"He has admitted that he cherished this hope," she told him, "but he would not tell me why. What have you done, Daman, to cause such purpose in him?"

Daman had ever been bold as a boy, and had grown bolder as a man, but now he looked as Glenys had never seen him before—discomfited and ashamed and wretched, all at once.

"I fell in love with his sister."

"His—?" Glenys had to find the nearest chair and sit down. "His sister? *You?*"

Daman nodded. "We met at a tournament, and I fell in love with her from the moment I set sight on her, for her beauty and sweet manner are beyond all words. Her name is Elizabet." He said it softly, reverently. "You heard him speak of her earlier. He must have known that nothing else could have brought me to my senses, save to hear her name. I loved her—*love* her—so deeply, Glenys. You cannot begin to know what a torment it has been to me, or how I have longed for her these months since we've been parted."

"I can scarce believe this," Glenys murmured, surprised. "You've said nothing, not a word. Oh, Daman," she cried with sudden understanding, setting a hand to her head and gaping at him. "You left her because of the Seymour name. Because of the magic."

He lowered his head. "Aye. I could not ask her, or any woman, to be my wife. You know that I determined that before. The madness must stop with us, Glenys, for how could we gift our children with the same curse that has plagued us every day of our lives? And how could I ever have explained it to Elizabet? She would have despised me, or, worse, become afraid of me. I could not bear to see that in her eyes. And so I...I left her. 'Twas best for her, for she will find another to love and wed, but I vow I have longed for her every moment, until I sometimes think I must go mad from the lack of her. I can only pray that she has put thoughts of me aside and set her purpose to finding another."

"Did you dally with her?" Glenys asked.

"I brought her no shame, if that is what you mean. I left her pure for marriage to another, at least in body if not in heart, for she said that she loved me, also."

"And you find it so impossible to believe that Kieran FitzAllen did the same?"

"Fully and completely," Daman replied. "He is neither a man of honor nor of truth, but a liar and scoundrel of great repute. And his conquests with women are too numerous to speak of. Why should he withhold from taking his pleasure with the sister of a man he wished to spite? He would think far more of just how perfect it would make his revenge, not only to make you love him, but to bring shame to you and all our family."

"But he did not do so," Glenys said, sighing. "I cannot make you believe me, yet it is true. I had no care for such things, but I can only now think how right Kieran was."

"Glenys, I've just told you that the man took you for revenge!" Daman protested. "Any sweet words of love that he gave you were lies, meant only to gain your trust."

"That may have once been his intent," Glenys admitted. "But somehow it changed. He loves me, Daman. I believe that with all my heart."

"How so?" Daman demanded angrily. "He's spent his life weaving lies, caring not who he's told them to or to what purpose. Why a-God's name should you believe him now?"

"Because no one else will," she replied simply. "Because he needs someone—even one person—to believe in him."

"Then you're a fool," Daman told her. "It saddens

me, Glenys, to see you come down to this. You were the most sensible among us, the most sane and trustworthy. Now you seem to have forgotten everything—even the safety of our family. Or will you tell me that now you've also begun to believe in magic, so that I am left alone to protect our aunts and uncles?''

"I think I have begun to believe," she murmured. "When we were at Pentre Ifan, a little man wearing a red cap appeared to Kieran, and called him Lord Eneinoig—the promised one."

Even Daman, for all his naysaying, checked at this, and stared at her.

"Lord Eneinoig? Kieran FitzAllen? That's impossible. And 'tis naught but a foolish legend, anywise."

"A family legend," Glenys reminded him. "One that we have heard all our lives. But Kieran FitzAllen could never have heard of it or found it out to use to his own purpose. I have thought it through from every side, and can only believe that it must be true. And if it is," she said, standing once more and facing her brother, "then Kieran is acceptable as my husband."

"Understand me," Daman said, his voice tight with ill-concealed anger, "you will never see Kieran FitzAllen again. There are no arguments you can make that will sway me to say otherwise. I will have him and his manservant taken to London, tried for kidnapping, and hanged."

Glenys took one step nearer, gazing into his eyes, unafraid.

"It will not be done. Once we're in London, I shall tell Uncle Aonghus everything, and he'll stop you. And if he does not, I'll go to the king myself and plead for Kieran's life, and Jean-Marc's as well. And, Brother, remember who holds the key to our family's wealth.

I've been the one to please both church and crown with tributes each year, and know full well which hands to warm with gold in order to obtain their freedom. Your efforts to have them killed will be for naught.''

Daman's expression was one of sorrow and dismay. "He's made you mad," he murmured. "I cannot trust that you will come to your senses before we've reached Metolius, and so I must keep you safe from your own folly. You will not come with us to London, Glenys. Nay, I will hear no arguments, not until you've grown sane again. You and Mistress Dina will remain in Wales, at Glain Tarran, until FitzAllen and his manservant have been put to death. My men will take you there now and keep you under guard. I will instruct the servants to listen to nothing that you say, and to keep you locked within the dwelling until I come for you. I am sorry, Glenys, but it must be this way. If I loved you less, I would not take such care. You may hate me for it now, but you'll thank me one day, once you've realized what misery I have saved you from."

For the next ten minutes, Glenys's fury raged unabated. She argued, she wept, she threw things at him and made every dire threat she could think of. But he remained unmoved, and, in truth, only grew more convinced that she was ill in her mind for having spent so many days in Kieran FitzAllen's company.

In the end, Glenys gave way, too exhausted and dispirited to go on. Her face, where Daman had struck her, ached badly, and she sat in the chair by the hearth, rubbing it with care.

"At least let me send a note to him," she said, closing her eyes wearily. "A farewell note."

Daman knelt beside her once more. "If it would soothe you, then write it out now and I'll give it to him. Does it hurt badly, Glenys? I wish to God that I had cut my hand off before ever striking you.''

Glenys moaned and pressed her hand against her swollen cheek. ''The pain is terrible. I can scarce bear it. I would have Dina deliver the note, so that she can tell me how Kieran and Jean-Marc fare.''

''Nay,'' Daman said firmly. ''I will take it.''

''Ohh!'' Glenys cried, pressing both hands on her face now. ''It aches so badly! And knowing that you could do such a thing to me is even more painful. I would be so greatly eased if only Dina could tell me that she had seen them with her own eyes. And spoken to them—at least to Jean-Marc. She needn't even go near Kieran. Please, Daman,'' she pleaded when he said nothing. '''Twould mean so much to me.''

He sighed and stood; Glenys waited.

''Very well,'' he said at last. ''But I must read the note you write, and Dina can spend no more than five minutes in the wagon with them. Guards will stand at the door the while.''

''It will be as you say,'' she said at once, dropping her hand and opening her eyes. ''Thank you, Daman. If you will find me paper and ink somewhere within this brothel, I shall write the note. And if you would send Dina in to me first, I would be even more grateful.''

The note contained only one word: *Godspeed.*

Glenys's name wasn't even signed to it, though Dina had thrust it into his hands, saying that it was from her mistress. Kieran supposed, gazing at the tiny scrap of parchment, that Daman would not let Glenys say more. In truth, he was surprised that she'd been allowed to write him anything at all.

Kieran lay back down in the straw, shackled both hand and foot, and with the small measure of freedom he possessed tucked the one-word missive into his tunic. His fingers, able to creep only partly into his inner pocket, touched the smooth surface of the little glowing stone. It was warm and comforting, something familiar to carry with him to prison and bear him company. Something to remind him of Glenys before he died.

In the far corner of the small, dark wagon in which they were confined, he could hear snatches of the fervent conversation taking place between Dina and Jean-Marc. She seemed to be trying to convince him to escape, and he apparently believed that he could not abandon Kieran. But Kieran would make certain that Jean-Marc was gone before they reached London. 'Twould be an easy thing for him to manage—they'd both escaped numerous imprisonments before now—and Daman wouldn't bother to search for a mere manservant. So long as he held the master, Daman would let Jean-Marc go without giving chase.

"You must come," Dina whispered urgently, casting a glance at the guard who watched through the single barred window. "We need your help. And 'tis the only way you can save your master."

"I can't leave him, Dina."

"Yes, you can," Kieran said wearily from where he lay, his head throbbing from the blow Daman had dealt him. "Never fear, Dina. Jean-Marc will meet you wherever you wish it."

"Quiet!" Jean-Marc set a finger to his lips. "He's listening." He jerked his head toward the guard, who did, indeed, seem to be trying to hear what they were saying.

"Time, mistress!" he shouted in at them. "Finish up."

"Jean-Marc!" Dina pleaded, grasping his hands.

"Dina, I love you, but I can't—"

"Oh, be quiet and kiss her," Kieran said irately. "You're making my head ache. He'll meet you, Dina. Tell Glenys it will be so."

Jean-Marc moved to sit beside him once Dina had gone, looking down at him with disapproval. "I'll not leave you alone," he stated. "I'll not leave at all, unless you come, too."

"You know I can't," Kieran told him, feeling both weary and sick. "Daman would chase us forever, and Glenys's name would be cast into scandal, and her family's as well. At every word of our whereabouts the rumors would start anew, never leaving her in peace. I couldn't do that to her. Never that, when she's spent so much of her life striving to keep her family safe from prying eyes. It's over, Jean-Marc. We've had many good years together, and I'm more thankful than I can say that you've been with me. But it's time for you to go on your own. And time for me to face a fitting punishment for all my sins."

"By the rood!" Jean-Marc swore violently, reaching down to grasp the front of Kieran's tunic and drag him upright, his chains clattering at the abrupt motion. "They'll kill you if they get you to London. You'll have no chance of escaping Newgate, and they *will* hang you. You must come with me when I go."

"I knew what risks I took with both our lives when I gave way to desire and lingered too long. Every sense and skill warned me. My only comfort is that you can so easily escape. I want you to live, Jean-Marc, and be happy with Dina. I want you to build her a beautiful manor house and have a dozen children and live like a king and queen. And, mayhap, from time to time, make certain that Glenys is well and happy. For the sake of our friendship, I would ask that of you.''

"I won't let them hang you," Jean-Marc told him stubbornly, giving him a shake.

Kieran sighed and gently pushed free of Jean-Marc's grip. "If I die, then Glenys will have a chance to live in peace. There will be rumors for a time, but they will soon fade. Daman will see to that."

"Kieran," Jean-Marc said with disbelief. "You don't know what you say. You won't be so foolish as to die for the sake of a mere woman, no matter what you may feel for her. I've known you too long to believe such a thing."

Kieran smiled and spoke to him gently. "Love is a frightening force, my friend. Ever remember that when you have taken your beloved Dina to wife." He reached out with his manacled hands and touched Jean-Marc's arm. "You must take every care. Set your mind on keeping Dina and Glenys safe, once you've escaped. Don't let yourself think of me."

Jean-Marc made a sound of disgust and pushed away. "If you think I'd go off and leave you after all these years, just to save my own skin, then you're far wrong." His voice was filled with insult and not a little hurt. "Oh, I'll escape, just as you wish, but only to help Dina and Mistress Glenys save your sorry neck. And because I can't bear to be in the company of a fool."

Kieran chuckled. "As you prefer it. I never was able to make you do what I wished. You're a terrible man-servant. But," he added more seriously, "an excellent friend."

Jean-Marc crossed his arms and looked away, grunting as if he didn't care at all about this. But Kieran knew better.

"I'll ask one last thing of you," he said. "Daman will have told Glenys about Elizabet, and she'll think that I took her only for that purpose, and that I lied to her about...everything. Tell her...tell her that I meant every word I said, and that I love her as I have never loved another, and that she gave me such happiness as I never thought to have. And a pleasant dream to carry with me into prison, knowing that she would have accepted me as her husband. Tell her that, will you?"

"Hah," Jean-Marc said gruffly, still not looking at him. "Tell her yourself," he advised, "when you see her in London, after we have you free. She'd rather hear it from you, anywise, and I couldn't speak such sap and nonsense without becoming ill, I vow."

Chapter Eighteen

"Up, you!"

A sharp poke with the blunt end of a long spear brought Kieran awake. Another poke encouraged him into an upright position, though he struggled against his chains.

It was dark and foggy outside. Kieran's head yet ached and his stomach rumbled from hunger. Neither he nor Jean-Marc had been given so much as a sip of water since they'd left Cardigan. Kieran's body was cramped from being in such close confines, and the manacles on his hands had badly chafed his wrists. The ones on his ankles weren't quite so bad; Daman had been thoughtful enough to allow Kieran to pull on his boots before the iron cuffs had been placed upon him.

"Come along!" Another ill-aimed poke. "Out!"

Kieran's mind came blearily to life as he gazed at the small opening of the door, where the man stood. Jean-Marc was nowhere in sight. Had he somehow managed to escape while the wagon was in motion? Without even bothering to tell Kieran farewell? But that was not to be wondered at. Jean-Marc had often been angry with him, but never so much as now. Kieran could scarce blame him. They'd been together so many years, as close as brothers all that time, and for Kieran to so suddenly send him off alone must have felt very much like abandonment.

He dragged himself forward on hands and knees, sliding bit by bit across the straw that had been placed down for a small measure of comfort and warmth, pulling his heavy chains behind him.

"Time to give the prisoners a breath of air, eh?" he said as he slid his legs through the door. "You'll have to help me stand, I fear, because I—oof!" The soldier pulled Kieran out of the small door opening with an abrupt tug, letting him fall on the ground, chains and all.

"Thank you," Kieran said dryly, picking himself up with no small difficulty—though he preferred that to being helped by Daman Seymour's men. "I'm most grateful for your kindness."

He was surrounded by soldiers, one of whom held Jean-Marc, who smiled grimly as Kieran looked at him. Kieran had known the younger man long enough to know what that particular look meant. The escape was coming soon. Silently, Kieran wished him well and saw that Jean-Marc understood. The slightest nod of his head returned the sentiment.

"Come along," the soldier who'd prodded him said, roughly shoving Kieran forward. "Sir Daman wishes to speak to you."

"What a happy coincidence," Kieran said pleasantly as he received another shove in the same direction. "I wished to speak to him, as well. I can only pray he has some wine for his guest. I'm parched after such a long, pleasant journey."

"Quiet!" his escort demanded. "None of your chattering, by Sir Daman's command."

What? Kieran thought with dim amusement. Did Daman think he'd try to charm his way free? Not that he hadn't done it before, but only when a pretty maid was present to let him go. Women were much easier to sway than hardened fighting men, he'd long ago discovered. And Sir Daman's were among the hardest soldiers to be found in England, a justly famed army, commanded by a justly admired knight of the realm. Kieran had always known it, even when he'd so foolishly dallied with that same man's sister. But Glenys...he couldn't have stopped himself even if her brother had been the all-powerful king.

There was only one tent in the encampment, hastily raised and still being tethered to stakes in the ground.

Kieran could hear Daman's voice within, and the murmuring of others. The soldier beside him raised his voice and announced, "The prisoner is here, my lord."

There was an immediate, telling silence in the tent, so that Kieran almost laughed aloud.

The tent flap opened and three fighting men walked out, all of them eyeing Kieran as they went. He nodded and smiled at each of them, and then, at their expressions, did laugh.

"Bring him in, Hubert," Daman Seymour commanded from within.

A nudge sent Kieran into the lamplit enclosure, which was being readied for Daman's use by two serving boys, who were rolling out a pallet and carpets and setting up a table and chairs.

Daman himself sat in one of those chairs, gazing at a map and a number of other documents. He was yet wearing his chain mail and gauntlets, but his helmet

had been removed. Kieran saw the face that had stayed
in his memory for so many months, since he'd seen his
sister Elizabet. He had met Daman Seymour only
twice, but the dark, aristocratic face was fixed in Kieran's mind. He was a handsome brute; Kieran had certainly never blamed Elizabet on that particular point.
His hair was straight and very black, and his eyes were
gray, like Glenys's, set beneath dark eyebrows that
tilted upward at the outer edges, giving him a con-
stantly thoughtful expression. Save for the eyes, Kieran
could see none of Glenys in the man.

He looked up from the map, met Kieran's gaze, then
instructed the soldier, "Release him and wait outside
with the chains. He will have them on again before he
is returned to the wagon."

Kieran gladly submitted to being unshackled and,
relieved of his burden, stood at full height and took a
moment to stretch his muscles before murmuring his
thanks. Hubert, the soldier, gave him an even-eyed look
before picking up the chains and tossing them over his
shoulder.

"I'll be just outside if you should need me, my lord,
along with the guards." He bowed and departed.

Daman chuckled and tossed the map aside, standing
to face Kieran. "My soldiers fear for my life because
of you," he said, clearly much amused. "They would
do better to fear for you, methinks."

"You are the one with all of the might on his side,"
Kieran confessed. "Apart from that, I have already decided that I would do naught to bring any further shame
to Glenys. Is she well?" he asked. "Where is she?"

Daman's mouth thinned. "I'll not speak of her to
you, save to say that she is safe and beyond your reach.
And that you will never set sight on her again. I will

keep her out of London until you've received just punishment.''

Kieran's heart lurched painfully at the words, yet he was glad to think that she'd not see him being hanged.

"Thank you," he said, and Daman nodded curtly. "I do have a request of you."

"What is it?"

"My family...those of both my father and mother...I'd not have them know of my fate until 'tis done. I would not have them so distressed.''

At this, Daman appeared surprised. "I would have thought, instead, that you would wish them to know. They might be able to save you, despite all. Your father and stepfather are far more powerful than I am."

"Your opinion of me is a lowly one," Kieran said, "but I am not so lost to honor that I would include either of them in my shame."

"Have you not done so in the past?"

"Regretfully, I have," Kieran admitted. "But I will not do so now. There is a compelling reason, which I have already told you. It would kill my sister Elizabet to know that the man whom she entrusted with her love had been the cause of her brother's death. I'faith, I would not have her know of your part in this at all, if't can be done."

The lamplight was dim, but Kieran could see a flush creep across Daman's cheeks. "Sit," he said, sweeping a gauntleted hand at one of the chairs. To one of his serving boys, he commanded, "Bring us wine, and some bread and cheese if you can find any."

He removed his gauntlets one after the other, placing them with care upon the table. Then he sat down opposite Kieran and looked him full in the face.

"I want the truth. You took Glenys because of what happened between Elizabet and me."

Kieran nodded. "Aye. I wanted to draw you out and take revenge upon you for the manner in which you had left Elizabet. I had heard that you were a man of honor, but after what you did to my sister, I knew you were not." Kieran couldn't contain the bitterness in his tone, all the anger he'd felt at Daman Seymour for so long. "I meant to give you a taste of what it was to have one you love dearly in the power of another, and then beat you senseless in a face-to-face contest." He glanced at the tent flap as it opened for the serving boy to return, a tray in his hands. "I didn't consider that I would be caught in a snare of my own making. You will not believe me, but I vowed that I would not seduce your sister."

Daman held up a hand to silence him as the youth approached, setting goblets and a decanter of wine on the table. There was a plate of roughly torn bread and a hunk of cheese that Daman himself pulled into smaller chunks and put before Kieran.

"Leave us," he told the serving boy. "Both of you, go."

Without a word, they bowed and were gone.

Daman filled Kieran's goblet with a shaking hand.

"Eat," he said. "I'm striving to think of why I should not kill you now. I know what manner of man you are and ever have been. Why should I believe that you didn't desire to make a whore of my sister, when that is just what you did?"

"Mayhap I will be the one to kill you," Kieran said tightly, "if I hear you speak of Glenys in such a lewd manner again. She is neither a whore nor shamed, and I'll let no one—not even you—name her as such."

"Do you forget the manner in which I found you?" Daman demanded. "Will you sit there and tell me to my face that you never shared a bed with her?"

"You're a God-cursed fool!" Kieran told him. "Aye, we shared a bed, and I will not deny that we shared pleasure, but Glenys is yet a maiden, as I'm certain she told you. Believe me or not as you will, but before you decide think upon this— would I, a man with so dark a reputation, make such a claim unless it were true? Knowing full well that it could so easily be denied by a physician? Consider that well, Daman Seymour."

Daman released a taut breath. "Be quiet for a moment and let me think. Eat in comfort, while you may. I do not know that we will set camp again before we reach London, and you will not be out of the wagon often."

Kieran drank some of the wine, grateful for it, and picked up a piece of bread.

"I would know what has become of my steed, Nimrod, and how he is being cared for. I want him returned to my father, Lord Allen, if't can be done."

Daman set his own wine goblet aside and gave Kieran a confused look. "I have no knowledge of your steed, and confess that I am sorry for it. I remember him well. A great black destrier, is he not? A fine animal."

"Aye, and a gift from my father. Surely one of your men has him. He is my most valuable possession, and worth no small measure to any who would take him."

"I will see if he can be found," Daman said, "but I fear he may have been left behind in Cardigan. If he is not here, I will send a man back to find him, for I agree he must rightly be returned to Lord Allen. A small comfort for the loss of a son, but I imagine he will not be oversurprised to know what fate befell you."

"Nay," Kieran agreed quietly. "I cannot think he will."

They were silent for a time, eating and drinking, until Daman at last cleared his throat and looked up. "You owe me naught," he said, sounding strangely nervous to Kieran's ears, "and, indeed, I am the man who is taking you to your certain death, but I would know...if you will tell me...of Elizabet."

Kieran sat back and regarded him for a silent moment. "Did you love her?" he asked. "Even a little?"

"Very much," Daman replied with feeling. "I have felt as if I were dying since leaving her, but there was no choice. I could not..." He fell silent.

There would have been a time, not very long ago, when Kieran would have spat in the man's eye. But now, having discovered for himself just how painful a thing love was, he felt a measure of pity for him.

"Glenys told me that your life had been ruined because of your family's peculiar ways. Is that why you left Elizabet without a word? Had you vowed never to marry?"

"Aye, that was why, but—" he shook his head slightly "—she knew that I was going. I told her how and why it must be. She wept to break my heart, but I knew that we must part. 'Twas all the best for her, for I never could have brought her such shame."

Kieran sat forward, blazing with anger. "You're a liar," he declared. "You've accused me of making a whore of your sister, of taking her maidenhead, but I found it impossible to leave her as you did Elizabet. Knowing how she suffered once you'd gone, so that she nearly died of it—I could not have done that to the woman I loved. Did you even know that you left your babe in her belly? Or did you leave her without caring to discover what had come of your pleasure-taking?''

Daman's eyes widened. ''A babe?'' he repeated faintly. ''That cannot be. Elizabet was a maiden when I left her. I told you...I could not leave her in shame. I *did* not leave her in shame.''

''God's mercy,'' Kieran said with disgust, ''you sound so sincere that I almost believe you. Almost. I was with Elizabet while she grieved for you and for the distress she had brought to our family. She told me that the child was yours.''

Daman stood, fury on his face. ''I tell you that it cannot be! I never lay with her, and never shared more than a few kisses and caresses. I vow by God above that I—'' He stopped suddenly and stared at Kieran unseeing, his expression slowly changing. ''Holy Mother,'' he said, then sat down. ''That last night, when we said goodbye...after she left me I drank a great deal to ease my sorrows...and then I sought my bed and dreamed of...*oh, God.*'' He gazed at Kieran with horror. ''She must have returned to my chamber, and what I thought were dreams were real. And if it is so, did she think that I was...that I would remember it aright? God's mercy.'' He stood up again, running both hands agitatedly through his black hair. ''Did she think that I had taken her innocence and *then* left her without care? I was gone before she had risen the next morn, thinking it best to go without seeing her once more. But I never would have gone if I'd realized what had passed between us.''

''Elizabet believed you had deserted her,'' Kieran

told him. "She became ill with grief at the knowledge that you could leave her in such a manner."

"I never would have done so!" Daman insisted. "God's truth, I vow it! I would have taken her to wife despite my misgivings, for I could not do otherwise and be an honorable man." He turned to Kieran and looked at him pleadingly. "You must believe what I say."

"Aye," Kieran said softly. "I believe you, for 'tis clear that you loved Elizabet. You could not have convinced me before I knew Glenys, but now I understand full well. What grieves me is Elizabet. She has suffered dearly for your mistaking the truth for a dream."

"Aye, but I must go to her as quickly as I can!" Daman said urgently. "She will be large with child now, if she has not yet brought it to life. We must wed as soon as may be." He began looking about the tent, picking up his gauntlets and his sword and helmet in a distracted manner. "Tell me where she is," he asked Kieran. "Please."

"She is with my mother and stepfather, mostlike," Kieran answered, adding gravely, "Lord Randall will kill you before asking why you've come. He left you in peace this long only because Elizabet pleaded with him to do so, and because he did not wish to make it known that she was with child. But if you arrive at his door—"

"Aye, aye," Daman said impatiently. "I know full well how it will be, but Elizabet will need me now. I'll deal with Lord Randall's anger when I see him."

"Daman," Kieran said, standing. "There is something else you must know. About the child."

Daman stopped pulling his gauntlets on to look at him. "It has not already been born?" he asked worriedly. "Nay, tell me it is not so. My own child, born out of wedlock? But that cannot be, for we have been parted not fully nine months." He took a step toward Kieran. "Has it come early, then? 'Tis a sickly child? By the rood, I must hurry—"

"No." Kieran set a hand on Daman's forearm, stopping him. "It has not been born." He didn't know how to tell him, save to simply do so. "Elizabet was very ill. It was a difficult time, especially the first three months and…she lost the child."

Daman's face drained of color. He stared at Kieran in stunned silence for a long moment, then abruptly turned away and lowered his head into his hands. Kieran moved back to the table, uncomfortably aware of how much sorrow he felt for the man. He remembered Elizabet's grief so clearly, and could not doubt that Daman Seymour was touched by that same inconsolable pain.

Daman spoke, his voice harsh and uneven. "'Tis because of my sin. My foolishness. God has visited a just punishment upon me. I only wish Elizabet and the child had been spared."

"Aye, you are a fool, just as I have been," Kieran said. "You threw away a sweet and true love because you lacked faith in Elizabet and in your own family. And," he added more softly, to himself, "I nearly did the same with Glenys."

"She must hate me now," Daman murmured. "Yet she must wed me. I will go to her at once and plead with her—nay, I will *tell* her how it must be. In time, she may come to forgive me, and if God is merciful, we will have another child together—mayhap many children." He turned and looked at Kieran. "I will no longer strive to have you hanged for taking Glenys, now that we are to be related by marriage. But you must still stand trial for the crime, and you may yet be condemned to death. You understand this.''

Kieran made a slight bow. "Fully and completely. I'm relieved, howbeit, that you will not distress Elizabet with your revenge. I'faith, let her think that another captured and brought me to London. It will be better.''

"Thank you,'' Daman said. "I begin to think that I may have misjudged you, Kieran FitzAllen. I wish, in all truth, that matters stood otherwise between us.''

Kieran smiled at him. "I would not be so quick to forbear just yet, my lord. Do you hear the commotion that has started up outside of your tent? I believe that my manservant has just made good his plan to escape.''

Daman's eyebrows rose. "What?''

"Aye, and if I am not mistaken, one of your men should be coming soon to tell you that he is gone and nowhere to be found.'' Kieran sat and picked up his wine goblet. "A difficult fellow to catch, is Jean-Marc. I would advise that you not bid any of your men to waste their time in the attempt, but you will doubtless do as you please.''

"He could not have escaped!'' Daman declared with disbelief. "'Twould be impossible with all my men guarding him.''

"Oh, Jean-Marc's talents are boundless,'' Kieran said happily. "He would find it but a simple manner to slip away, I assure you.'' He began refilling his goblet with an easy motion. "But there is more. If I understand his intentions aright, he has gone to lend Glenys and Mistress Dina his aid in some scheme they have developed, with the intent of setting me free.''

Daman gave a bark of laughter. "Then he is a fool!

My sister and her maid are safe at Glain Tarran, guarded by a dozen of my finest knights. He'll not be able to get to them, and they'll assuredly not be able to get out to meet him.''

Kieran sighed and sipped his wine. A voice outside the tent begged for admittance. Daman, gazing at Kieran with a frown, bade the man enter.

It was Hubert, casting a glance from Kieran to his master, looking very uncomfortable.

''My lord, I fear I bear bad news. The other prisoner—the manservant—has disappeared. We've searched the camp, but he is not to be found.''

Daman scowled at Kieran, who merely nodded and smiled.

''How did he escape?'' he demanded.

''My lord, I do not know,'' Hubert said sorrowfully. ''No one knows. We've questioned every man who had the watch of him, but they all claim that the lad simply...disappeared.''

''It is as I told you,'' Kieran noted proudly. ''He's a thief of great repute, held in the highest regard amongst his fellows. Weaned to it, you see, from his birth. That's how the best thieves come about.''

Daman glared at him. ''I need none of your rattle now.''

''My lord, there is worse news, I fear,'' said Hubert in quaking tones.

Daman turned slowly to stare at him. ''My sister and her maid have escaped from Glain Tarran?''

Hubert nodded. ''I fear, my lord, that it is so. A rider has just arrived from the estate, bearing those very tidings. I'm sorry, my lord.''

''How did they escape?'' Daman asked in a deadly voice.

Hubert shook his head. "'Tis only known that they rode away on a great black destrier—"

"Ah," Kieran nodded. "Nimrod."

"—and a smaller gray mare."

"That would be Strumpet." Kieran picked up a piece of bread. "I'm glad to know where they are."

Hubert gave Kieran a look of much aggravation before returning his attention to his master.

"Chase was given at once, my lord, but a thick fog quickly covered the area, and they could not be found. Indeed," Hubert added with a measure of embarrassment, "the men became lost themselves, and could not find Glain Tarran for some hours. That is what delayed them in sending word to you, Sir Daman."

There was a deafening silence as Daman gazed at the man, his fists clenching and unclenching.

"A problem, is it not?" Kieran said intemperately. "Whether to chase Glenys or go to Elizabet." He sighed aloud. "I would not wish to be the one to choose."

"As you will be in prison," Daman reminded him tautly, "which is, I vow, the only safe place for such a knave, you will not have the trouble of having to decide."

"Nay, but I do have an idea where you might find both women at once," Kieran said.

Daman sent Hubert away. When they were alone, he cautioned, "'Twill make no difference to you if you should tell me what you know. You will yet go to prison."

"I am full aware of that. 'Tis Glenys I care for now. I'd not have her harmed in any manner."

Daman's face reddened, and then, suddenly, he swore long and loudly, impressing Kieran with the breadth of his knowledge. At last he fell silent, breathing harshly, gazing at Kieran as if he'd like to kill him then and there.

"You love Glenys?" he demanded.

"I do," Kieran replied calmly.

"God curse you, then," Daman said. "For you can never have her."

Kieran nodded and looked away. "I know that full well. You may wed my own sister safely, matched in family and name. But I will not be allowed the same privilege, for I was not born to it. But I will tell you this, Daman Seymour. If I were free to marry Glenys, I would do so, not caring what you or your family, or even the church or crown, might say of it. You see how wicked a man I am."

"Aye, as wicked as any man I ever knew," Daman agreed angrily, "and yet my sister says that she loves you, and swears that she will have you without any more care for what is right than you have. God curse you!"

"I know," Kieran said with every sympathy. "Love seems not to care for those things that the law and church hold so dear. I can only tell you how sorry I am. There's naught else to be done."

"Then tell me where I may find her," Daman said, "so that at least I can make certain of her safety."

Kieran set his wine goblet aside and sat forward.

"You would do well," he began, "to seek out my sister, Lady Eunice of Hammersgate. Glenys will have gone to her for help, and together, I believe, they will go to my mother."

Chapter Nineteen

Being imprisoned in Newgate wasn't quite so bad as Kieran had thought it would be. A number of his former acquaintances were prisoners, as well, and he spent his first two days pleasantly occupied in discovering how each of them fared, though this was accomplished only during those few hours when he was allowed into the prisoners' common area. Otherwise, he was kept alone in a small chamber, considered far too dangerous a knave to be placed in one of the larger rooms with other lesser thieves and criminals. And so it was that he spent most of his time either pacing or sitting in his bleak cell, left alone to think upon his own thoughts and regrets.

Although not entirely alone. He'd reached into his inner pocket during the first hour of his imprisonment and found, to his complete surprise, that the small glowing stone had company. The queen piece, which he was certain he'd not had upon him in Cardigan or at any time during his journey to London, was suddenly there.

"Now, how did you come to be here?" he asked, gazing at her with the help of the glowing stone. She responded with a brightening of her glowing, golden eyes. "'Twas not wise, milady. If the guards discover either you or the stone, they'll take you, and I've little way of keeping you safe. But we must pray that it is not so, for I admit that I am glad to see you."

Her eyes glimmered from gold to blue, and he smiled.

"We must likewise pray that Daman will return to London ere long, so that I can return you to him and thence to Master Culain. You will be eager to be with him once more, will you not?"

More blue—he had realized long since that this indicated a particular happiness in her.

"Aye," he said with a sigh, "I know full well how you feel. I miss Glenys just as greatly." He ran a finger lightly over the top of the queen's smooth wooden head. "Do you think she is well? And safe? 'Twas such foolishness for her to run off and try to save me. But that is how she is, very brave and very foolish."

The blue eyes began to turn golden again.

"You think me harsh?" Kieran asked, stretching his legs out on the dirty straw that comprised his bed. "I did not mean to be, but—this you must admit—both Glenys and I were foolish to dream that we could ever come together in perfect union. 'Twas a most sweet dream, all the same, was it not? If't is the last I have in this life, I'll be glad of it."

Weary, he leaned against the wall behind him and strove to make himself comfortable. He dared not lie down, else the multitude of rats and vermin in the prison would crawl over him during the night. Not that he would be able to gain much rest, even if he did manage to fall asleep. The prison was continually alive with noise, either from the prisoners—men, women and children packed together in various cells—or the guards, getting drunk, taking their turn at the watch, clattering up and down the stairwells. And then, too, there was ever in the back of his mind that he was going to be executed. There was little chance that Glenys could rescue him. Her family would be furious that she'd been taken; they'd press for his death on all sides. He deserved such a fitting punishment after the wastrel life he'd led, but he couldn't deny that he wasn't looking forward to either the hangman's noose or the executioner's ax. Kieran only hoped that he'd behave more properly in death than he had in life, so that his family—and Glenys—would have no cause to be ashamed.

"I must make certain that you are safely with your lord before that time," he told the queen once more, who seemed to be watching him intently out of her glowing eyes. "He would be grieved to know that we had gotten you safe away from Caswallan, only to lose you in such a foul place as Newgate. But never fear, milady. I shall think of the way, if I've enough time for it. Pray God that I do."

Her golden eyes shimmered with light. Kieran yawned and tucked her safely within his pocket. He took up the glowing stone and said, "I would have your company the night through, for both you and our lady queen give me great comfort, but I fear the guards will see your light and take you from me. Best to be as quiet as you can for now. And you need have no fear. When I find the way to get Her Majesty to safety, I'll send you back to Metolius, as well."

The little stone stopped glowing at once, and Kieran rubbed a gentle thumb over its cool surface for a few moments, sitting in the darkness, before pocketing it with the queen piece.

He yawned again and closed his eyes, thinking of Glenys to keep despair at bay. He'd never particularly enjoyed being held captive. This was the longest he'd ever endured it, and before, he'd always had Jean-Marc to bear him company. Thinking of Jean-Marc presented a whole new set of difficulties. Would he be all right on his own? They'd been together for so many years and had complemented each other so well, but there had been times, often, when Kieran's education and upbringing had served to smooth over those areas in which Jean-Marc was somewhat lacking. In all of their business dealings, especially, Kieran had been the responsible one. He'd invested their funds and managed their wealth and— He opened his eyes and sat up. Jean-Marc didn't even know how to go about gaining possession of his own money. He could neither read nor sign his name. God's mercy, what would become of him?

Kieran stared into the darkness for a long time, possessed by the ungovernable fear that Jean-Marc would be utterly lost without him, until he at last began to think more clearly and remember just how capable a fellow Jean-Marc was. He was a far better thief than Kieran, a far better scoundrel in every way. I'faith, Kieran had it all turned around. He was the one who needed Jean-Marc, and not Jean-Marc who needed him. If Jean-Marc wished to get his hands on his own money, he'd simply break in and steal it. And then, Kieran thought, sitting back and closing his eyes again, he'd settle down with Dina in some distant part of England and build a fancy manor house—fancy, because Jean-Marc had a taste for fine things—and they'd live quietly there and raise many fine little thieves who would all look like Jean-Marc. Mayhap they'd name one after Kieran, a particularly roguish lad. The thought made Kieran smile. He turned his head against the wall to make himself more comfortable, and slid into sleep.

He was wrong to think that he would not slumber deeply, for he did, and dreamed deeply, as well. A most pleasant and striking dream.

He and Glenys were married, the lord and lady of a vast estate set on a cliff overlooking a wild, beautiful sea. They had children—boys and girls, equally wild and beautiful, some with hair like the sunset and some golden—laughing, charming, delightful creatures one and all. The queen piece came to life of a sudden, and all else faded away. She was beautiful and regal...and she bowed to him, calling him by the name that Glenys had said. Lord Eneinoig. She swept a hand toward the sea, but it was no longer simply water; it was people. His and Glenys's children and their children and—he could scarce believe his eyes—a vast array of his descendants, all very fine and seemingly endless. The sight filled Kieran with inexpressible pride.

He came awake to the light of dawn creeping through the tiny window high in the wall, finding himself lying flat upon his back. He stared at the ceiling for a long, thoughtful moment before saying, "God help me. An Abraham dream. I must be losing my mind."

"Eh?" another voice said. "What's that? Abraham?"

A face came into Kieran's view, someone standing over him, gazing down at him. The face possessed bright blue eyes, an elfin face and a long, white beard. It was smiling.

Kieran blinked and then scrambled upward to sit against the wall, his heart pounding as he strove to push away the sluggish remnants of slumber.

"Who a-God's name are you?"

The fellow straightened to full height and gazed at Kieran with amusement. He was tall but slender, delicate in both form and face, and dressed in elegant purple robes.

"I'm Aonghus Seymour," he said. "And you are Kieran FitzAllen. Not Abraham." He chuckled.

"Aonghus Seymour," Kieran repeated stupidly, wondering if something was wrong with his brain. Surely he'd not heard the man aright. The next words out of his mouth, however, were, "Is Glenys well? And safe? Is she in London?"

The elderly man smiled gently and said, "Not yet. But I've come to fetch you on her instructions. You're to come home with me to Metolius."

"Nay, I'm to be hanged," Kieran told him. "Or otherwise executed. I kidnapped her. But I am glad you've come, for I've something that belongs to your brother, Glenys's uncle." He reached into his inner pocket and withdrew the queen piece, holding her out. "She's in perfect health. We've taken the greatest care of her."

"Oh, good," Aonghus Seymour said with pleasure. "Culain will be so glad to have her returned to him. But you must give her to him yourself, so that he can render his thanks. Come now, Master FitzAllen, for I've left my niece, Mistress Helen, waiting in the guardroom, and God alone knows the trouble she might cause if left there too long." He turned and walked out of the cell, nodding to the two scowling guards who waited on the other side of the door.

Shaking his head to clear it, Kieran stared for a moment, then hastily rose to his feet and followed.

"My lord—Master Seymour—I fear you don't understand aright." He set a careful hand on the older man's arm to make him stop and listen. "I kidnapped Glenys. Took her against her will and dragged her halfway across England. That's a crime punishable by death."

"Aye, and so it is," Master Aonghus said agreeably, patting Kieran's hand in a comforting manner, "but I fear Glenys will be most displeased with me should I allow such a fate to befall you. And you needn't worry, for what happened between the two of you was just as it was meant to be. We knew it from the start. And now, here you are at last, come to be with us at Metolius. My dear sisters can scarce wait to meet you, I vow. They're full overjoyed at the very thought. I've had such a time keeping them from coming to get you themselves. But we did have to wait for Glenys's missive, of course," he said more confidentially. Leaning forward, he whispered, "We must be careful to let her think 'twas her own idea, you see. She doesn't like it when we know things before she does. But I'm sure you understand that full well, knowing her as you do."

"Ah…yes," Kieran agreed with confusion. "Of a certainty."

"Good lad," said Master Aonghus, patting Kieran's hand once more. "Now come along and let us deal with this tiresome business of getting you free. Although I should not be surprised if Helen hasn't already managed the entire matter." He cast a glance back at

Kieran as they began to climb the tower stairs. "She's very much like Glenys. Good-hearted, but managing."

Kieran laughed. "I am forewarned then, sir."

They made their way to the main guardroom, where Kieran took one look at Mistress Helen and decided that if anyone could convince the Newgate warden to set a prisoner free, it was she.

Blond, vividly green-eyed and dressed all in black, she was the sort of woman whom a man had a hard time not staring at. The sort of woman who was stunningly beautiful—and knew it. The sort of woman who exuded an animal sensuality both openly and with great assurance. To look at her was to be riveted by the promise of pleasure that flashed in those green eyes, and, worse, to find oneself lured into their depths. Kieran, less susceptible to the powers of certain women than most men, was able to shake himself free of her hypnotic gaze. The other men in the chamber, apart from Master Aonghus, weren't so fortunate. They surrounded Mistress Helen like a pack of frothing idiots, gaping openly and uttering complete nonsense.

Ignoring them, Mistress Helen pulled her elegant black cloak more tightly about herself and glided forward, moving as if she were floating, rather than walking.

"Here you are, Master FitzAllen. I began to think you'd not come at all. Sergeant," she said, casting a glance at one of the men, who hopped forward at her bidding, "my uncle will sign the required document. Please hurry."

It was all done so easily that even Kieran, who had experienced any number of near escapes in his life, could scarce believe it when, only minutes later, he was riding in the very coach that he'd taken Glenys in, driven by the same servants, John and Willem, that he and Jean-Marc had left tied in an alleyway.

His disbelief continued when they arrived at Metolius and he found himself standing in a grand entryway, surrounded by Glenys's family, her two elderly aunts and other uncle, all of them hugging him by turns as if he were a long lost son at last come home to them. There wasn't a word of reproach for what he'd done to their niece and her maid; there was only welcome and gladness.

Still in a daze, he was bundled up several flights of stairs to a chamber that had been made ready for him, where a tub filled with water sat by a blazing fire, and servants were waiting to tend him. He was bathed, thoroughly scrubbed, then rinsed and dried and wrapped in a fine silk robe. Food and drink had been set out for him, and once he'd sated his ravenous hunger he was led to a large, curtained feather bed, which he lay upon with gratitude, falling asleep at once.

It was dark when he woke again, feeling much the better for food and rest. His mind was clear and he knew where he was, at Metolius, with Glenys's family. Why he was there was yet a mystery, but he'd learned long ago not to question fortune when it smiled upon him.

His clothes had been laid out for him, but the manservant who'd been waiting for Kieran to rise pleaded with him to accept the new garments that Master Aonghus had supplied. Kieran readily acquiesced, expecting that the fit would be imperfect. But much to his surprise, the finely crafted leggings and velvet tunic fit him perfectly, almost as if they'd been tailored just for him. The servant confided that they had been. Master Aonghus had ordered an entire wardrobe to be made only a week after Mistress Glenys had left. The garments had been waiting in this chamber for many days now. Kieran had looked at the young man with disbelief, but he had assured him that was the truth.

"Master Aonghus wishes to speak with you, Master FitzAllen," he added once Kieran had finished pulling on new soft half boots that were as comfortable as his old, battered pair. "If you consent."

"Give me but a moment," Kieran replied, running his fingers through his overlong hair and then rifling through the pockets of his old tunic before following the man out the door. "Will you take me to Master Culain first, please?" he asked. "There is something that I must return to him without further delay."

Master Culain, as well as Glenys's two aunts, was sitting in the richly furnished great chamber that Kieran had passed earlier on his way into Metolius. They all rose at once to greet him, the uncle having been sitting alone at a chess table, and the aunts from where they'd been by the fire, gazing into a wooden box.

"Oh, you've come down at last!" one of the aunts declared happily. "We hoped you'd awake in time for the evening meal."

"Won't it be agreeable to sit together at last?" the other, her exact twin, said, smiling up at Kieran. "Oh, isn't he handsome, Mim? Hasn't our Glenys done well for herself?"

"Quite, quite handsome," Mim said. "Won't it be nice to have such a lovely man to escort us when we go out, Wynne? We'll be the envy of every woman who sees us!"

They both giggled and attached themselves to Kieran on either side. He found himself thoroughly charmed.

"Leave him be, now, girls," said Uncle Culain, his

blue eyes stern as he moved to take Kieran's hand in greeting. "He's only just arrived. Give him time to rest and gain his strength before Glenys returns. Now, lad." He looked at Kieran hopefully. "Do you, perchance, have a liking for chess?"

"Indeed, I do, sir," Kieran replied honestly, "and I should be glad to match you sometime very soon. For now, I am required to speak with Master Aonghus, but I wished to return this to you first." He pulled the queen piece out into the open, holding her on the flat of his palm. Her amber eyes twinkled up at him. "I cannot deny that I shall miss you, Boadicea. I'm glad that I was able to do this one thing for you—to return you safely home."

He gave the piece to the other man, who took her up with shaking hands.

"Oh," he murmured, his blue eyes shining with sudden tears. "I never thought to see her again. How good of you to bring her back to me. Thank you." He reached out to touch Kieran's arm, his gaze fixed upon the queen piece, whose eyes had gone brilliantly blue. "Thank you." He turned away and wandered out of the great chamber, murmuring indistinctly to the chess piece, not stopping to bid his sisters or Kieran farewell.

"Oh, that's wonderful," Aunt Mim said happily, wiping her own eyes. "Isn't it, Wynne?"

"'Tis very good to see Culain with his favorite again," Aunt Wynne agreed. "He's missed her so very much."

"I fear I have something that belongs to you ladies, as well," Kieran told them, and produced the glowing stone. "I am equally loath to part with it, for this sweet creature gave me much pleasure during my journeys

with Glenys. It faithfully gave us light on many a dark
night, and I was grateful to have the care of it.''

"Oh, Mim," said Aunt Wynne, "aren't we fortunate
to have Kieran with us? Such a good, kind heart he
has. No, Kieran, dear, you must keep the stone.'' She
folded his fingers back over the smooth white rock. "It
has become your own, and will give light to no one
else now.''

"Yes, dear," Aunt Mim agreed, nodding. "You
must certainly keep it, else it will pine for you, and
that would be terribly sad. You do wish to keep it, do
you not?'' she added with a note of anxiety.

"Very much," Kieran said at once. "I thank you
with all my heart.''

"Such a *wonderful* man," Aunt Mim sighed. "He'll
be so good for Glenys. Just what she needs.''

"Oh, yes," said Aunt Wynne. "Exactly what she
needs. We never could have chosen a better. And *so*
handsome!''

They beamed at Kieran, who pocketed the stone and
thought that he could easily get used to this kind of
adulation.

"But Aonghus will be waiting for him," Aunt Mim
said suddenly. "We'd best let him go.'' She reached
up to kiss Kieran on the cheek. "Hurry now, dear,"
she said, just as if he were a favorite nephew. "We'll
see you at the evening meal.''

"Yes," Aunt Wynne said, reaching up to kiss his
other cheek. "We'll see you then, and we'll have *so*
much to talk about! Hurry on to Aonghus. I'm sure he
must be anxious to speak with you.''

Kieran thought them two of the sweetest ladies he'd
ever met, and was perfectly happy to let them dote
upon him. He kissed each of their hands and bowed

regally before heading for the door and the waiting manservant, leaving the two sisters giggling with pleasure.

The manservant led Kieran down a long hallway, then another, and finally down a flight of stairs until they reached what looked very much like a cellar door. The manservant bent, took hold of an iron ring set in the door, and pulled it open. A cloud of reddish smoke, smelling faintly of gunpowder, rose into the air.

"M-Master Aonghus awaits you below, sir," the manservant announced, coughing and waving a hand in front of his face.

The smoke cleared sufficiently for Kieran to see the tiny steps that led down to the chamber below.

"Very well," he said, and taking a deep breath, began the descent. The stairway seemed to have been fashioned for a child, so small and short the steps were. Kieran was obliged to traverse them sideways, else he would have tumbled to the floor below.

"My lord?" he called as he made his way into the smoke, which grew thicker and more pungent with each step. "Master Aonghus?"

"Is that you, Master FitzAllen?"

Kieran began to cough. "Aye!"

"A moment, lad, and we'll have this cleared."

There was a familiar flash of tiny glittering purple stars, and the red smoke faded almost at once, soon disappearing altogether. Kieran found himself standing in the midst of a strange, cavernous chamber lit by dozens of glowing stones similar to the one he had in his pocket. Master Aonghus Seymour, looking very much like a wizard in his purple robes, stood behind a long wooden table lined with various small, lidded jars fashioned of glass, pewter, stone and brightly colored pottery. Wooden hooks on the wall behind the elderly man held dozens of leather pouches, bulging with what Kieran supposed were powders and other dried elements.

"You desired to speak to me, Master Aonghus?" Kieran asked, making a slight bow.

"Indeed," his host replied. "Come and sit. There's a table and some chairs here." He led the way to the chamber's farthest corner, which was also quite dark. However, as they neared it, glowing stones set on shelves came to life, while those behind them dimmed. Kieran stopped to look back.

"Does it make you uncomfortable, Master Fitz-Allen?" Master Aonghus asked. "They will be happy to come forth again, if you wish it."

"Oh, nay," Kieran assured him, taking his own stone out of his pocket and setting it on the table. It instantly joined its brothers and sisters in putting off a gentle glow. "I'm used to them. I have one of my own now, you see. A kind of pet."

"Ah, very good," Master Aonghus said with a nod as he turned away to fetch a nearby wine decanter and two goblets. "Mim and Wynne quite love them. And spoil them, as well."

Kieran grinned at the other man. "I believe I understand how that comes to be. I find myself rather attached to mine."

"Glenys found that most vexing during your journey, I would vow," said her uncle. "Sit, please. This is very good wine. Glenys has it brought to us from Italy each year, in great quantity. I don't understand such things," he admitted, filling each of their goblets, "so 'tis a fine thing that she is so practical and capable in nature. We would be in dire circumstances without her.'' He set the stopper on the decanter and looked up at Kieran, who was yet standing. ''She makes our lives possible, if you can understand such a thing.''

''Aye, I understand full well,'' Kieran murmured, his heart giving a painful thump. ''You need say no more, Master Aonghus.''

''Oh, but I must, for there is a great deal more. Please, Kieran, sit, so that I may do likewise. My knees are not as strong as they once were.''

Kieran sat at once, waiting until his host was likewise seated before sipping from his wine goblet. The wine was, indeed, quite good, just as promised, but it tasted like sand in Kieran's mouth. He almost wished he were back at Newgate, awaiting death. What would his life be like when he was sent out of this place, away from Glenys forever? He supposed he could seek out Jean-Marc and they could take up as they had done before—but nay. That was a time already done with. Jean-Marc wouldn't need his thieving former master as a shadow to dim his new life with Dina.

''Do you love Glenys?'' Master Aonghus asked suddenly, watching Kieran.

''Aye,'' he replied without hesitation. ''Very much so. At least, I believe 'tis love. If not, it is some kind of maddening sickness that seems to have robbed me of sense and reason. A torment beyond all others.''

Master Aonghus laughed. ''I have never heard love better described. But how is it that this has happened? Glenys is not a great beauty, and you, I think, must be far more used to having the loveliest women upon your arm. Helen told me the sort of man you are.''

''Did she?'' Kieran said, with immediate affront directed toward Mistress Helen, which faded when he realized that he had taken her measure, as well, upon their first meeting. Aye, he and Helen understood each other. They were very like. "T'faith, I do not know how my love for Glenys came about. I only know that 'tis there and cannot be changed. I've tried, please believe that I speak the truth, knowing full well that we cannot be together under the law. And I would not ask her to be with me otherwise."

"Can you not explain even a little better than that?" Master Aonghus prodded gently.

Kieran drank deeply from his wine goblet, then set it aside, wiped his mouth with his fingers and for a long moment was silent and thoughtful. At last, it came to him.

"You say that Glenys is not beautiful, and this is, in certain senses, true. But neither is she foolish or vain or...like so many other women. She is a rare gem set among so many more common jewels. Like the Greth Stone, I suppose." He smiled, feeling foolish. Master Aonghus looked at him encouragingly, and Kieran went on. "I have lived a poor life, my lord. I'm probably the worst man living on God's earth. Bad through and through. But women like me because of my face and form and charming manner. I have taken whatever I pleased because I could have it almost without effort, and have been taken in like manner because I was a man to be enjoyed and then sent away. No woman wished to keep me forever. Only for a time, for being a bastard and a thief do little to recommend me as a husband, despite the nobility of my parents. Only as a lover have I been sought, and in that regard I was held as valuable. A man to be desired. But it was not so with Glenys." He uttered a laugh. "She saw nothing in me to like, no matter how I tried to please. Indeed, she despised me at first, which I admit I deserved, taking her so against her will and for my own purpose. Oh, aye, she hated me then.'' He gave a sorrowful shake of his head.

''But in time she liked you better?'' her uncle pressed, filling Kieran's wine goblet anew.

''Somewhat. I had already fallen in love with her by then. Her face—those lovely angles—I found entrancing. I could read all her thoughts just by looking at her,'' he admitted with a grin, which Uncle Aonghus returned with a nod. ''I told her what a wicked man I was—though God above knows she'd already discerned the truth of that—and yet she cared for me despite it all. She came to love me,'' he said, with all the wonder that he ever felt upon thinking of it. ''And then I found that I could not keep myself from her.'' He looked away, frowning. ''But I should have. My only comfort is that I brought her no shame. I beg that you will believe me, Master Aonghus. Her husband will find nothing lacking in her.'' The words were painful to speak, for he could not bear to think of her with another.

''Of that I'm certain,'' said Master Aonghus. ''Tell me, please, Kieran…do you speak any Welsh?''

Kieran shook his head. ''Nay. I wish I did. Glenys speaks it so well. I found it most…'' *Sensual,* he almost said, but refrained, finishing the sentence instead with, ''lyrical.''

''Do you believe in the old ways?'' asked Uncle Aonghus.

''Do you mean magic?''

The older man shrugged. '''Tis a way of saying what we hold as being most natural, but I will agree to the word.''

Kieran had to think upon that for a moment. ''Aye,''

he answered at last. "I think I do. When we were at Pentre Ifan, I saw an elf...or some such creature. He tried to steal the queen piece, and then bit me when I fought to regain it. I yet bear the scar." Kieran held his hand up to show his host. "He called me by a strange name."

"Aye," Master Aonghus said. "Lord Eneinoig. Did Glenys tell you what it means to our family?"

"I do not even know what it means to anyone," Kieran confessed apologetically.

Master Aonghus sighed. "You will be obliged to learn *Cymreag*, Master Kieran, before long, I vow. 'Tis your fate. Will you not have more wine?" He moved to pour the red liquid into Kieran's half-empty goblet. Then he sat back and sipped from his own glass. "*Eneinoig* means 'promise'," he said presently. "There has been a legend in our family for centuries past, telling that a 'promised lord' would come from outside the Seymours to give guidance and power to future generations. He would be named by those creatures whom we yet believe in—the faeries at Pentre Ifan, among them. This man would be called Lord Eneinoig, christened thus by those who would choose him."

Kieran straightened in his chair. "My lord, I fear that you are mistaken. I'm not this man you speak of."

Master Aonghus looked at him with full sympathy. "I'm sorry if you don't like it," he said, "but you are. The Seymours do not question the determination of those who know better."

"Glenys told you of it?" Kieran demanded. "She wrote you?"

"Nay, she did not," Master Aonghus told him. "I learned of it in quite a different manner, before you left

Wales, I believe. That you have been chosen is most clear, the evidence strong. You may reject it, but in doing so, you will reject much.''

Kieran tried not to laugh, but couldn't help himself. He set a hand to his chest and said, ''But I'm a thief, a knave. You cannot know how so, my lord. If I have been chosen, then 'tis a mistake. It must be.''

''This is what you thought when you knew that Glenys loved you?'' Uncle Aonghus asked.

''Aye, of a certainty.''

''Then I think,'' his host said gently, ''that you are quite wrong, about both Glenys and your choice as the promised lord. Tell me, did you find Glain Tarran pleasing?''

''I never set sight upon it.''

Master Aonghus sat upright. ''Never set sight upon it! Glenys did not take you there?''

''She said it was not always evident,'' Kieran explained. ''I did not take it amiss, I promise you.''

''But you should have seen it!'' Master Aonghus insisted with some indignity. ''''Tis your own estate now, your seat of power. You are the head of the family, being deigned thus by the powers. 'Tis your right to see your own estate. And all the rest.''

Kieran stared at the elderly man, wondering if he had perhaps suffered a mental illness, and thinking of how greatly that would distress Glenys and add to all her burdens.

''Master Aonghus,'' he said in his most careful, soothing voice, ''you must be very calm. I will be perfectly glad to do as you say, whatever you say, but you must remain quite easy.''

''My lad,'' Uncle Aonghus said, ''you do desire to have Glenys as a wife?''

"More than I wish to save my own life," Kieran told him. "But you know as well as I that 'tis impossible."

"'Tis not, my lord Eneinoig. All you must do is accept what you have been claimed as. 'Tis as simple as that. You assuredly have charm and skill enough. That is the most required of a lord. Glenys," said her uncle, "will take care of the rest."

Chapter Twenty

How could he say no? Even if he knew full well that he wasn't a proper man to be lord over anything, the temptation to gain Glenys was far too overwhelming for a man such as he was—weak, desperate and needing her so badly.

And so he agreed to be the Seymours' Lord Eneinoig—their promised lord—and even went so far as to agree to giving his and Glenys's future children the Seymour name, rather than his own, though he would continue to use it out of respect for his father. Privately, Kieran determined that he would do his utmost to be the best lord he could be. And also to pray mightily that God would keep him from mucking it up. The rest, as Uncle Aonghus had advised, he would leave in Glenys's capable hands.

As far as Kieran could tell, Glenys's aunts and uncles only seemed to want him to be charming and entertaining—or that was what pleased them all just now, anywise. Since he happened to be skilled at these things, 'twas an easy matter to please them. He only had to be himself, and they loved him, especially Aunts Mim and Wynne. He spent much of his time in their company, escorting them about Metolius, one elderly lady on each arm—through the gardens, to the great room, to the dining chamber, and even, twice, outside of Metolius to attend Mass at St. Paul's.

They had introduced him to their special box, which both intrigued and alarmed Kieran. Seeing the various objects it offered up at each opening, he understood just why Glenys wished to keep her family as far from prying eyes as possible. Anyone seeing the box and the joy it gave the elderly aunts would conclude that it was the work of sorcery, and off they'd be dragged to the nearest stake.

With much encouragement from the ladies, Kieran took a turn at opening the box. A very old, odd-looking key came up, the sight of which made Aunt Mim gasp and Aunt Wynne faint dead away. As it had quite obviously distressed them both, he put the key back into the box at once and closed the lid. This, unfortunately, made Aunt Mim faint, too, and Kieran found himself, along with Uncle Culain and most of the household servants, on the floor, striving mightily to revive them.

The first thing they did upon being roused was to open the box. Aunt Mim brought up what appeared to be a child's toy, made of a strange, ironlike substance and tiny soft wheels. It was bright red and had the words *Hot Wheels* on the side; Mim put it away at once. Aunt Wynne's effort was likewise disappointing, as she brought up a tiny silver spoon, which she dropped back into the box with a cry of distress.

"I'm most sorry," Kieran apologized. "I didn't know whether you wished to have the key or not, for it seemed to distress you both. Now, I perceive, you are distressed that it's gone. Let me try the box once more and see if it returns."

"Oh, nay, it won't," Aunt Mim said sadly. "It appears only once every hundred years and—"

Kieran flipped the wooden lid open with one hand. The key lay inside. He held it up to show them. "Here it is," he said with relief, placing it in their waiting hands. "Mayhap it appears several times in one day, every hundred years. This must be the right day. What does it open?"

Considering the reaction the key's presence had wrought, it rather amazed Kieran that no one, not even Uncle Aonghus, could remember what, exactly, the key was for. They only knew that generations of Seymours had been searching for it without success, until that day. It was, Kieran concluded, another one of their legends, of which there were many. After a fitful discussion, which ended with them determining that nothing could be done with the key, it was put—somewhat reluctantly—back into the box, where it disappeared. Temporarily. Every time Kieran opened the box, it was there. Day after day. Always there, but only for him. The aunts were overjoyed, but Kieran found it rather dull. He had hoped to bring up something more interesting, like the little red Hot Wheels.

Mistress Helen put in an appearance late each afternoon, since she always slept late into the morning. She was polite to Kieran and her relatives, always ready to enter into conversation or lend her aid in directing the servants, but otherwise she remained aloof. She had taken over the care of the many Seymour business ventures in Glenys's absence, and spent most of her waking hours in driving about London, talking to bankers and merchants and the captains of the several Seymour ships. She was always dressed in unrelieved black, always looked somewhat bored, and always disappeared once darkness fell. This seemed not to bother her relatives, but Kieran's curiosity was roused, especially by the green-eyed, ink-black cat that suddenly appeared at nightfall and roamed the vast dwelling throughout the many dark hours, though it was never to be seen during the day. Kieran had his suspicions, but there were some matters that were so far removed from his experience, and too disturbing, that he simply didn't let himself dwell upon them. He also stayed as far away from the cat as possible. It make his hair stand on end, just looking at it.

When not occupied with escorting the elderly ladies, Kieran spent several hours over the next few days playing chess with Uncle Culain, with the queen piece, set in a place of honor on the side of the chess table, watching. They took turns talking to her—Kieran was glad that the rest of the family found this to be perfectly normal—and she had never appeared, to Kieran's eyes, so pleased and content.

He also tried his hand at helping Uncle Aonghus in his cellar workchamber, an experience he enjoyed thoroughly, especially when he learned how to create interesting explosions. More than once they ascended the cellar stairs covered in powder, grinning happily and very pleased with themselves. Uncle Aonghus declared Kieran a natural with elements, but warned him that Glenys would be displeased if they set anything on fire.

Kieran, who became increasingly impatient as each day passed, didn't worry overmuch about whether Glenys would be angry about anything—he simply wished to see her again and be assured that she yet loved him. It was not that he was unhappy at Metolius; far from it. He was cosseted and spoiled and treated like a prince by one and all—even John and Willem, who had kindly forgiven him and Jean-Marc for what they'd done. But, delightful as it all was, there was an incompleteness without Glenys. Kieran worried about whether she was well. Whether Daman had been angry with her when—and if—he'd run her to ground. Whether she, too, wanted to be with Kieran again. Whether she even knew that her missive had arrived in time to keep him from being hanged. He didn't like the thought of her worrying over that.

"When will she come?" he asked longingly one afternoon, gazing out one of the tall windows in the great room. "Something must have gone amiss to keep her away so long."

Uncle Aonghus set a comforting hand on his shoulder. "Soon, she will come. The longer she is absent, the sweeter your reunion will be."

Kieran laughed. "I'd be happy to forgo greater sweetness to simply *have* it."

Two days later advance riders began arriving at Metolius, bringing news that set Aunts Mim and Wynne to scurrying. A large number of guests were coming, they said, though no one seemed to know precisely who they were or exactly how many, but rooms needed to be prepared to accommodate them all and additional stores of food and drink must be stocked.

Mistress Helen received the news of so many unexpected guests almost without comment. She calmed Aunts Mim and Wynne and then set about directing the servants, in her usual bored tone, in making preparations.

Kieran tried to stay out of the way as best he could, spending most of his time either walking about the front courtyard and looking out of the gates, or standing by the tall windows in the great chamber, watching and waiting. He was tempted to sneak out of Metolius in the dead of night and find his way to one of his former haunts in London, the sort of place where information could be bought and sold. Surely one of the scoundrels who frequented such places had heard, during his or her travels, of Glenys or, more likely, Jean-Marc. But Kieran decided not to pursue this plan. For one, it would be a poor return of the Seymours' kindness to him if he should unwittingly get into some manner of trouble, and for another, he had a feeling that the blasted black cat would follow him, and he didn't want it—her—making him feel guilty the following day for practicing such guile.

When Glenys finally arrived, it was in such an abrupt manner that Kieran could only stand at the window he'd been gazing out of and stare. She came galloping through the courtyard gates riding atop Nimrod, her hair unbound and flowing behind her, her skirts flying and her expression filled with exuberance and laughter. She slid down from Nimrod's back without help from the servants, and then ran at once up the stairs toward the entryway doors.

Kieran had sprung into motion by then, and by the time the doors were flung open he was there, catching Glenys up in his arms and crushing her tightly.

"God be praised," he said, turning about in a full circle, feeling her arms squeezing hard about his neck. "You're here at last."

"Oh, Kieran, such a time I've—" she started to say, but the moment she pulled her face back to look up at him, he kissed her. And kept kissing her, over and over, until she was gasping for air. She laughed and grinned up at him happily. "I'm sorry I was gone so long. I had much to do."

"Did you?" he murmured, kissing her again, more gently this time. "I hope it's all done with, for I plan never to be parted from you again. We're to be married. Your uncles say so. And so do your aunts. And even your cousin, Helen."

"I know," she said, then laughed, bubbling with pure joy. "So does your father. And your mother. And your stepfather. And all your brothers and sisters—you have such a large family! I was worn almost to naught bringing them all together."

Kieran stared at her. "Together?"

"Aye," she said, nodding. "They'll all be here soon. I came ahead because I could not bear to be kept from you any longer." She reached up and kissed him.

With some difficulty, Kieran pulled away. His head was buzzing. "They're coming here?" he asked faintly. "*All* of them?"

"Yes, is that not wonderful? They've come for the wedding. And because I wasn't certain whether Uncle Aonghus could free you from Newgate. I didn't know then that Daman had turned aside from insisting upon your immediate execution. Your father sent at once a dozen of his finest knights to Newgate to keep you from being hanged, though he wanted to go himself. I wouldn't let him, of course, for I needed his aid in other matters. He was much relieved when they returned and reported that you'd been released and taken to Metolius, as was I. Oh, Kieran," she said with even greater enthusiasm, ignoring his attempts to speak, "there was such an unfortunate scene when Daman arrived at your stepfather's estate. He nearly killed him! Your stepfather nearly did, I mean to say. But your dear sister, Lady Eunice, put herself in front of Daman and reasoned until your stepfather came to his senses. And now—'tis so wonderful—your sister Elizabet and Daman are betrothed! My aunts will be so pleased!''

Kieran's head was spinning. He held more tightly on to Glenys to keep from losing his balance.

"Daman and Elizabet are betrothed? But—"

"And so are Jean-Marc and Dina. I'm so sorry that you weren't present to witness their vows, for I know you would have liked it very much. But your stepfather insisted that it must be done immediately following Daman and Elizabet's betrothal, for he said he'd had enough foolishness from the both of you, and he'd be damned if he'd let either of you go on in such a feckless manner. We will be present for both weddings, and that will be some measure of recompense, will it not? Oh, Kieran, all has come about so well. We are the most fortunate of all God's creatures."

"I am," he told her, "but do you truly wish to take so great a risk with me, Glenys? I cannot say what manner of husband I will be." He searched her face intently. "I would not have you regret, in time to come, that you gave yourself to me so fully. I have been a wicked knave all my life, as I'm sure my vast family told you."

She lifted a hand to cradle his cheek. "They told me only that they love you, and that I will be most fortunate in being your wife. Your father described the estate he had given you in greater detail, as well as all your inheritance. Why did you let me think you so poor, when, in truth, you possess both land and fortune?"

"I began to tell you that last day at Berte's, for that was all I had to offer of any value—at least you would not think that you must live as the wife of a thief, treading in such wayward places as Berte's or Bostwick's.''

"May God forbid it," Glenys murmured fervently. "I will be content to live with you anywhere, Kieran FitzAllen, but I'll not raise our children in brothels and taverns.''

Kieran laughed. "Then I think we must do as you have ever done, and spend part of the year at Metolius and the other at Glain Tarran.''

"But what of your own estate, in Derbyshire?"

"I believe I will make a gift of it to Jean-Marc and Dina, if my father will not mind too much.''

"I do not think he will mind anything, now," she said. "He is very pleased to know that we will be wed. As are your mother and stepfather. Is it not strange that we believed we should not be allowed to wed, yet all who love us are very pleased, indeed? 'Tis like a miracle.''

"Nay," he said, kissing her, "'tis magic. For how else could a rogue such as I am hope to wed so fine a lady? You're taking a wretched fellow for a husband, Glenys, but I love you, and will ever do so.''

"As I love you," she murmured. "And you are not a wretched man, Kieran FitzAllen. Far, far from it. You are the man who took me prisoner and taught me so many wonderful things, and gave me so much happiness. You're the man who taught me to believe in magic, when I had denied it for so long. Nay, that is not a wretched fellow, but only a rogue and scoundrel and knave—" she smiled up at him, "—and all mine.''

The ardent embrace taking place in the entryway was observed with full approval by Glenys's aunts and uncles, as well as by her cousin Helen, who wore one of her rare smiles. Outside, the clattering of horses and carriages filled the courtyard as a small army of visitors began to arrive. And yet Kieran and Glenys, entwined in loving embrace, seemed not to hear any of it.

"They are perfect together," Aunt Mim said, sighing happily. "A most handsome couple."

"Oh, indeed," Aunt Wynne agreed. "He is truly the only man for our dearest Glenys. They shall be so happy. I do hope Daman doesn't find it unbearable that his sister should be the one to continue the line."

"It could not have been Daman," said Uncle Aonghus. "He is a very good lad, and we would assuredly have no other in his place, but he is so practical in his nature, far more than Glenys. He would never cherish the old ways, as Kieran will do. I'faith, Kieran is far more suited to what will come than even he knows. He has had many adventures before now, but there are many more to unfold."

"My queen has approved him," said Uncle Culain. "That is important."

"Glenys approves of him," Helen interjected. "That is even more important. He will be good to her," she added with purring satisfaction. "I only wish that I might find myself so fortunate."

"You will," Uncle Aonghus assured her. "In time, my dear. Be patient."

"That I am," said she, "above all things. But now the guests come, and Glenys and her betrothed seem not to notice. 'Tis amazing how they manage to breathe in such an ardent embrace. His parents will be shocked to enter Metolius and find them thus."

"Oh, give them another moment," begged Aunt Mim. "They are so pretty a sight. 'Tis such a happy ending, is it not, Wynne?"

Aunt Wynne nodded, wiping tears from her eyes, but

her brother Aonghus chuckled and said, "'Tis not an ending, my dears, for either Kieran and Glenys or our family. 'Tis but the beginning. And," he added sagely, "a very good one, too."

* * * * *

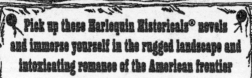

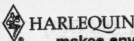

CALL THE ONES YOU LOVE OVER THE HOLIDAYS!

Save $25 off future book purchases when you buy any four Harlequin® or Silhouette® books in October, November and December 2001,

PLUS

receive a phone card good for 15 minutes of long-distance calls to anyone you want in North America!

WHAT AN INCREDIBLE DEAL!

Just fill out this form and attach 4 proofs of purchase (cash register receipts) from October, November and December 2001 books, and Harlequin Books will send you a coupon booklet worth a total savings of $25 off future purchases of Harlequin® and Silhouette® books, AND a 15-minute phone card to call the ones you love, anywhere in North America.

Please send this form, along with your cash register receipts as proofs of purchase, to:

In the USA: Harlequin Books, P.O. Box 9057, Buffalo, NY 14269-9057
In Canada: Harlequin Books, P.O. Box 622, Fort Erie, Ontario L2A 5X3
Cash register receipts must be dated no later than December 31, 2001.
Limit of 1 coupon booklet and phone card per household.
Please allow 4-6 weeks for delivery.

I accept your offer! Enclosed are 4 proofs of purchase. Please send me my coupon booklet and a 15-minute phone card:

Name: _____

Address: _____ City: _____

State/Prov.: _____ Zip/Postal Code: _____

Account Number (if available): _____

---

097 KJB DAGL
PHQ4013

Bestselling Harlequin® author

JUDITH ARNOLD

brings readers a brand-new, longer-length novel based on her popular miniseries *The Daddy School*

Somebody's Dad

If any two people should avoid getting romantically involved with each other, it's bachelor—and children-phobic!—Brett Stockton and single mother Sharon Bartell. But neither can resist the sparks...especially once *The Daddy School* is involved.

"Ms. Arnold seasons tender passion with a dusting of humor to keep us turning those pages."
—*Romantic Times Magazine*

Look for Somebody's Dad in February 2002.

HARLEQUIN®
Makes any time special®